The
SINGAPORE
FILE

by Tom Cassidy

As the distant glow of headlights from a solitary vehicle drew closer Diamond's pulse revved to over a hundred. Moments later the automobile rolled into view at the end of the clearing and drifted past. The same car returned, unhurried, entered the parking area and proceeded to a spot on the far side opposite Diamond's car, well positioned for a quick getaway. Its lights doused, an infrared night-vision scope panned back and forth around the entire locale paying special attention to windows and doorways and confirming Diamond's identity. A cigarette lighter flashed twice and Diamond responded with his signal. He stepped out and approached the other car. Its right rear door swung open and a burly man with wire-rimmed glasses and dark clothes stepped out and allowed him to enter. He squeezed inside between the two thuggish-looking men, recognizing only Nicholai in the front passenger seat.

The bald, ox-faced man to Diamond's left maintained a blank forward stare as he took breaths through a mouth that reeked of decayed teeth marinated in cheap vodka. Resting on his stomach, clutched in his left hand, a dark pistol with a silencer pointed at Diamond's chest. Unseen on the other side, the man with the wire-rimmed glasses rolled a spring-loaded syringe back and forth in the palm of his right hand, poised to plunge the lethal dose of chemicals into Diamond's neck, sending him to an instant oblivion. The callous enforcers awaited only their command.

A hidden microphone captured every spoken word. "Are you carrying any weapons tonight, Mr. Diamond," Nicholai asked as the ogre with the fire breath continued to pat Diamond down, and concluded with a menacing clutch of Diamond's scrotum.

"No, no, nothing" Diamond responded as he squirmed, his voice edgy.

INTRODUCTION

What kept me motivated to write *The Singapore File* were three things. First, the Republic of Singapore is a great country in many ways and deserves more notoriety in today's world. Second, the environment for me as a naval intelligence officer working in the US Embassy as assistant naval attaché for three years was nothing short of outstanding. Lastly, I wanted to touch on some possible misconceptions about embassies, diplomatic life, and military attaché work.

Several individuals who read my manuscript prior to publication commented that it did not read like the spy-thriller novel they anticipated; it was more of a non-fiction series of personal events. True. The storyline for the most part is authentic and based largely on reality though names were changed, and some characters and situations made full use of literary license. I also resisted adding high-speed car chases, plastic explosives to blow up everything in sight, and a brainy hero with endless ammunition in his pistol's magazine, etc., as do some fanciful novels in bookstores today. My story is close to what it was like to be the assistant US naval attaché in Singapore, 1976-1979.

My cameraman/photographer son, Michael, created the book cover, and my wife, Jean, endured endless questions from me as well as providing sanguine advice. I hope the overall result provides you with a few enjoyable hours enmeshed in the adventure.

TC

1

A bottle-a-day addiction to gin had turned Constance Diamond into nothing short of a besotted bitch. Without provocation she would telephone her husband, Steve, at the US Embassy in Singapore to initiate the argument du jour, slurred and indecipherable, as if he did not already have enough weighing on his mind.

The infighting had an effect on the Diamonds' normally submissive household staff as well. The shy but toiling Malaysian amah, the scrawny turmeric-infused Indian cook, and the saluting pith-helmeted gardener of mixed lineage, innocent victims all, found themselves caught in the demeaning crossfire. Finally, to avoid the endless berating and barrage of expletives they upped and left in unison one day without as much as a final goodbye or the collection of their well-deserved wages.

Diamond tried to control his anger while considering all options. He seldom spoke to Constance aside from an offhand remark about her disheveled appearance, the messy household, or his indigestion from a snack she sometimes left on the kitchen counter.

It was not an exaggeration to say it had been a particularly bad Friday at the office for Diamond. There were more than the usual number of complaints from his supervisor and run-ins with co-workers. He arrived home late and full of angst; there was no exchange of greetings.

Constance slid a plate of something the length of the dining table. "Try this, Baby, I think you'll love it. Go ahead, try it, you'll see."

Up close, the offering looked and smelled like cat food and

it set him off. "Get this shit out of here!"

She responded by sweeping everything into his lap. He lashed out—she swung back. He sprang to his feet infuriated. A wildly arcing butcher knife carved thin air as it whooshed by him. He counterattacked and caught her squarely on the temple with a powerful punch. She bounced off the stove and crumpled to the floor. Adrenalin pumping, he hovered above her intolerable stillness. Turning her over he placed one foot on her throat the other on her chest and found unsteady balance like a high wire acrobat. Mere seconds passed before he cut loose, leaping and stomping in frenzy.

"See, I told you, I told you. I told you to shape up but you never listened. You tried so hard to destroy me, but it didn't work, did it? I told you to shape up, but you ran your mouth off, you never shut up." he screamed from a trapdoor blown open then slammed shut deep inside his warped mind. Pushing down one conclusive time in triumph, blood gurgling from her now terribly silent mouth, he shrieked again, "You tried so hard to destroy me, yes you did. Get up you little piss-ant. You had it coming, you're not listening!"

Still panting with rage, he grabbed her heels and dragged her lifeless body to the back porch, booting the inquisitive cat aside as it tried to rub against his leg. The telephone began to ring. It seemed to grow louder and louder like a screaming air raid klaxon, but single-mindedly he retrieved a hacksaw, hammer, duct tape and pliers from his toolbox, a bucket and sponge, and a knife from a pantry drawer. Humming the Seven Dwarfs' song, "Heigh-ho, Heigh-ho," he stripped naked, grabbed a beer from the refrigerator, and began.

The puzzled feline repositioned nearby, watching wide-eyed, tail twitching, mute witness to the surreal madness. Fantastic hallucinations flashed through Diamond's mind. He saw Constance's severed hands grappling with feisty-finned bottom feeders and he the ever circling, zebra-striped, underwater referee, which forced a twitchy smile onto his cheek.

Out of the corner of his eye, lights tracked across the wall. *Who in the hell?* It looked like headlights from an automobile pulling into the driveway, but he was not expecting visitors. On hands and knees, he scurried roach-like into the living room, pulled the curtain aside for a peek, and saw a car backing out into the street. *Just some idiot turning around.*

"Open wide for Stevie-poooooh," he mocked in falsetto as if dispensing a spoon of cereal to an infant. Extracting her teeth with the pliers was easy, twist-twist-pull "one", twist-twist-pull "two—three—four" and so on he counted aloud as he dropped each one precisely into an empty coffee cup. The molars were more of a challenge, but that was when the hammer came into play. With the thud of each sadistic blow and brutal levering with the claw end her head flopped and twisted, her jawbone splintered and cracked, blood splattered everywhere, across his face, upon his lips, the bludgeon nearly slipping from his grip.

"Up, up you go, head down, down, come on now you can do it, don't worry about your hair." Pushing and pushing, grunting and shoving, bending and twisting her legs could not drive her in deep enough to close the freezer's lid. Furiously hurling a bag of ice, T-bone steaks, containers of ice cream, and packages of vegetables over his shoulder he tried again. This time she folded bottom-up deep inside the frosty hideaway. The dial was cranked to coldest. He summarily closed the top, hopped upon it, and sat savoring the last swigs of his beer, eyes shut, shaking as though rabid, tinctured sweat showering down.

The panorama was scattered food, broken dishes, and furniture strewn along a trail of gory footprints. The porch looked like a pointillist canvas of some neo-Impressionist artist, splatter patterns and intensities of tiny crimson dabs were everywhere, ceiling, walls, and floor. A graphic snapshot of the fatal relationship was a single red rivulet, which traversed across and down the freezer's front to its drip-by-drip ending. It would take days to clean the place. But Diamond was pleased to see his furry little four-legged friend had already pitched-in and not surprisingly his headache was gone ... for now, so it was time to find a spoon and cool off with some ice cream before it completely melted.

2

Two months later and over 9,000 miles from Singapore in Washington, D.C., it was a routine end of the week Friday afternoon. Throngs of federal workers, defense contractors, and other employees hustled to conclude business, close files and offices, and head home to the Maryland and Virginia suburbs or catch flights from area airports before traffic got too backed up on the I-495 beltway.

US Navy Lieutenant Commander Dalton Kane was a solitary exception. He sat alone in Defense Intelligence Agency (DIA) office spaces quietly scanning lines of data in a stack of computer printouts and scribbling occasional notes. It was June 18, 1976, his last day before departing with official orders to the Republic of Singapore on a three-year assignment as assistant naval attaché.

Kane was not yet well known throughout the naval intelligence community. None-the-less, he was a rising star having been promoted early to Lieutenant Commander for outstanding duty onboard an aircraft carrier during the Vietnam War. An avid reader and student of military history, his analytical prowess was also a direct consequence of an uncanny memory for details. He seemed particularly adept at analyzing volumes of data and then postulating outcomes and conclusions, which seemed to have a higher than normal probability of coming true. He was also good at "reading" people, and he would find out how valuable those subtle nuances of non-verbal communications were in his new assignment. On a personal level he was friendly, but guarded. Only his parents knew about the tragic loss of his fiancé in an automobile accident on the day of his graduation from college and the lingering effect it still seemed to have on him.

US Army Lieutenant Colonel Jerry Doyle, Kane's Defense Attaché School section leader entered the room. "Dalton, I'm glad you're still here. I just took a call on the secure line from a Janis Crowell at CIA. She wants to talk to you tomorrow at Langley. She left her callback number and wants to know your availability as soon as possible."

"Who? Janis who?" Kane didn't know anyone by that name and a meeting this late would be difficult since he was less than 24 hours from catching his flight and he still had last minute packing and several errands to run. Puzzled, he inquired if Doyle had any inkling what this was all about.

"I don't know and she wouldn't say. I tried to elicit more information, but she was less than forthcoming with details. She specifically asked for you, though, and she knows you're leaving tomorrow. She said the meeting wouldn't take long. She offered to have you picked up at 8:00 AM at your motel, and then deliver you to the airport in time for your flight. Look, if you're too tied up here, I can pass your reply back to her."

The call from a mystery woman proposing an unspecified last-minute meeting at CIA headquarters piqued Kane's interest and he answered contemplatively. "Uh, yes, that would be helpful. Please tell her I'll be waiting at the Best Western in Alexandria with my luggage, and I accept the offer of a lift to Dulles airport afterwards."

3

Earlier in his career, Kane had participated in periodic forums on naval topics at CIA headquarters, so he was familiar with a few of the office spaces there. However, the next morning he was escorted along polished corridors in an unfamiliar wing, stopping at a shaft of light from a partially opened doorway, the adjacent sign lit in bold red letters reading "Top Secret Briefing in Progress."

Inside the small conference room, a hushed conversation halted. The three people present, two CIA and one FBI, were introduced, coffee and donuts offered, the door closed and locked. Crowell, a robust woman in a navy-blue suit highlighted with a gold cartouche pendant had a distinctive alto-pitched voice, a firm grip, and glasses that did not obscure dark semi-circles of fatigue under her eyes.

They sat under a halo of lights at a conference table, three facing one. "Before we press on, I want you to understand you can halt these proceedings if at any time you are troubled with what I am about to discuss with you. All you need to do is stop me, sign a non-disclosure agreement and another form I have in here, and you can be on your way with no hard feelings. I assume that's alright with you Lieutenant Commander Kane?"

"Yes, of course, that's fine."

"And feel free to ask questions at any time. Also, my apologies again for the extremely short notice. So let me get straight to the point. There appears to be a serious problem at our embassy in Singapore. That's why I invited you here, to determine if you would be willing to assist us in a counter-espionage matter of some importance. Now I know this would be new to you; however, timing is everything and we have reason to believe you are the right person for this. If you agree you'll need a polygraph even though I see you had one not long ago and that formality could be taken care of immediately following this discussion."

A synaptic *"wow"* ricocheted through Kane's brain and he impulsively answered in the affirmative, "Absolutely, I'd like to help."

"Good," Crowell replied without flourish as if his answer had been anticipated.

However, Kane knew this was beyond the normal scope of US military attaché duties. To clear up the point he inquired if DIA and Navy had already approved the CIA's tasking of him.

"No, approval has not and will not be requested due to the sensitivity of the operation. No one else will be briefed into the effort at least for the time being. Only a small group of people, including those present, has the need to know. There is precedent for your participation though and I have the pertinent references available for your perusal should you wish to review them later."

She continued. "In the last few months our NSA and the UK's GCHQ have collected some intriguing bits and pieces of communications intelligence from the Russians. A portion of this cache can be categorized as operator error, some indiscretion and mistakes with hardware and materials and such. Subsequent in-depth analysis has revealed among other things oblique reference to an entity alluded to as "Bernard" and this Bernard's activities at an unidentified location. At first, we weren't sure whether this was a real person, a pseudonym for a real person, or a cover name for an organization or operation, so we began down multiple paths, ever wary of deception. Then there was some timely collateral information we believe was inadvertently disclosed by a Russian representative at a UN International Law of the Sea Convention conference in Brussels. These seemingly disparate elements began to coalesce and finally came together. Earlier this month British MI-5 forwarded a tantalizing new piece of the puzzle, a vital geographic data point provided by a Russian defector. As a result, a hypothesis has emerged suggesting a clandestine source, a mole within our embassy in Singapore, someone working for one of the Soviet Union's intelligence services, the KGB."

Then, as if the implication of her point might somehow have escaped him, she reached again for her coffee cup, raised an eyebrow, and nonchalantly re-stated it. "It's quite possible you'll be shaking hands and chatting with this person, this spy, whoever it is, soon after your arrival there."

Kane listened with rapt attention as Crowell went on. "Our Singapore Chief of Station, Dirk Eggleston, is already on the case and with your presence there will be just the two of you engaged on site for now. No one else, not Ambassador Adele Lipka nor your naval attaché boss, Captain James Grusk, or anyone else in the embassy has knowledge of our effort. We're trying not to arouse suspicion from the other side so everything must appear business as usual, status quo. It's one of the reasons we selected you. The timing of your official orders to the embassy was perfect, and your outstanding record as an intelligence officer as well as your performance in the attaché course a definite plus. More assets may be added to the embassy staff in the future as needed, but for now the burden is on Eggleston's shoulders, and in a matter of hours yours to a slightly lesser extent as well."

"Also, as you are probably aware, the military attachés and the other DoD employees move in different social circles than do State Department personnel. Plus, you have different functional duties and are relatively isolated on a separate floor of the embassy. Therefore, Eggleston doesn't have cover for access to the attaché office on a continuing basis. But don't misunderstand. I'm not saying this Bernard is in the attaché office, although some of our analysts believe he is. What I am saying is we think you will be in the best position to find out whether he's there or not."

The coffee relieved Kane's dry mouth and enabled another question. "I believe Bernard is a masculine name of French origin. Is there any relevance to that?"

"No, probably not, but we're confident it is an alias. There's no one by that name, first, last, or even a solitary 'Bernie' working at the embassy right now. And as to the name being French, well, it leads nowhere, the name probably selected at random as is the normal case, and it wouldn't be unusual to see other aliases as we move forward. And while the KGB may be referring to this individual as Bernard, Bernard himself or herself could be using some other alias."

"Herself?"

"That's right, the gender of the name may not accurately represent the gender of the actual person. For now, our profilers are divided. Most feel Bernard's male, probably college educated, and well positioned in the embassy. In actuality though, he could be almost anyone there and at this early stage of the investigation virtually everyone is under suspicion, some obviously more so than others are.

"Could he have accomplices in the embassy?"

"Good question. It's a possibility, but at present we have no evidence."

"How long do you think he's been at work?"

"That's difficult to say," Crowell answered while motioning for the coffee, "the time line being little more than conjecture at this point and each case is different. But if you stand back and look at what we have, the suggestion is not long, if we're lucky."

"You said virtually everyone is under suspicion, some more so than others, so who in particular is under closer scrutiny?"

"There's no evidence of merit pointing to any specific individual, but it's fair to say right now we're focused more on Americans based on the nexus of information, more so than the lower occupational level Singaporean employees. And just because you're relieving Lieutenant Commander Morrison and Captain Grusk will be retiring from the naval service in another six months or so doesn't diminish either of them as suspects. Morrison is returning to another DIA assignment in Washington and Grusk, an aviator with an up to date background investigation, could go to work almost anywhere with some US aerospace contractor on a classified program. Now with that being said, Eggleston may have a new lead changing everything by the time you land there. I want to add we don't know whether Bernard is someone who woke up one morning in a mid-life crisis and decided to become a traitor, or at the other extreme it portends of an orchestrated recruitment-in-place penetration by the Russians. Either way great harm can be done."

Crowell resumed, trying to keep within the allotted time. "I think you'll like working with Dirk Eggleston, or 'Eggs' as some of his friends call him. He has the background and expertise to help conclude this the way we'd like to and you might also be interested in knowing he's quite the sportsman and a crack shot with a variety of weapons including a blowgun." She must have noticed the incredulous look on Kane's face because she imme-diately elaborated. "Obviously he doesn't carry one now, but the skill was picked up in the jungles of Malaysia some years ago I believe."

After another fast-paced thirty minutes of questions and answers, Crowell checked her watch and Kane took the cue. "I wish we did have a more time, but I think you've answered all my questions except for the endgame. How do you envision this playing out?"

"Assuming probable cause is established an arrest warrant would be issued for violations of Title 18 United States Code, the sections on Conspiracy to Commit Espionage, Transmitting National Defense Information, and perhaps other sections, Acts, and Executive Orders depending on what we have. And since there is an extradition treaty in place with Singapore it could be relatively simple, arrest and processing according to the treaty and delivery of Bernard back here to the states for trial. That's the simplest, best case scenario for us."

Crowell placed several typed sheets of paper on the table. "You'll need to read and sign these. Look them over carefully because you can't take any copies with you. This one cites the legal basis and authority to conduct the operation and the sec-ond one spells out our organizational relationships, which you asked about and shouldn't find troublesome. The last one relates to security and classification. We'll alert Eggleston right away. He'll obviously have much more to pass along once you get your feet on the ground. And there's just one more thing I must mention before we finish here."

"What's that?"

"I don't anticipate this will get dirty. I hope not, but you never know. Occasionally things can go awry because cunning people are often unpredictable. Therefore, I can't rule out the possibility of heightened personal danger for you as a direct participant."

"I understand there's risk. I'm okay with it."

Crowell studied Kane's face for a silent moment weighing her ultimate decision. Then she nodded almost imperceptibly, "We can proceed to the polygraph whenever you're ready."

Kane reviewed the documentation and after his successful polygraph and the application of his signature to more forms he met briefly with Crowell again. She pumped his arm vigorously, wished him a safe flight and concluded with, "Good hunting, Lieutenant Commander Kane, I'm counting on you. We'll be in touch."

Later, while waiting in the airport terminal to board his flight to Singapore, reality set in and Kane wondered half-daringly, half-apprehensively just what entanglement his patriotic fervor might have drawn him into.

4

What Janis Crowell left purposely unmentioned while briefing Kane was that Bernard's existence also represented an opportunity for Dirk Eggleston to resurrect what remained of a tarnished CIA career. A few like Crowell viewed the Angola blemish on his otherwise exemplary record as a single instance of bad judgment, and it was a result of her effort on his behalf and an eleventh-hour reprieve at the highest levels of the Agency that his career resuscitated. Supporters hoped he could get back on track with some productive years at a small post like Singapore. However, with a spy now apparently thrust into his lap the critical spotlight shown back on the CIA's Singapore chief of station, his abilities and fallibilities.

Eggleston was a wily veteran with guts, a man of action, and the type of individual you expect and need in a line of work like his. Fit and trim in his mid-forties he could also turn on the wit and charm if he had reason to do so. Quite a few of the embassy staff had endeared themselves to him because he seemed to relish being a buffer to the embassy's imperious and narcissistic number-two man, Deputy Chief of Mission (DCM), Jonathon Bass, known by some as "FMB" (Field Marshall Bass) behind his back.

Fluorescent lights were on the earliest and off the latest in Eggleston's office. Frequently before sunup he was on long distance calls, screening and approving certain classified reports drafted by his staff, or reading and highlighting portions of intelligence message traffic received overnight. If you weren't on his calendar your only chance of catching him was the few minutes in between a private get together with the ambassadress and when he returned to his office to check-in before heading out again to some other scheduled event. At other times, he was so occupied he had breakfast and sometimes lunch from the embassy's cafeteria delivered to his office. Alternatively, he exited into the city to be sequestered with Singapore government officials for hours on end.

In the evening, he attended the most important parties on the diplomatic circuit, sojourned to one of the other US embassies in the region, or made the requisite periodic trip back to Langley and Washington. But every now and then he would literally disappear, no published itinerary or return date, his secretary mum, seemingly unconcerned, and then he'd re-surface a day or two later and no one ever asked questions.

One could tell the bullet that ripped a hole through his thigh and nearly took his life during covert operations supporting UNITA rebels during the Angolan Civil War in Africa in 1975 still bothered him. Even though he managed to battle back through an arduous physical rehabilitation and a tough review board to resume his work, the undertone from a few of his more vocal detractors persisted: The hit man was a lousy marksman, the gun sight should have been leveled on Eggleston's balls.

Water cooler scuttlebutt was accurate in that his wounds were suffered during a midnight bedding of a foreign female agent killed in the incident, and the occurrence also contributing to his ongoing second divorce, rumored nastier than the first one. The official account of the attack stated that after he and his *femme de nuit* were struck through the window of his hotel room with multiple gunshots he recovered just long enough to grab his customized Colt model 1911 pistol from the nightstand as he crashed to the floor and rolled to the window. There he unleashed rapid fire, a full magazine of bullets in the direction of the hit-and-run assailant before losing consciousness and nearly bleeding out.

Moments after the din of gunfire jolted the dozing contract security guards to their feet, they found empty cartridge cases, a dropped AK-47 assault rifle, a fresh blood trail leading into the alley, and a warm human corpse succumbed by two instances of .45 caliber torso ventilation. Eggleston's deadly display of marksmanship under duress was even more note-worthy because he returned fire left-handed, his more dexter-ous right hand having been nicked in the initial spray of AK-47 lead. As was normally the case the hit man lacked identification, but was almost certainly associated with the socialist Popular Movement for the Liberation of Angola (MPLA), or if not them, some other proxy for the Russians or Cubans.

Late in the afternoon at the embassy in Singapore Eggleston signed off the last piece of correspondence destined for the next outgoing diplomatic pouch to Washington, delivered the com-pleted paperwork back to his secretary with his compliments and dismissed her for the day.

Returning to the privacy of his office he opened a file cabi-net drawer, removed a crystal cocktail glass and a handful of ice from a bucket, broke the seal on a new bottle of Johnny Walker Black Label, and poured. Sitting at his desk and tilting back in his chair with his feet propped up, he squinted at the calendar, checked his watch, and loosened his tie. Refocusing through the window at the city lights and darkening sky he took a gulp, and another. Thoughts began to stream: *His ruinous divorce; the spy, Bernard; the Soviet Embassy's KGB resident, Yuri Lubachev, that crafty bastard; the rogues' gallery of embassy spy suspects; and the imminent arrival of Lieutenant Commander Dalton Kane.*

5

From birth Steve Diamond was unwanted, neglected, and abused. He never knew his father. His mother, Tina, purchased bargain-basement groceries and rented cheap rooms with welfare checks and paltry sums received from a posse of sordid-looking johns. Much of Diamond's adolescence revolved around conflict with rival street gangs and engaging in petty crime. Returning home late to find a place to sleep he often heard brutish sounds of sexual pleasure reverberating through the walls, a slap, a beer bottle sent smashing, his mother's muffled voice silenced with a threat, and a protracted crescendo of bedsprings.

School provided a measure of order and discipline, a needed sanctuary. Young Diamond stayed late and alone as long as the teachers would permit, immersed in the fantasy of words and images in the books. Eventually he read almost everything in the school's library and against the heavy odds of a troubled life his regimen slowly transformed into scholastic achievement. But controlling an enormous range of emotion was never-ending. He could reverse in seconds from the heights of euphoria to the depths of unhappiness and anger, and without supervision he revealed a lack of conscience and respect, instigating arguments and fighting for no apparent reason. If not receiving accolades for another "A" he was often on detention. In high school his principal once referred to him as a "villain savant" whose escapades would someday land him in jail or worse. Then again, they understood the root of his problems and he was gifted with a high I.Q. So, with the help of teachers who went out of their way to assist him, he received a scholarship to a small college and stayed out of serious trouble there, or more likely just never was caught, and was well on his way to receiving a bachelor's degree with honors, as improbable as that may seem based on his beginnings.

Maturing early to slightly over six feet tall with broad shoulders, wavy black hair, penetrating brown eyes, squared jaw, and dimpled chin, Diamond was ruggedly handsome and he knew it.

It was pure luck he met the latest love of his life. His girlfriend at the time had found another roommate, Constance Baron, and moved into a classy apartment in a trendy area of the city. Diamond learned Daddy was a wealthy commercial real estate developer in the Phoenix, Arizona area who doted on his little girl, a plain Jane physically, but adorned with designer clothes and accessories and who spent weekends on ski trips in a new Corvette. The situation became more intriguing with each meeting and Diamond calculated Constance Baron would do very nicely, very nicely indeed.

Within a month he orchestrated an amicable breakup with his girlfriend and carefully avoided both young women for a time thereafter. However, he continued to monitor the movements of his new darling from a safe distance and when late spring thawed the slopes, he made his move. He conveniently ran into Constance at a campus bookstore and invited her for coffee, where he cautiously launched a well-planned courtship resulting in their engagement only two months later.

Deeply in love, Constance urged Diamond to arrange for her to meet his mother, Tina, though his stomach lurched at the thought. But when he realized he could delay it no longer he reluctantly sent Tina some money with instructions to spend it on a new dress, shoes, manicure, and whatever remained to pay for transportation to the chosen restaurant.

Tina arrived at the appointed time and place, her thinning grey hair dyed jet-black, a polyester print dress stretched like a drumhead over her boney frame, lipstick askew, and the scent of Old Spice aftershave in the air. After spending an inordinate amount of time in the ladies' restroom she returned to initiate a wacky monologue on her bladder infection and the evening went quickly downhill from there. But with Constance's overindulgence in martinis, becoming totally blitzed and passing out face first on her steak, she would not remember much about that first encounter with her soon to be mother-in-law.

Following graduation from college, an extravagant Scottsdale, Arizona wedding without Tina, and a Mediterranean honeymoon on Daddy, Diamond ,was successful testing for and securing employment at the US State Department in the Foreign Service. The young couple settled into Washington, D.C.-area life, but tension reigned as they made new adjustments and unpleasant discoveries in each other. Constance learned her husband was subject to sudden bouts of unreachable depths of depression and frequently muttered furiously over some perceived injustice. During these "spells" as she came to view them, and sometimes after brief, but terrifying nightmares he would scream, wakeup, and look at her with a blank stare as though she were not there.

Constance drank heavily when stressed, became belligerent, and regularly humiliated her husband in public. She was also superficial and self-absorbed, incapable of functioning without servants, and insatiably extravagant. Luckily, for both, Daddy's hefty stipend continued and as far as Diamond was concerned it was enough to make the marriage work for him.

6

Tina loomed on the periphery. Aware her son had "married up" she badgered him for money as soon as he returned from the honeymoon and what started out as rent and grocery assistance soon encompassed expectations of card room and off-track debt subsidies. She repeatedly telephoned him at work demanding cash to repay her neighbors for God knows what. Quietly closing his office door Diamond cupped his hand around the mouthpiece and paced back and forth at the end of the cord, emphatically reiterating that Constance was still away and he had no extra money, no payday for another week. Then, as Tina's tone became shriller he promptly hung up. Moments later, telling the secretary he was not feeling well, he left the office and spent the remainder of the afternoon checking out waitresses at a nearby coffee shop.

The next day after work and a stop by the dry cleaners to pick up his laundry he headed home and that's when he saw her, his mother, sitting splayfooted, staring off into space, a grocery bag full of personal effects at her side on one of the benches flanking the entrance to the exclusive apartment building. *Geez, she must have ridden in on the Greyhound bus!*

Smiling through clenched teeth he approached and bent to kiss her cheek, trying not to speculate how long it had been since she bathed. She frowned and launched into a rant. Cutting her off, he said, "What we need is a little wine and pastitsio." The old gargoyle lit up, as he knew she would, and so he solicitously patted her hand and slipped his arm around her shoulder to help her to her feet.

Halfway to Baltimore he turned into a shopping center and made a quick stop at a liquor store before crossing the parking lot to a Greek cafe where they enjoyed fragrant and familiar dishes. He was able to distract Tina enough to slip slugs of vodka into her retsina. He would need extra shots himself if his credit card maxed-out; it did not.

Tina was nodding off as they reached her block of shabby houses. He helped her inside and offered to stay until she fell asleep. His head ached as he looked around the depressing scene, a scene he was accustomed to, a sight he had been careful never to let Constance see. In the malodorous kitchen a bare incandescent light bulb illuminated a dripping faucet and clogged sink, countertops piled high with dirty dishes, countless pill bottles, a webbed bag of molding oranges, and a foraging legion of ants. In the living room, a sagging couch shrouded with stained pillowcases and *Inquirer* magazines renewed more unpleasant recollections of times past. A rabbit ears antenna adorned with aluminum foil strips for enhanced reception was tipped-over atop the small TV set. He opened a window for some much-needed ventilation and while standing there in a flood of mawkish memories he heard shuddering sounds of sleep coming from Tina's bedroom.

Working quickly in the darkness back at his car he took off his blazer, removed the plastic sheath covering a cleaned shirt, wadded it up, and stuck it in his pocket along with the pint of vodka. Quietly re-entering the house he listened, the slumbering grunting and snorting, her gasping breath, a welcome sound. He covered a pillow with the plastic, tiptoed into the bedroom, then ever so carefully onto the bed, straddling her, using his knees to pin her arms to her sides, and pressing the pillow tightly over her face until he finally felt her relax. She hardly struggled; it was over in less time than he anticipated. He spat on his handkerchief, wiped down the opened liquor bottle, pressed her fingers around it, and let it drop to the floor. Then removing the plastic bag, he replaced the pillow on the couch and let himself out. There was no remorse.

The next day he placed a call to Arizona and had a long conversation with Constance, reconciling most of their differences at least for the time being. She finally gave in when he begged forgiveness, telling her it was impossible for him to get along without her by his side, in a way true.

7

Diamond poured fresh coffee in the kitchen. Almost a week and apparently no one had found his mother's body. Now if he could just control Constance. But he learned a painful lesson while she was gone. He could not live as he wished without her and her father's generosity and so he would have to walk a fine line.

Constance was at the breakfast table concentrating on the morning newspaper's comic section and nibbling on peanut butter and jelly toast. The telephone rang and Diamond crossed the room quickly to reach it first. Constance watched as he listened and almost immediately he turned pale, his knees buckled, and he pitched forward to the floor. Constance leapt from her chair and pried the telephone from his fingers.

"Who is it?" she asked.

"It's me" the voice roared, "What happened to my Stevie-pooh?"

"Tina, let me call you back in a minute, he—he's not feeling well!"

Constance turned him over, lifted his head, and looked into glazed eyes. Listening to his heart and feeling for a pulse she dialed "O" and asked the operator to please send an ambulance right away. The emergency crew arrived, asked a few questions, gave her directions to the hospital, and wheeled him out. She ran to the bedroom for her purse and car keys and then remembered his mother. She put the telephone to her ear and dialed, "Tina, are you okay?"

"Hell, I don't know...went to bed Tuesday and didn't wake 'till Thursday. Soiled my bed, splittin' headache, feelin' shaky, took a cab to the hospital, musta drank too much, gave me buncha tests, lotta pills, and stuck me. Said I musta had a stroke or somethin'. Anyways, I'm home now, feelin' better, and I need money cuz I gotta buy food and stuff."

"Don't worry, I'll send some right away and try to rest. Let me know if you need someone to stay with you for awhile."

Awake and talkative when Constance entered the hospital room, Diamond was adamant his medical records were not to be shared with the State Department and the doctors replied it would probably not be necessary at the present. In a brief conference, Constance was informed her husband needed a complete workup and must keep the current levels of medication in his system until this was accomplished. Discharged the next day, Diamond left with several bottles of pills and an appointment for a return visit in two weeks. There was no reaction or comment, only a blank stare when Constance told him his mother was apparently recovering from a mild stroke.

8

Diamond performed only marginally satisfactory at best at the State Department even during training; he was definitely not a team player. He did excel on one small research project, but failed to achieve the recognition he thought he deserved. Well into his second year without any encouraging signs of a promotion, seething anger and paranoia were building over perceived injustices. Several of his contemporaries were on the fast track to the next higher pay grade, although he knew he was much better than that clique of Ivy League "asskissers" as he called them directly to their faces.

Aware an overseas posting was an avenue out of Washington, Diamond watched for openings and in January 1976 he bid on an embassy assignment in distant Singapore. Surprisingly, or perhaps not, he secured the new job with the help of behind-the-scenes officials who wished to see a dogged personnel problem disappear. The couple passed the orientation and suitability screening for the overseas post, packed up, and left.

Predictably, a few weeks after their arrival in Singapore as the novelty of the new job and environment began to wear off the couple's spats returned and the marriage continued to spiral out of control. The final countdown began at a birthday party gathering of several of Diamond's office mates. In one group, wives were talking about a nest of poisonous snakes found under a neighbor's back steps. While polishing-off her third alcoholic beverage, Constance interjected she had encountered a large rat in their garage and if her husband, she laughed, could get up the courage she wished he would kill it too.

Standing nearby, Diamond smiled awkwardly, shrugged

his shoulders, and finished his beer. Then as the conversation turned to other topics and the group migrated toward the buffet table, Diamond took Constance by the arm and marched her to the exit with hardly a notice from the other celebrants.

"Hurting me you fffucking ape," she protested.

"Inebriated again, everyone's noticed. You smell like you bathed in Tanqueray."

"Fffuck offff" she slurred, wrenching her arm free, and launching skyward what remained of her drink as they stepped outside.

In the downpour, he pushed her into the car and threatened her to remain there. Then into the darkness they sped away. The deluge overpowered frantic wipers and fogged windows further diminished visibility as jolting fusillades of thunder and lightning surged to the ground. Sodden tropical foliage slapped and swiped the vehicle, losing its way then overcorrecting across the centerline, just missing a sudden flare of headlights from the opposite direction. Braced over the wheel Diamond strained to see ahead while fending off the next attack. Constance lurched menacingly closer, her foot vying for the accelerator, her fists pummeling in a drunken rage.

9

Trapped in tourist class for most of a day on a packed airliner with only the briefest refueling stop is punishment. Regardless of how many times Kane snacked, imbibed alcohol, fiddled with the air vent, stretched legs, read books and magazines, chatted with flight attendants, re-hydrated, completed crossword puzzles, tried to sleep, used the toilet, or watched another B-grade movie and contemplated over and over the spy, Bernard, the flight remained endless discomfort. A persistent irritant was the large fellow seated directly behind him who seemed to be on a mission to snore his way across the entire expanse of the Pacific Ocean and thus into the Guinness Book of Records.

The PANAM 747 finally touched down at Singapore's Changi International Airport close to 10:30 PM. Setting foot in the main terminal Kane proceeded to follow the signage for foreign arrivals. Most of the terminal's shops and restaurants had closed for the day. Passing a barbershop he wondered if it was the infamous one of a few years earlier where unwelcome, long-haired hippies were given the option of paying for a government regulation buzz-cut permitting them to stay for a short visit or, if choosing to remaining unshorn, re-boarding the next plane out of the country.

The gauntlet of checkpoints including immigration proved no challenge for his black diplomatic passport and he breezed on through.

The baggage carousel shuddered to life moments after his arrival in the claim area. He glanced back and forth between the cascading luggage and the dozens of faces jostling for position on the other side of the plate glass barrier wall for Lieutenant Commander Charlie Morrison, the officer he was relieving. He spotted Morrison in the background, a head taller than anyone else, and the only African-American present. A few minutes later after a wave through Customs with two suitcases in tow and a briefcase tucked under his arm, they met.

"Wow, Charlie, you didn't have to turn up the heat for me," Kane joked as they shook hands and Morrison relieved him of a suitcase.

"Well, Dalton, it's pretty much like this all the time. The humidity makes it seem hotter than it really is, but you'll get used to it. So how was your flight?"

"It seemed like forever."

They headed to the parking lot and Morrison continued. "You'll have to pardon the cliché, but I have some good news, some bad news, and some interesting news. The good news, besides you being here, is we got a call yesterday your household goods shipment arrived and your change of address must be working because you've already received a mound of mail on your desk. The bad news is my mother is not doing so well back in Kansas City. She was hospitalized last week with a stroke and complications, so I've had my orders modified to leave on Saturday."

"I'm sorry to hear about your mother," Kane responded with genuine concern while another part of him processed first impressions of Charlie Morrison: The eye contact; the conviction in his voice; his grip; and his casual confidence.

"Thanks for your concern, but unfortunately it means we have only two days of turnover instead of the two weeks I had planned for. Sorry about that, but I'm sure the rest of the crew will bring you up to speed on anything I don't cover. The interesting news is a Russian we believe to be KGB who I spotted earlier in the main terminal. You'll see the KGB resident, Yuri Lubachev, out and about occasionally, but rarely this guy or for that matter any of the other KGB minions."

Minutes later they were on the freeway headed toward the city. "I've put you up in a small hotel, the Rajah Brooke; it's walking distance, about four blocks to the embassy. It's named after a butterfly labeled in honor of Sir James Brooke, the first Rajah of Sarawak."

"*Trogonoptera brookiana*" Kane replied.

"What?"

"That butterfly, they're huge and beautiful. I saw one once in a collection."

"Oh, well, anyway, the place is clean, your temporary living allowance covers the cost and the Ministry of Defence has vetted it for us. You'll be fine, but there are many other good choices around the city if you want to make a change. Also, I heard one of the embassy's houses, the smallest one, is being vacated, so if they don't tear it down to build a larger one and if you happen to get a call from Davidson Peeler, the embassy's General Services Officer (GSO), offering it to you definitely give it some consideration."

They discussed the rigors of the compressed turnover schedule, embassy and attaché office personnel, Singapore Ministry of Defence contacts, office boat operations, and enjoying Singapore in general. "It's great" Morrison said. "There's something different happening every day and with almost every telephone call, and a regular boat ride around the harbor if nothing else is a breath of fresh air."

"By the way" he continued, pointing to a dent clearly visible on the hood of the attaché office sedan, "don't park near any coconut trees, especially during the monsoon seasons."

Morrison kept checking the rearview mirror and changed speed and lanes unnecessarily several times, which alerted Kane of a possible problem. "Is someone tailing us?"

"I'm not sure. There's a car behind us keeping pace. It's been there since the parking lot. Who knows, it's probably someone like us, picked up a visitor, and now they're inbound to the city. When you're on an island only 26 miles long by about 14 miles wide serendipitous things happen from time to time."

"Okay, he's going to pass, take a look." As the large dark sedan pulled even with them it swerved unexpectedly and struck their vehicle with a glancing blow before accelerating away. "Shit! He sideswiped me!" Morrison yelled above the squealing tires as he wrestled the steering wheel to regain control. They kept their eyes on the sedan's fading taillights as long as they could, hoping it might get snarled in heavier traffic near the city and they could catch up, but it disappeared into the night.

"That's a fine welcome," Morrison said disbelievingly. "I thought it would be an uneventful trip, but now it may require an incident report. We'll see what Captain Grusk has to say. I saw two people in front. What did you see?"

"Two in front and possibly a third one in the rear. It looked like a Russian Zil, big and boxy, maybe a limo, but I couldn't be sure. It happened so fast I didn't get the license number, but I don't think the plate was the larger dimension of a diplomatic license plate," Kane added.

"No way that was an accident, no way," Morrison muttered.

They arrived at the hotel with the black and green butterfly mosaic over its entrance a few minutes after midnight. An alert porter pushed a luggage dolly curbside before they could get the car doors opened, "Lieutenant Commander Kane?"

"That's me."

"A very good morning to you, sir, and welcome to the Rajah Brooke Hotel. Is your luggage in the boot?"

They took a moment to check the dent and scrapes on the door and fender and the missing mirror while the porter loaded Kane's gear and left for the lobby.

"We've got a lot to cover, but it's late and you look beat. Why don't you get some rest if you can, grab a late bite of breakfast, and come in about 9:00 AM? We should have most of the morning flaps taken care of by then and you and I can get right to work. They take US currency in the restaurant or you can put the meals on your room tab.

"In the morning go two blocks north and two blocks east on Hill Street; the embassy is on the left; you'll see the flag. Have the Marine guard call me from the lobby and I'll come down to get you. No uniform tomorrow, civvies are okay and bring your orders so Warrant Officer Masters can process them. If you happen to get up early and need to stretch your legs you might check out those tailor shops I mentioned over on Coleman Street."

"Will do Charlie and thanks for the lift. I'll see you tomor-row morning."

The room was clean and cool. The walls were decorated with several framed butterfly pairs and a tall pink orchid stood in a vase on a small rosewood desk. A telephone handset sat on a stand next to the bed. Kane unscrewed the telephone's mouth-piece for a quick, suspicious look inside. Then he conducted a close angle scan of the room's walls for any telltale bulge, a possible indication of an implanted listening device or pinhole camera lens. He found none. He fell backwards into bed shortly after 1:00 AM. The ceiling fan was perfect on low speed and within minutes he was asleep.

of the presentation, pausing to launch two perfect smoke rings, the second passing through the first, he handed several pieces of paper across to Kane who immediately recognized the silent duplicity. The first few pages were a 'Who's Who' in the Soviet Embassy, including names, mug shots, and covert action photographs of KGB bigwigs and other suspicious Russians in and around the city.

The last two handwritten pages read, "This is what I need from you" and contained a number of items:

For starters, just be the new attaché. Get acquainted with your office mates over the next few weeks and try to be invited into their homes. Any indications of sudden or unusual affluence or living beyond means?

Any observed tension or stress in your office mates, drug or alcohol problems, sexual abuse, blood pressure medication, chain-smoking, homosexual traits, unexplained absences from work, anything out of the ordinary going on?

Anyone seemingly going out of his or her way to develop your friendship? Any radical, anti-US viewpoints? Anyone quizzing your political beliefs?

Anyone showing unusual interest or skill with cameras or electronic gadgetry?

Who are the bachelors dating, Singaporean girls? Others? Names and addresses. (FYI, your two Army sergeants are bachelors.)

Any on-site documentation of past security violations in your office? If so, what was missing, what happened? I need the results of your classified inventories and classified material destruction reports for the past three years. Any discrepancies? Who were the witnesses and what were the dates of the destruction events? What were the destruction methods and where was the destruction accomplished?

I need annual and sick leave records covering the past 3 years. Who went where and when?

Discretely check the page counter on your copy machine at the close of business and first thing the next morning. FYI, the Marine guard keeps a log of afterhours arrivals and departures. When you return to work the following day, check to see if the combination lock on your vault door is set exactly where it was when you left it the previous day.

Check co-worker desks, files, wastepaper baskets, etc. for anything interesting.

Anyone in your office (besides yourself) speak Russian?

If you develop a "detective's hunch" about something you think we should be pursuing let me know.

I may need your help with the installation of some surveillance equipment.

If you need to talk, call me here on my direct line. The number is in the embassy directory. However, if I don't pick up after three rings, hang up and try again later. Never leave a message related to this operation on this phone and never call my flat about this unless it's a real emergency. There are plenty of reasons for us to get together in the conduct of normal business here in the embassy, so routine contact and periodic conversations are no big deal. As necessary, we can always arrange a special meeting at the water fountain, men's room, etc. If needed, we can rendezvous in the city, but there are surveillance risks there too.

Finally, there's nothing new to add to what was discussed with you by Janis Crowell. My advice: Be active, but be patient and observant. Things can happen when you least expect them to.

Kane finished reading and returned the papers, pointing to several lines, and tapping his wristwatch to ask the unspoken question, how soon do you need it?

Eggleston mouthed a large, but silent "NOW", and then addressed aloud the final graphic concluding in a normal tone of voice with, "Any questions?"

"No sir, I think you covered everything."

"Well then, since the season is rapidly approaching, let's talk NFL football. If there's one thing I miss it's sitting in front of the television on a Sunday with a six-pack of beer and a pepperoni pizza and watching my Bears beat the hell out of somebody."

As he spoke, he handed across a billfold-sized leather case, a lock picking set containing two tension wrenches and five picks.

Kane returned the case with a whisper, "Have one", followed by his louder comment, "They won't take my Packers this year." This prompted an energized debate about college draft picks, off-season trades, and the strengths and weaknesses of both squads. While rattling off quarterback statistics Eggleston inserted the 13-item tasking paper into the shredder. Kane watched it disappear, pulverized into corpuscular bits of unintelligible confetti as Shirley Bassey sang.

17

Back at the attaché office the remainder of the items on Morrison's list were tackled: Personalities on the MINDEF staff and other senior officers and "up and comers" in the Singapore Army, Navy, and Air Force, and a review of the periodic U.S.—Singapore joint exercises in the South China Sea. Finally, there were the personalities in the foreign attaché corps, and the Russian and North Korean intelligence cadres. Neither the Russians nor the North Koreans had military attaches officially accredited to Singapore, but they did have other individuals under diplomatic cover with different job titles who were obviously accomplishing military intelligence-type work.

Kane watched and listened for signs of deception as Morrison spoke about the KGB resident, Yuri Lubachev. Facial decoding and body language were not an exact science, but no "red flags" emerged to raise doubt about Morrison's honesty and integrity. Kane was captivated at hearing more on how bourgeois Lubachev seemed to be, no doubt a façade to go along with his official cover as the Soviet embassy's cultural attaché. Nonetheless, if you saw him speeding across town in his green Fiat convertible, top down, designer sunglasses, ascot fluttering in the breeze, you might mistake him for an Italian movie director. Or, if you saw him at a party with the jewelry, the reptilian leather shoes and silk sport coat, drinking, dancing, and laughing with the women, you assumed he might be a social director from a visiting cruise ship. Kane detected nothing to raise his suspicion of Morrison during the presentation, and the information about Lubachev correlated with that which he had received from Eggleston.

There was not a lot to report on the North Koreans. They had their own small circle of friends, including the Russians, and they only went out in public in pairs or greater numbers for security reasons. Occasionally, a small group would go to the only Korean restaurant in one of the larger hotels. However, they were always fixtures at events hosted by the government of Singapore, such as the National Day celebrations. Two men always showed in the haute couture of Pyongyang: suits and neckties at least 25 years out of style in the West. Each one displayed a large picture of "The Great Leader", Kim IL Sung, on their lapels, and they both stationed themselves in opposite corners of a room facing one another. This was done so #1 could rat on #2, if #2 was seen talking to someone like, God forbid, an American. Stone-faced and braced for some imaginary inspection they said nothing unless addressed, but when it came time to dine, stand back. In tandem they were at or pushed their way in front of ladies at the head of the buffet line, itself speaking volumes about their social ineptitude and sorry political-economic situation.

At 4:45 PM, someone from up front yelled back to the vault to "pick up on line two." It was William Ross, the colorful Aussie warrant officer from the Australian High Commission calling about the possibility of a boat run on Monday morning. Morrison talked and joked with him for a minute and then passed the telephone. Kane had planned an extensive familiarization tour of the harbor, straits, and shipyards on Monday and it would probably extend well into the late afternoon. If the Aussie wanted to come along, fine, but he declined so Kane told him they would probably be going out again on Wednesday and he could join up then.

18

The Saturday morning exodus from the Morrisons' hotel to the airport was uneventful except Jill was a little late with some last minute shopping. But Captain Grusk's driver, Omar, as stoic as ever, navigated safely to the airport on time. After a handshake and a hug, and a distant wave goodbye, the Morrisons vanished in a phalanx of luggage-toting travelers streaming to their international departure gates.

In the car, Omar inquired if Kane was returning to his hotel.

"No, take me to the embassy." Kane wanted to get a feel for the office with no one around and take some initial action on Eggleston's list.

Even though the embassy was closed on weekends there was always work to be done. Five cars were in the employee parking lot and the ambassador's armored limousine was near the front entrance. In the lobby, the Marine guard informed Kane that Sergeant Weber was at work inside the attaché office.

"That must be 100 words per minute," Kane said as he stepped behind a startled Weber.

"Whoa! Sir, what are you doing here? You should be sight-seeing or soaking up some rays at the beach."

"I probably should be Weber, but I need to spend a little time on some background reading in the vault and getting my act together for my first boat run around the harbor Monday morning."

"Well, I'll be here for another half hour or so. This contract modification needs to be on Colonel Chang's desk by 8:00 AM Monday so he can deliver it to MINDEF by 9:00 AM."

A short time later Weber appeared at the vault door to

inform Kane he was departing. "Remember to tell the guard when you leave so he can reset the alarm, and don't work too hard, sir. I'll see you tomorrow at the ambassador's Fourth of July party."

"Right, Weber, see you there." Kane gave him five minutes to clear the building and then he went up front for a look around. He lingered in Captain Grusk's doorway for a moment before entering. The office contained the usual government executive furniture, a sizeable mahogany desk accommodating a large calendar, a wingback leather chair tucked behind it, a waste basket, a coffee table displaying popular military journals, two comfortable-looking leather chairs opposite, a safe, and a large American flag in a stand. Kane spent several minutes on hands and knees with a penlight looking under all the furniture for hand-written words or numbers, which might be safe combinations or other cryptic information, but he found only furniture manufacturers' information.

Mounted on the wall next to the window was a large white board showing several senior Singaporean military officer names and future dates. The other walls displayed a visual history of the captain's career in naval aviation including photographs and plaques from former squadrons, squadron mates, and four different aircraft carriers. Scattered on the desktop were several defense-related magazines, a familiar hand-carved mahogany ink pen set from Subic Bay in the Philippines, and a half-consumed mug of black coffee. Also present was a framed 8x10 photograph of smiling people, presumably sons and daughters and their children. The desk was locked, the "IN" box and wastepaper basket empty. The "HOLD" box was half-full and by the yellow tinge on the edges of some of the papers it appeared they might have been there for some time. Kane extracted a pencil from his pocket and used the eraser end to lift a few pieces of correspondence to view content. He didn't know exactly what he was looking for, but there did not appear to be anything out of the ordinary. Noticing where the dial was set, he tried the 4-drawer safe—locked—then returned the dial to its original position and wiped it clean. The safe's sign-off sheet appeared to be properly filled-in and double-checked daily with the initials "CM", Curt Masters, the operations coordinator.

Kane moved to the window and pressed the edge of the venetian blind for a look outside. A tall office building stood directly across the street. A terrorist there on an upper floor with a scoped rifle would have a deadly easy shot through any windows on this side of the embassy.

Colonel Silver's office was slightly smaller. The smell of burnt tobacco was immediately traced to a pile of Winston cigarettes smoked down to their filters and mashed in a desktop ashtray. In addition to airplane photos and squadron plaques much like Grusk's office, Silver's desk held several stacks of correspondence most with office routing slips attached. Shuffling through the top few inches Kane found only administrative minutiae, nothing classified or important. Silver's "IN" and "OUT" boxes were empty, but his "HOLD" box was nearly full of information and clippings from newspapers and periodicals concerning the Republic of Singapore Air Force (RSAF). On the desk along with a family photo was a partial draft of a letter to the Pentagon related to a logistics course for the RSAF. A page by page spin through the colonel's Rolodex provided nothing of interest, no obvious code words, no safe combinations, and likewise, as in Grusk's office, nothing significant on the underside of his furniture. The waste basket contained five empty Coke cans and an old invitation to a party at the Thai naval attaché's house. The whiteboard behind the desk had the words "UNCLASSIFIED, DO NOT ERASE" written across its top in bold letters. Displayed on the board was information possibly pertaining to an RSAF program, including dollar amounts and fragmentary quotations from MINDEF officials, plus a zigzagging graph. The 4-drawer safe was properly secured and signed-off. Kane deduced Colonel Silvers was working hard on important projects involving the RSAF at the expense of more mundane attaché office administrative work, and keeping the cleanup crew out of his way as well.

Colonel Chang's office was in total contrast. Various paperwork and bound documents were neatly stacked and indexed with notes and tabs for quick reference. His desktop was neat and clean and included a family picture presumably his wife and two children. The office walls held photo snapshots of old friends and outfits mostly from Vietnam, where he had spent three tours of duty according to the inscriptions. The bookcase was dust free and the desk chair inserted evenly into its slot. The adjacent white board listed neatly printed reminders about deadlines, meetings at MINDEF, and social events requiring his action. A clean coffee cup was turned upside down on a paper napkin and a shoeshine kit hung on the coat rack near the door. Safe secured, dial turned to zero, and check-off sheet filled-in, Colonel Chang was one squared-away Army Ranger and besides being a highly effective attaché and good paper-pusher according to Morrison, he was in excellent physical shape. He had a chest full of medals including a Purple Heart and one of the highest in precedence, a Distinguished Service Cross, for extreme gallantry in actual combat.

Needing to locate office personnel records, Kane went to Warrant Officer Masters' work area. As the operations coordinator one of his jobs was to process administrative actions like leave requests, so the files Kane sought were likely located somewhere in the vicinity of Masters' desk. There appeared to be three possibilities, the desk itself or two four-drawer filing cabinets standing nearby. In an office of only fourteen people, counting the Singaporeans Janie Tan and Naseer and the attaché drivers, leave was not something that came up on a daily basis. The annual accumulation of leave requests for such a group probably wouldn't consume more than a single file folder and since leave records weren't classified there was no requirement to store them in a security container, so Kane proceeded to the filing cabinet without a locking mechanism.

Bottom drawers are usually the least convenient to access. In many offices these store Dead Sea Scroll vintage files, occasionally-needed hand tools, paper punches, extra government calendar holders, and miscellaneous other and often obsolescent office equipment. There may be an area in the upper drawers for personal items as well. Kane suspected the personnel files he sought, if they were in this file cabinet at all, would be in one of the upper drawers. He reached for the handle of the first drawer then moved to the second one and opened it. He was not surprised to see the contents in alphabetical order with files beginning with the letter "H". He walked his fingers to the "L's" and saw "Leave, Military/Civilian." Bingo! All the files going back five years were there.

As the copy machine warmed up, he waded through the records. Office personnel traveled quite a bit, some trips to the US, but most within the region: Kuala Lumpur, Penang, Fraser Hill, and Genting Highlands in Malaysia; Bangkok, Thailand; Hong Kong; Manila, Philippines; and Bali, Indonesia. There were also vacation trips to tea plantations and small towns in Malaysia plus visits to Australia and New Zealand. Leave requests typically contained names of the travelers, inclusive dates of their leave, destination addresses, plus contact/hotel telephone numbers. All the information needed to be checked out in the hunt for Bernard.

From the vault Kane retrieved and copied the classified inventory files, placed the copies in an envelope, and hid it in his personal safe for retrieval Monday. Then he returned the original files to the exact locations where he found them.

Kane's first fishing expedition hadn't turned up anything damning or even suspicious. However, it did add to his base-line of knowledge about office operations and co-workers, and perhaps he wouldn't be so uneasy sifting through everyone's business the next time around.

19

It was getting close to noon on Sunday, time to get ready for the Fourth of July Independence Day celebration at the ambassador's residence. A festive Hawaiian shirt and light-weight khaki trousers seemed to be the right combination for the event. Kane then dug deeper into his suitcase for the bag of mementos. The Defense Attaché School recommended attachés bring with them to their new assignment a bit of Americana, a trinket to use as an "icebreaker" when meeting foreign contacts for the first time. After searching high and low through nearly every store in Alexandria, Virginia Kane finally came across the perfect item: stars and stripes bowties. The flashy little items were ideal conversation starters and timely, so he purchased the store's remaining stock of thirty ties.

The Grusks, with Omar at the wheel, were waiting in the car. Following an introduction to Mrs. Grusk, Kane apologized for his shortsightedness in not having any special gifts for the ladies. The bright red, white, and blue bowtie was an instant hit with the captain though and he immediately clamped it on the collar of his pastel-colored tropical shirt above a pair of jumping swordfish. They all laughed at the garish combination.

It was good the grounds at the ambassador's residence were expansive. There were several hundred people already mill-ing around when the Grusk party arrived. Of course, all US embassy employees were welcome and each staff element had its quota of foreign guests to invite. Attaché office guests were primarily from the MINDEF staff, the Singapore Army, Navy, and Air Force, and members of the foreign military attaché corps. Although Kane had not yet had the opportunity to meet many people outside of the US embassy, the time had arrived.

The first to be introduced were the attachés from Malaysia, Indonesia, and Thailand, and their wives. Right away Kane noticed they looked cooler than he, probably because of the natural fabrics and sheerness of their shirts and blouses, the women's ensembles complete with fancy ankle length batik print dresses. The men saw Grusk's bowtie and immediately asked where he obtained it. It was obvious they wanted one and Kane had already reached into the bag to make the presentations. The French naval attaché and assistant naval attaché were next and then they left to show-off their new wardrobe accessories.

The food was nothing fancy, just 100% American—grilled hotdogs and hamburgers, corn on the cob, watermelon, ice cream, and apple pie. Most of it had been shipped-in specifically for the event.

The Grusk party headed toward Ambassador Lipka and her husband who were stationed in the receiving line. Kane presented the ambassadress with a tie, which she graciously accepted, turned, and gleefully untied and replaced her husband's necktie with the festive new one.

In the meantime, Captain Grusk rounded up the Australian and New Zealand Attachés and their wives and brought them over to meet Kane and more bowties were in order following those introductions.

The ties were a much bigger hit than Kane ever imagined they would be and since he had already given away a bunch, he decided clip one on his own collar before he ran out.

More introductions, more bowties: Major Wee, the MINDEF Liaison Officer; one of the missile patrol boat Captains; several other officers from the Singapore Army, Navy, and Air Force; and the remainder of the foreign military attachés all received ties. Of course, he had to give one to Colonel Chang and Colonel Silver too, and he found it difficult to say no to several other Americans, including Dirk Eggleston. Kane stuffed two ties into his rear pant pocket, one reserved for Chief Sanderson and the other one for Naseer.

With only a few ties remaining, Kane met the British Naval Attaché, Captain Alistair Brett and his wife, Brenda. He always liked engaging Brits in conversation. Their broad education and total command of the language made them so grounded, cerebral, and expressive.

"What is this?" Captain Brett asked as Kane pressed a tie into his palm during their handshake.

"Well, sir, it's a little extra something to help us celebrate our independence," he chided. There followed a brief moment of silence and Kane could tell by the twinkle in the Brits' eyes a retort of some kind was being formulated.

Brenda spoke first, "But Lieutenant Commander Kane, there are far too many stars on this tie."

"True, but we're looking to acquire additional real estate for development so perhaps you could recommend a new territory for us to investigate."

"Oh, no, we're not too good at that, are we?" Captain Brett responded and they all laughed aloud as Brenda helped her husband attach the tie to his shirt collar.

Captain Brett inquired if Kane had settled in, where he was staying, and if he was already inundated with invitations to social events. The Bretts, reportedly two years into their three-year assignment had grown weary of the diplomatic social scene. According to them, the downside of a small island and proportionally small diplomatic community was rubbing shoulders with the same attachés, embassy crowd, and Singaporean officials, five or six nights a week, for months on end to varying levels of tedium. In theory there was always a new topic to insert into the conversation and information to gather and report. In reality, though, it was sometimes difficult to find a new subject since yesterday and no wonder alcohol consumption was high in the diplomatic corps. Captain Brett added, "But you should definitely plan to go to the French Embassy's Bastille Day celebration on the 14th." And in a lower voice he attached, "It's the one thing the French do well."

"Yes, sir, I intend to go and I've already responded to the RSVP."

20

Steve Diamond's head was elsewhere as he sped through traffic to the Fourth of July celebration. Constance had been missing from his side in recent weeks because of her "bad luck fall and sprained ankle" as he had made it known. However, he knew her permanent absence was a much bigger problem from here on out because his latest fabrication, her sudden trip to Europe, would hardly last forever. Suddenly, he shouted "frozen ass" blasted the car's horn and zipped past the parking attendants into the ambassador's compound following the signs to overflow parking.

Diamond tossed-back an ice-cold Bud, inhaled a hot dog slathered with everything, and then tried to bleed off a foaming, mustard-flavored belch as he stepped into the receiving line for the requisite greeting with Ambassador and Mr. Lipka. He arrived there several couples behind the new assistant naval attaché, the fellow he had previously met while getting a cup of coffee in the cafeteria. He watched as Kane presented a patriotic-looking bowtie appreciatively received by the ambassadress. As Kane finished and stepped away another person approached him clamoring for one of the little ties.

All the to-do about the bowties gave Diamond an idea and he chuckled to himself. *Perhaps the worrisome Russians would lighten up and stop being such pricks if I obtained one of those ties and crammed it in the dead drop next time, along with the film of course.*

Diamond weaved his way through the crowd and as he progressed the embryo of the new plan of action proposed by the KGB, a plan featuring the ambassador's secretary in the starring role, grew larger in his mind. Blackmail was always in the KGB's playbook and he was tasked to obtain compromising material on Ms. Feldman, photos or otherwise, as soon as feasible.

Ambassador Lipka often joked that her secretary could easily take her place and no one in the embassy would ever notice, and this prompted Diamond to consider his new challenge with greater caution. Even with his heretofore-limited contact with her, he knew Ms. Feldman's intellect exceeded his usual prey so he must act carefully so as not to arouse her suspicion. Searching her out in the crowd, Diamond complimented her patriotic attire and initiated idle banter. She was a gifted conversationalist, familiar with all of the usual topics.

"I heard you have relatives in Greece. Have you visited there?" she asked.

"Relatives in Athens, yes, and branches of the infamous Diamondis gang are still hiding out there in caves" he said with a grin. "Constance and I spent some time with my aunts and uncles and then we headed off to the Greek islands for the remainder of our honeymoon. If you're an ancient history buff you could spend a lot of time in Greece. The Oracle at Delphi was particularly interesting to me and we loved the beaches at Mikonos." And the conversation with Ms. Feldman continued along those lines for a while longer, much to Diamond's satisfaction.

21

The following Monday, checking the ambassador's schedule and noting her departure at 2:00 PM Diamond stapled together correspondence concerning a regional trade issue. It was as good an excuse as any to go up to the ambassador's office. In presenting the papers to Ms. Feldman, he said they were "No rush, but FYI for the ambassador." She thanked him and smiled. He inhaled deeply and sighed, "Do I smell fresh coffee?"

"I just prepared a little. Would you like a cup?"

"Desperately. Mondays are an absolute zoo and another shot of caffeine just might keep me going until they unlock my cage."

He sat in the reception area and she joined him moments later carrying steaming coffee mugs.

"What's the latest from Constance?"

Diamond held his breath and reply, staring at the floor, seeming to formulate an answer and then he slowly emoted, "She left me," adding he had not told anyone because he was not ready to deal with it. Then shifting to Ms. Feldman's compassionate eyes, he confided she was the only person he felt comfortable in speaking freely.

As he suspected, she was sympathetic. She touched his hand and reassured him she would keep it to herself. They spoke of other matters and after a few minutes he looked at his watch, apologized for dumping his troubles, thanked her for the coffee, and left.

Thursday afternoon presented his next opportunity for a repeat visit and on Friday he decided to boldly ask if they might dine together Saturday evening to which she hesitated at first, but then agreed. He arrived at her flat carrying an unexpected basket of Greek food and later that evening with the empty wine bottle turned upside down in the ice bucket, the lights dimmed, and the music turned down low, she foolishly obliged his desire for carnal dessert.

Hidden under her little sundress he discovered a most exquisite body lavishly endowed with soft lush curves and pale silky skin lightly dusted with freckles. Intoxicated by her fragrance and impassioned by her sexual aura he was unstoppable, taking her breath away repeatedly and blissfully over the next several hours. It was so unlike her; she could never explain why she gave in so readily to his advances.

But when she asked him for a secret dinner date the following Wednesday, he decided to up the ante for a change of venue; he needed a go at Ambassador Lipka's office. So, he followed her invitation with one of his own, a weekend at an intimate beach resort only a few hours drive up the coast into Malaysia.

Back at his residence, Diamond opened the safe and pawed through Constance's jewel cases in search of an appropriate bauble. *Ah, perfect, a gold bracelet in the Greek key pattern.*

At the resort, Ms. Feldman offered fitting appreciation for the lovely bracelet and within days Diamond was able to initiate his first brief incursion into the ambassador's private office. He called in advance to make sure the ambassador was away, the appointment schedule clear, and Ms. Feldman was so disheveled after their quickie on the ambassador's jam-packed desktop, it took her six minutes in the ambassador's private bathroom to repair the damage—plenty of time to accomplish his clandestine photography at the next opportunity.

Ms. Feldman re-emerged dressed, hair combed, and makeup refreshed, but with a puzzled look. "I can't find my panties." Diamond smiled, reached into his front pant pocket, and pulled out a pair of pink ones. "These?"

After that first time Ms. Feldman's passion for office sex seemed to soar off the charts. She was mesmerized, couldn't get enough of him, and incredibly she didn't seem to care if they were caught, a discovery that would surely cost them both their careers, not that it made any difference to him though.

Yet the regular, mind-blowing trysts with Ms. Feldman were becoming less exciting and more like work to Diamond even though her feelings for him grew more genuine with each encounter. The payoff, literally, in continuing the relationship was the gushing praise and money he received from his delighted KGB handler. The Russians were so cautious in the beginning, though, Diamond almost gave up on them and considered going to the North Koreans instead. On two separate occasions in the middle of the night and at great personal risk he sailed duct-taped manila envelopes bulging with originals and copies of classified cables, internal memoranda, and other sensitive reports over the wall into the Soviet Embassy's compound. Finally, following his third delivery and a flurry of communications between KGB officials in Singapore and Moscow, he overcame their suspicions.

22

In a close quarters city-state like Singapore it was not easy for a known or suspected KGB operative, particularly a relatively tall Caucasian among a populace of generally shorter Asians, to shake surveillance for any length of time day or night and find safe venues to meet. The Singaporeans, Americans, British and others had good human and technical surveillance capabilities and Singapore's Internal Security Department (ISD) and the police had scores of ad hoc informants throughout the island. The stakes were enormously high for Diamond and the KGB whenever a rare face-to-face meeting was called. Locations and times were always altered to help keep the worthy opposition at bay; diversion, deception, and disguise were standard operating procedures.

At a recent after dark face-to-face in a hotel room, Diamond's KGB case officer, Nicolai, reassured Diamond he was pleased with the product. Actually, the KGB's First Chief Directorate in Moscow was more than pleased, but down at the operational level Diamond was difficult. He had a mercurial temper, tended to be flippant and unreliable, his tradecraft erratic, and overall seemed to have trouble comprehending the risk to himself as an instrument of the KGB.

Sometimes even simple precautions seemed difficult for Diamond to carry out. For example, no one jaywalked in Singapore because it was against the law and rigorously enforced. Yet, in wending his way to service a dead drop site, Diamond might dart across a busy street with automobile horns blasting at him rather than quietly melding into the crowd at a crosswalk and waiting for the light to change. Running after taxis and yelling at the top of his lungs to hail one was another attention-getting blunder and on one occasion KGB contact was aborted because of this. Every so often reportedly for his health, but seemingly for his own nefarious pleasure, Diamond would pace the city's sidewalks. He'd make stops at markets and shops, sometimes drawing attention by arguing with merchants and making purchases of a seemingly nonsensical nature. Once he purchased a large stalk of perhaps a hundred ripe bananas, hoisted the load to his shoulder and marched off.

Prearranged dead drops were the principal method of indirect clandestine exchanges of documents, film and payments between the KGB and Diamond. But some signals used to prompt the servicing of a loaded dead drop were on occasion less reliable in Singapore than some other places. It rained often, often hard. A chalk mark placed on an exposed surface could be washed away in seconds. The same for a mark gouged in the soil with the heel of a shoe near an exhibit at the Jurong Bird Park site, or pebbles arranged behind a certain potted plant at the Botanic Gardens. Singaporean fastidiousness presented challenges as well. A soft drink can, a cigarette butt, a flower, or some other innocuous item placed as a signal a dead drop had been loaded and was ready to be cleared might end up in a trash container if spotted by any of Singapore's civic-minded citizenry. Colored tacks or pins stuck in certain tree trunks at the arboretum in the Botanical Gardens or small pieces of adhesive tape placed on metal railings or posts at specified bus stops seemed to meet visual requirements and work satisfactorily most of the time. For the moment, however, dead drop servicing signals were being exchanged in real time over the noon hour while Diamond sipped a cool drink at a small sidewalk café.

Besides information lifted from his own office, Diamond became competent with several KGB cameras: A rollover camera integrated into a normal looking 3-ring notebook and a miniature camera, the match box-sized F-21 with its 28mm/f2.8 lens. Both were used to photograph classified messages and US position papers on various treaties and security agreements under negotiation in the region, Navy ship and military aircraft visit schedules, and military equipment sales proceedings to name a few, all of which crossed Ambassador Lipka's desk on a regular basis.

Still, exactly how was this happening? The ambassador being the busy woman she was often did not have time to fumble with the closing of her safe before dashing off late to her next appointment. In these instances, she imprudently delegated the task of securing classified materials and locking up her office to her faithful secretary, the dependable Ms. Feldman. But Judith Feldman's infatuation with her handsome lover made her the perfect unwitting accomplice to espionage. If anything classified was left out in the open, she only needed to be out of sight for a few minutes in the bathroom and Diamond could photograph several dozen or more items. He merely ran the spine of the camera-notebook back and forth across the documents. Inside the spine, wheels activated the tiny hidden camera along with a battery-powered light source. Moreover, his criminal act was never detectable by the roving Marine security guard because everything in the ambassador's office was always locked up tight during the regular security rounds.

23

Singapore's provenance, importance, and enduring prosperity are due to a great extent to its position adjacent to the Singapore and Malacca Straits, the shortest, most navigable water route between the Pacific and Indian Oceans.

With a significant portion of the world's sea trade and oil shipments passing within sight of Singapore it was not surprising the country developed as a crossroads for international commerce and became one of the world's busiest seaports during the latter part in the twentieth century. Additional infrastructure like shipbuilding and repair, manufacturing, banking, the development of an educated workforce, a stable government, and enlightened leadership turned this place, slightly smaller than the area of present-day New York city, into an influential island-nation and important US friend and ally in Southeast Asia. From a naval intelligence standpoint Singapore presented a unique sea level viewport for information on foreign navies and merchant fleets of the world drawn there on business or just steaming past.

Early Monday morning Kane arrived at Clifford Pier. He stood for a moment admiring the final seconds of a watercolorist's wash of pink sunrise giving away to a hazy cerulean blue sky before waving his arms overhead for attention. The unmarked white boat, which had been slowly circling in the anchorage, headed in to pick him up. Naseer's boat handling skills were immediately evident as he swung the craft deftly alongside and stopped it dead in the water a foot from the pier. Kane stepped easily onboard with camera case in hand. Sunglasses, polo shirt and shorts, and a new pair of deck shoes were his uniform of the day. He intended to ask questions about the harbor and get to know the boat's capabilities as they cruised the anchorages and shipyards. He would take routine pictures of ships and port facilities, anything of interest to update the database. After an exchange of greetings and presentation of the last bowtie to Naseer they headed into the Eastern sector of the harbor among the many merchant ships at anchor where the engines were shut down in order to explain the 38-foot boat's features and capabilities.

Many merchant ships were extracting cargo from their holds. Winches whirred and whined, steel cables strained taut and bulging cargo nets hoisted sacks, boxes, or pallets filled with goods for local consumption or transshipment to other world-wide destinations. Booms swung the loads outboard and lowered them onto awaiting lighters or barges where crews stepped lively, pushing and placing the cargoes into the right places to maximize payloads. Other strings of heavily loaded lighters, waves splashing over their gunwales, were in tow toward the wharf area to be off-loaded, their cargoes warehoused. In his professional reading Kane learned a warehouse in Singapore was not a warehouse; it was a "godown." The term was born of the British East India Company era when immigrant coolies and laborers carried heavy loads on their backs and were prodded by English speaking bosses to keep moving and "go down, go down" off the barges and into the buildings to deposit their sacks of tea, coffee, spices, and other commodities of the day.

A siren blared and red lights flashed as a Singapore Harbor Police boat sped close by toward the strait. Kane swung around and observed a passing freighter had slowed its transit. He saw people on deck dropping armload-sized cardboard boxes over the side to a small, dark boat. As the Harbor Police approached to within several hundred yards of the ship, the boat with its apparent contraband loaded sped away toward Indonesian territorial waters. At that point the Harbor Police boat broke off the pursuit and the merchantman picked up speed and continued its passage.

"What was that? Smuggled weapons or drugs?"

"Bad things" was Naseer's only response.

They set a course toward Keppel harbor passing near the container port where huge gantry cranes were off-loading two large container ships, one from Sweden, and the other from Germany. Minutes later they passed beneath red cable cars making their circuit between the tourist attractions on Sentosa Island and the main island. In Keppel harbor they stopped near the Keppel Shipyard entrance. A busy shipyard is a noisy place and this one was no different. Metal on metal scrapping, grinding, hammering, cutting, banging, the revving of auxiliary engines, and workers yelling to communicate above the deafening racket was present in maximum decibels. Four large dry-docks were filled with vessels under repair. One of them, a big cargo ship, had its rudder and screw removed. Other ships' hulls were being painted with anti-corrosion red lead or receiving final coats of their livery colors. Several ships had scaffolding in place around masts where new radar, communications antennas, and other electronic equipment were being installed. Smaller ships and tugboats were alongside the piers in various stages of maintenance and repair. Kane studied the activity with the binoculars for a few minutes, cross-referencing the ship's names with the ones he could find on the shipping list.

They reversed course, south of Sentosa Island, and headed toward the less crowded Western sector anchorage area.

"Let's see how fast she'll go."

Naseer nudged the throttle handles forward. The engines roared and the boat's wake slowly flattened out as they picked up speed and began to come up on plane.

"How fast do you think we're going?"

"Maybe fifteen knots" Naseer yelled back.

It was not great speed, but enough to keep pace or even overtake most ships of interest since the speed and interval of ship traffic in the strait was monitored and regulated for safety.

Kane scanned the horizon and as he did, he saw the largest commercial sailing vessel he had ever seen, perhaps 150 feet in length with the lines of a Middle Eastern dhow. It was under tow to the harbor, lowering large lateen-shaped sails, riding very low, only a couple of feet of freeboard, and laden with four large mounds of canvas-covered cargo.

He pointed and passed the binoculars, "Where's she from?"
"Indonesia."
"What's she's carrying?"
"Charcoal."

The Western sector anchorage had hazardous and quarantine designated areas and another area for ships under repair or awaiting access to various shipyards. The largest vessels present there were Liquefied Natural Gas (LNG) and Liquefied Petroleum Gas (LPG) carriers, which were nothing more than gigantic floating gas tanks. They were out there in the remote areas for obvious reasons. If one of them ever blew up it would sink or severely damage anything close by.

They continued northwest along the coast until they came to Jurong where more ships were in various stages of repair and overhaul and others were waiting their turn. Kane observed the activity for a while and then they continued up the coast as far as the village of Tuas before doubling back. At this point Naseer inquired if Kane was hungry and since it was already approaching noon, they decided to cut the engines and drift while lunch was being prepared.

As the water heated in the teapot Naseer produced a precooked bowl of rice and an array of canned goods including a tin of mutton curry from Australia, "Good and not too hot for you." In his other hand, chili sardines from Thailand. "These are hot, but maybe you try?" They sat on the shady side in Captains' chairs, ate, and talked while tranquilly drifting in the current.

Once Naseer got started he was a real talker and Kane was an avid listener. He was Muslim, born and raised in Malaysia, growing up near the Australia, New Zealand, and United Kingdom (ANZUK) headquarters at Butterworth where he trained and worked as a lorry mechanic. He had immigrated to Singapore ten years earlier and had been employed in the US embassy for about six years. He recently moved his family from an older area of the city where the government was tearing down substandard housing into one of the new government housing projects. The move to the high-rise was both good and bad; good because it was new, affordable, and convenient to the

mosque and work, but not so good because the unit he quali-
fied for was small, one bedroom and a bathroom for his family
of four. Privacy was a concern. When it got too hectic, he just
retreated along with other male friends to the sanctuary of the
mosque. He enjoyed working for the embassy because the pay
was good and he loved the boat. Sometimes his son helped out
with bigger jobs like sanding and repainting the deck or cleaning the engine compartment. Naseer said he liked Kane's prede-
cessor, Charlie Morrison, and Warrant Officer Ross, the Aussie.
"He drinks beer, big ones."

"Do you ever fish out here?"

"Sometimes, but too many ships now and water not good,
you go far for fish."

Later in the afternoon, after spending the day on the boat,
Kane arrived back at the attaché office where Janie Tan stopped
him at her desk.

"Commander, you received four telephone calls and some
mail, these look like invitations. Would you like me to return
of any of the calls? Major Wee and Philipe from the French
Embassy would like to hear from you this afternoon."

"Yes, Janie, make the calls, thank you."

It had been a very educational first day in the boat thanks to
Naseer. Kane learned a lot and it was refreshing to think about
a few things other than Bernard.

24

Kane had either seen from a distance or been in direct contact with Steve Diamond almost every day since his arrival at the embassy including meeting him in the cafeteria the first day and again while handing out bow ties at the ambassador's Fourth of July party. This day was no different, as they both just happened to exit the embassy at exactly 5:30 PM.

"Hey there, so how was your day, Lieutenant Commander Kane?"

"It was interesting including my first boat trip around the harbor. And your day, Mr. Diamond?"

"Just call me Steve. Like all days here, another one of torturous paper work and incompetent supervisors, and it's not over yet. I'm off to the Raffles now for a meeting with some bean-counting Singaporeans about an upcoming trade seminar. We'll have the usual drinks and dinner and then they'll want to discuss every aspect to the nth degree 'til midnight. They're obsessed with plans and details."

"That's a coincidence, I'm moving into the Raffles tomorrow myself."

"I thought you were already settled."

"Yes, that was the Rajah Brooke. It's comfortable and convenient, but the Raffles is a once in a lifetime experience and it's only a few dollars more and a couple of blocks farther away, so I thought I'd give it a try."

"Great, so you'll have to join us tonight. You might be able to endure it for a few minutes and then break away when you get bored. You probably know most of our people and I'm sure the Singaporeans won't care. I'll even buy you a Singapore sling from the Long Bar; it's where it was invented you know. A real sailor can't pass on an offer like that."

"Well, I was going lay low tonight, but you talked me into it, and I haven't had an authentic Singapore sling yet anyway."

"Great, then ride along with me."

"Okay, thanks."

"You're a bachelor, right?

"I am."

"So, what do you do when you're not cruising around in that yacht or escorting the ambassador to those VIP parties and impressing all the ladies with the white uniform, the sword, and that macho gold rope thing wrapped around your arm?"

"The aiguillette, well, I'm getting back into golf. The game's good for making contacts, and I'd also like to try some fishing in the area if I can find the time."

"Ah, the G-word. I can't wait to relieve you of some of your hard-earned cash."

"You're on, just give me a little time to get ready with my new clubs."

"Play any tennis or squash?"

"I've played them, but not much. I don't think I own a tennis racquet anymore."

"So how do you keep in shape?

"Jogging, calisthenics, a few weights, and martial arts off and on."

"Found any women yet?"

"Oh, I've met a few, but I've been so busy I haven't had time to follow-up. Yourself?"

"Oh, no, I'm a happily married man, no little rug rats yet, but I think that's next. It doesn't hurt to look though and some of the local women, 'straits born' as they're called, are quite attractive as you know. We'll have to play golf soon. I know all the people at the best clubs, so make sure you call me when you're ready."

"Just give me a week or so."

"By the way, you haven't purchased an automobile yet, have you?"

"No, and I'm in no real hurry since I don't have a permanent place, but I have been checking the bulletin board outside the cafeteria in case something good pops up."

"I purchased an older Bentley limo a few months back. Believe it or not the Malaysian Sultan of Johore once owned it. It only needs a little detailing, but it has low mileage and runs just fine. I was going to bring it back to the states and have it totally restored, but I recently decided against doing that. If you want some really classic wheels at a good price, I can make you a sweet deal. Let me know if you want to see it."

25

Kane's first few weeks at the embassy were history and he was in a busy rhythm, boat operations, drafting maritime-related intelligence reports, night and day official social events, and of course his other task. His relationship with Eggleston seemed good, collegial, even though they didn't see each other as much as he had anticipated due to their mutually busy schedules. So far Captain Grusk appeared pleased with Kane's productivity too, and Chief Sanderson and Naseer also gave impressions of liking his laborsaving ideas and delegation of authority allowing them to take care of the routine and mundane without asking permission.

26

The 14th of July Bastille Day gala at the French embassy was in full swing when Kane arrived there. Hundreds of people strolled the gardens and lawn of the large, gated compound. The night air was a very still, inky black illuminated only by tiny twinkling lights and the occasional flash and pop of fireworks. On a distant terrace, colored strobes scanned enthusiastic, gyrating couples, and the musicians were clearly determined to earn their pay. Mosquito coils glowed and smoked, but had minimal impact on their voracious opponents and bare-shouldered women slapped and swatted, abandoning any pretext of decorum.

Kane was informed open collar shirts were acceptable protocol for all outdoor events because of the climate. Jackets, ties, and full-dress uniforms were required only at official dinners and receptions held in thoroughly chilled posh clubs and hotel ballrooms. His clothes were already clinging though, the new silk shirt a sweaty mistake he vowed not to repeat.

He took in the bubbling champagne fountains, crepe kiosks, and the long tables laden with every conceivable delicacy as he made his way through the crowd searching for familiar faces. Chatting briefly with guests, he noted it would have been helpful if all had worn nametags—not done at these soirees.

A pass again at the champagne and he re-filled his glass. *Veuve Cliquot?* Surely not, but he was almost certain it was. Proceeding to the hors d'oeuvres, he popped a handful of tiny dried anchovy-like fish into his mouth and savored the flavorful tang while behind him a woman voiced a surprised observation.

"I have never seen a European gentleman eating *ikan bilis* quite like that."

Kane turned and looked up, and up. A tall, exotic Eurasian woman in a red cheongsam smiled down, her glossy black hair wound in a large bun and delicate hands were accentuated with long red nails. Distracted, Kane swallowed then responded, "American, I love to travel and I always try everything the local people eat."

"Have you been here long?" she inquired.

"Into my third week now and I've just moved from the Rajah Brooke hotel into the Raffles. So veddy British, reminds me of my one and only childhood school year in England."

"Indeed. I was schooled in the UK as well. My father was British and we spent years there, but I never got used to the cold."

They touched briefly on the museums, galleries, and theater. An animated conversation ensued, punctuated by laughter over shared stories of characters and situations unique to London and its neighbors.

Such an interesting man, she thought. *I haven't laughed so much in ages. And those typical American teeth, white, straight, flawless.* She recognized his costly Italian shoes too; she had the same in stock at her business. But it was then she felt, rather than saw, the disapproving stare of her escort for the evening, a middle-aged local merchant. She excused herself, but with a lingering soft-eyed look she added, "I have a shop on Orchard Road called Aurora, do stop by."

"Aurora—I'll remember," Kane replied, standing a bit taller.

With a dazzling smile she glided away to rejoin her friend. Kane watched as she slowly melded into the crowd, an unfettered view of the entire package from astern including those stiletto heels and shapely long legs, and a concluding glance back in his direction. *Aurora, oh yes, I am watching.*

A recharge of his champagne glass and then Kane paused to observe more of the activity. The Frenchmen, civilian officials and military attachés alike possessed all the social skills, but they were particularly suave and deferential with the female guests. A formal greeting included a kiss on both cheeks and preceded commentary on how lovely they looked. A snap of the fingers brought waiters and valets flying out of nowhere to care for their every need.

A disco beat drew Kane's attention to the dance floor where he found an attractive and willing partner from the Finnish Consulate. Her spoken English was perfect; her name was Nikka, and she had all the moves.

"I see you like zee good things," voiced the French assistant naval attaché who came up behind Kane in his dress white uniform, gold aiguillette, chest of medals, and two giggling young damsels clinging to his arms.

"Indeed I do, Philipe," Kane said as they shook hands. "This is fabulous, the champagne, the caviar, the slide show of Paris and the countryside, and last but not least these beautiful women. *"Bon soir, Mesdames"* he proffered as he looked from side to side at Philipe's companions and slightly bowed.

"Bon soir Monsieur" returned in stereo.

"I take all zee credit for zee beautiful women, especially my lovely friends here, zee twins, Giselle and Sylvie. The food it came to us by air on UTA and we took a beeg pay cut to get it for you, just look at our Navy compared to yours," laughed Philipe as he held high his flute of champagne for a community toast. *"Salut."*

Philipe and the twins downed their beverages, leaned unsteadily to port, to starboard, laughed, and reeled away while supporting each other as best they could. Sandwiched comfortably in the middle and taking complete license as both a Frenchman and host, Philipe alternated amorous pecks on the twins' perfumed and slightly perspiring cheeks and necks.

Several familiar faces were in the line for crepes Suzette and Kane joined in right behind his British acquaintances, Captain and Mrs. Brett.

"You were right about this party, captain. Our 4th of July get-together pales in comparison."

"Yes indeed, it's on the scale of the Queen's Birthday Party. Everything is top hole, eh what? Say, was it you I saw on the dance floor a few minutes ago, the disco music I believe?"

"Yes, I was out there."

"And who was your lovely partner?"

"Her name is Nikka. She works at the Finnish consulate and I met another lady this evening I would hope to see again as well."

"Oh?"

"Yes, her name is Aurora and she has a shop..."

"It must have been Aurora Booth. I know her, a lovely lady. Her late husband, Harold, a countryman of mine, was a petroleum engineer. He was killed last year in a dreadful helicopter accident in a remote area of Sumatran jungle while surveying for an exploratory drilling site. Her shop is in the telephone book. If you ring her up you can mention my name if you like."

"Oh, Alistair, let him work at his own speed," demurred Brenda, half listening while watching the delivery of bubbling hot escargot along with a baguette of freshly baked bread to nearby guests.

"But she would be such a good companion for him."

"I know my dear, you've always been smitten by her."

Somehow, between the eating and drinking, Kane managed to find and say hello to Ambassador and Mr. Lipka, and then he saw and chatted with Eggleston, the Grusks, Changs, and Silvers, and interacted with several of the foreign military attaché corps officers and people from MINDEF. By chance, he also said good evening in Russian to Yuri Lubachev as he and a male companion brushed by, but Lubachev acted as though he did not hear the greeting.

Throughout the evening Kane met a number of foreign business executives and entrepreneurs with interesting import-export products and backgrounds. He made a point to exchange business cards with those traveling to Vietnam, Laos, China, and Cambodia.

Kane started to leave the festivities around midnight after sampling a final, irresistible glass of exquisite Bordeaux and dancing one more foxtrot with a French lady who spoke minimal English, but knew her way around the dance floor. As he thanked her and made his way toward the exit a female arm reached through the crowd and grabbed his shoulder.

"Monsieur, you are American, no?"

"Why, yes, oui."

"Pleez dance with me."

The tango was not exactly in Kane's repertoire; however, her vise-like grip and that final glass of wine told him he needed to give it a whirl or run the risk of upsetting US-French relations. There were a few cheers and light applause from her friends as she led him to the center of the dance floor. It is a very sensual dance, the tango, marked with abrupt pauses and postures, and his partner's lack of sobriety over-emphasized these to say the least, and Kane had difficulty keeping his composure while concentrating on his own inexpert footwork. As the music ended, she took a teetering bow to an ovation from the sidelines then spun and flung herself into his arms, luckily, and smeared a passionate goodbye kiss on his cheek.

The revelry on the embassy's grounds continued into the wee hours of the morning. While the French ambassador's tipsy entourage and most of the other diplomatic officials and guests retired, several dozen diehard and totally smashed French men and women stayed on to sing the Marseillaise, their national anthem, and toast France over-and-over again. Eventually, all the wine was decanted and consumed and the chorale grew hoarsely quiet. None of the troupe was vertical or awake at daybreak. Overall, it was quite the celebration.

27

With thunderstorms causing occasional power outages throughout the island Diamond did not want to run the risk of a thawed-out corpse stinking his place if the freezer was off for any extended period of time. For this reason, he mulled over new locations for Constance's final resting place.

Burial in the backyard would be quick and easy. He could just dig a hole and plant her in the middle of the flowerbed now that the gardener was gone. But there were several large dogs next door and with their acute olfactory sensors he thought it best not to risk a canine excavation of the gravesite if they got loose one day while he was at work. A short drive across the causeway into Malaysia was a possibility as well. He could dump her on an anthill in the jungle and after a week of ravaging insects and animals there would be nothing left but bones. He rejected the idea of thawing, dismembering, and disposing of her piece by piece in the garbage. He likened it to cleaning fish; too time consuming, too messy. He finally concluded deep-sixing her intact offshore was the best option and just let the deep-sea diners have their way with her. However, he realized the logistics of secretly transporting and dumping a frozen 135-pound body at night at sea would be no small feat.

One possible location from which to embark upon such an expedition was a remote peninsula on the Northeast side of the island where the road ended, Punggol Point, on the Johore Strait. Virtually uninhabited except for a small enclave of fishing cottages and a rustic seafood restaurant, it seemed the ideal spot and the water would be calmer there, easier to launch a boat. So, Diamond decided to sample the cuisine and reconnoiter the area.

The restaurant was small and quaint with a few old folding chairs surrounding salvaged wooden industrial cable spools as tables, which were placed here and there across the beach. A tattered menu with a variety of seafood dishes was offered, but the reputation of the establishment was based on the chili crab dish, so he ordered it and a cold beer.

There were no houses nearby; the closest ones were a hundred yards or more beyond the restaurant. There were no streetlights. The five fishing boats he could see hauled up on the beach behind the restaurant had sets of oars conveniently stowed alongside them. One of the smaller boats looked just about the right size for him to handle. There were no regular business hours for the restaurant; they just blew out the torches and lanterns and closed down when the last customer departed. Diamond noticed the crashing waves and realized he needed to check on the tides and find a day in the middle of the week when business was slow and the shoreline calm.

The tasty-looking dish arrived on a circular, pizza-type pan. Red chili sauce was drizzled all over. He used the accompanying mallet to smash the claws and extract the crabmeat and the bread to mop up the sauce. It was messy, but delicious. He had it all over his face and hands and when it began to drip down his chin he was reminded of Constance.

The next evening, he opened the freezer for the first time since that eventful night. Rapping his knuckles on her buttocks he smiled, she was hard as a brick. It was a struggle getting her to the top. He managed to prop her on the rim and stepped aside to ease her to the floor, but she slipped away. The resounding crash shook the entire porch and made a good-sized dent in the flooring. He partially wrapped the body in a plastic tablecloth as best he could and taped it together with the last few feet of duct tape. A pathway cleared to the door, he went outside, unlocked the trunk of the car, and pulled loose the wires to the trunk light, no need to call attention to his work.

He wrestled her onto the dolly, which he had borrowed from the embassy's mailroom. The wheels squeaked with each revolution under the strain of her weight as he proceeded to the door then slowly, carefully, down one step at a time to the car.

As he lifted her at an awkward angle and levered her over the bumper into the trunk, he felt a sudden twinge of pain in his lower back, "Damn." He let go and she hit bottom with a thud. The noise triggered barks from the neighbor's yard along with four-legged running and growls followed by investigative sniffing under the fence.

Traffic was light, but he drove cautiously, arriving at his destination around 11:00 PM with his headlights turned off. Parking about a hundred yards short of the restaurant, he shut off the engine and waited and listened for a few minutes longer with the windows rolled down. After his eyes adjusted to the darkness and to confirm no one was around he exited the car and walked closer to the restaurant. No one was there. He returned to his car and drove onto the beach, but he stopped short when he felt the sand pulling at his wheels. The boats were 30 yards or more away and although he did not relish the idea of bearing her that distance and pulling a boat to the water's edge with his back bothering him there was no other choice.

She had begun to thaw a little, some surface moisture here and there, just enough to make her slippery. It was much more difficult getting her out of the confines of the trunk than it was dropping her in because of the close quarters. Finally, he managed to lift her and in doing so he pulled his back muscles again. It was painful, but he had to press on. He was making slow headway staggering toward the line of boats, but his forearms, biceps, and chest developed a hellacious frostbitten sensation and the sandy footing was unstable. At once he lost both his balance and his grip and sprawled in the sand on top of her. It was at that moment he had another feeling—she had not finished exacting her revenge. He got to his feet, brushed off, and dragged her the remaining distance to a boat where he struggled once more to load her up.

No fun, but no insurmountable problems so far. The moonlight was minimal, perfect, and the tide was going out, so the surf was reduced and navigable. He pushed off in the boat, hit his shin hard while scrambling aboard, and inserted the oars into the oarlocks. After making several trial strokes he remembered the cement blocks and chain assembly he had strung together to sink her; it was still sitting in his garage.

Upon nearing what he thought might have been the half-way point in the strait he began to tire and it was very dark, so he stopped. He hoped there would be enough current there to sweep her further out to sea before daylight. The little boat pitched and rolled as he stood up. He took a step aft then crouched and shuffled his feet into position astride her in order to lift and push her over the side. He gave her a mighty heave-ho and she dropped in like a depth charge, making quite a splash.

The boat rocked, his foot slipped, his balance lost, and backward he fell into the sea. He choked on several unexpected gulps of saltwater as his clothes were weighting him down. Without a life jacket he worked hard to tread water while removing his shoes and then swam a few yards back to the boat, which was drifting away. He tried unsuccessfully to get onboard, nearly swamping the craft several times in futile attempts. As he held on to catch his breath, he tried to reorient himself to the shoreline and looked over his shoulder into the darkness in vain for the missing oars.

While clinging to the boat in near zero visibility he thought he saw something break the surface nearby...perhaps it was nothing. Moments later something touched him from behind, a slight tap in the middle of his back like an initial probe from a nocturnal predator searching out an easy meal. A chill shot up his spine to his scalp and he yelled out, "OH NO, NO!" in anticipation of what was coming next. He turned and thrashed violently trying to protect himself by kicking and splashing, his legs churning as fast as he could move them, actually propelling him partway up and out of the water nearly enough to get back onboard the boat. "No, No!" Despite his efforts his right foot made sudden and painful contact with something large. "No, go away Constance, go away!" He pushed her back, turned, and kicked and paddled vigorously with one arm while holding onto the boat with the other. But now more than ever a mauling by some abyssal creature looming up from the depths was in his head.

Even with the boat for an assist it took him more than half an hour to make it back to shore because of the rip current. He was shaking and exhausted when he finally released his hold on the boat and crawled the last few yards onto the beach. He rolled over in the sand and lay there for a few minutes before he began to take inventory. His shoes were gone, his shin was raw and sore, his right big toe, the one he had kicked her with was painful, and his back was killing him. He patted his front and back pockets. Somehow through it all he had retained his billfold and car keys.

Finally, he was rid of her. Only two more actions in his plan remained, the vacation, and the promulgation of the lie. He had cleared his work calendar of major events for the next two weeks so he would ask for some time off for a relaxing retreat with Constance. He would say they had made reservations in the Genting Highlands, Fraser's Hill, and the Malaysian capital, Kuala Lumpur. According to his story, in Kuala Lumpur, Constance decided to scoot off to Europe for another one of her shopping sprees. It was an impulsive decision and he was unsure just when she might return, probably when her money ran out. In the meantime, he would persevere at work, take care of the cat, and wait for her return.

That was his story. He knew it had flaws. He wondered what would happen if he ran into someone he knew during the trip or at the hotel and they inquired of Constance's whereabouts. And what about her parents? They were already suspicious in not hearing from her. Fortunately, they sent letters and made long distance calls, so he could continue to type and forge replies and tell them lies. Maybe he should have made it look like an accident and let her body be found. No, maybe he shouldn't have killed her at all, or perhaps she went missing in Europe.

He considered finding and taking someone else on the vacation, someone who looked similar to Constance, but thinner, and better sex. The idea though, as appealing as it was, added complications to his already dangerous scheme. He knew he needed to be more careful. Someone could check the records of his wife's departure from the airport in Kuala Lumpur and find out she never departed. And how long could she remain gone? And there would be no long-distance telephone call records to support his assertions. It was all just too much to worry about.

28

They were underway in the boat around 8:00 AM Monday morning. Kane provided Naseer with the day's mission, ship photos in the Eastern anchorage and then the bi-weekly cruise up the east coast past the village of Bedok into the mouth of the Johore Strait as far as Changi before doubling back.

As they progressed along their route, Kane, as usual, made notes and scanned ships and shoreline facilities near and far through the binoculars. The current seemed stronger than their previous run through the area and there was more flotsam to avoid due to a storm system, which had begun to influence the southern portion of the South China Sea. Several large, whole trees floated by along with many bottles, cans, and ubiquitous plastic items. Naseer cut back on the throttle on the lookout for partially submerged logs, which could damage the hull, bend a shaft, or break a propeller.

A flock of seagulls was having a noisy picnic on a carpet of seaweed about a hundred yards abeam to starboard, so as a brief matter of interest Kane suggested a course change to check out the commotion. On approach the gulls flew off to a circular holding pattern as Naseer reversed the engines in order to halt the boat's advance. They sat at idle surveying the site. A large seaweed clot trailed around a sizeable tree limb holding yards of tangled fishing net and a faded red float. Also snared in the clutter was a Styrofoam lid from a cooler, a Tiger beer can, plastic bottles, a length of 2x4-sized lumber and something else, which caught Kane's eye.

"What's that?" From his observation point he motioned toward the light-colored patch on the water's surface.

Naseer squinted, trying to make it out.

"Let's go around the other side for a closer look. I'll get the boat hook."

"It looks like a mass of hemp rope, or a coil of fishing line, or YOW!" Kane yelled after he poked the object with the pole and it submerged slightly. It was blond hair attached to a human head. The buoyant corpse slowly resurfaced as Kane stared in abject disbelief. The lifeless body was suspended vertically, but face down in a fetal position with the back of the head and top of the shoulders just below the surface. The flowing hair and body size suggested an adult female; however, the low center of gravity made it difficult to maneuver the deceased for conclusive identification. He tried once to guide it closer to the boat but the pole slipped off and the body tilted back to its equilibrium, releasing a plum-colored cloud in the water from the facial area. Raw bite marks from the gulls and other pelagic creatures checkered the pale skin on the back, shoulders, and upper arms. The fact the body was floating and showed signs of *rigor mortis* suggested the person might have died very recently, perhaps within the last day or so.

In the short period of time the discovery had occupied them the current quietly swept their boat further out into the strait and there was no one was around except for the occasional passing merchant ship. *Where were the Harbor Police when you really need them?* Kane wondered as he looked for help in all directions.

It occurred to Kane he should consider it a crime scene. Regardless of whether it was or was not, though, he decided not to try to haul the body out. The boat's freeboard was too high for one person to lift that much weight over the side and by the wild look in Naseer's eyes he could not be counted on for any help—one corpse was one too many dead bodies onboard the boat. Kane considered holding the body by the hair or securing it with a rope and slowly towing it back to the harbor until they encountered the Harbor Police. However, during the towing process he considered any evidence on the body might be altered or lost.

The radio was worth a try. "Tuna, tuna, this is sardine, over."

Again, "Tuna, come in, this is sardine, over. Come in tuna, this is sardine, over. Damn it, tuna, we need a better radio, over."

The speaker crackled to life moments later with Chief Sanderson's voice cutting in and out for a few seconds, "Sar... over...Sardine, this is..."

"Tuna, this is sardine. You're breaking up. We need help. Send Police boat ASAP to our position off Changi. I repeat, send Police boat ASAP to our position off Changi. Tuna, did you copy? Tuna, did you copy, over?"

"Sar...rog...out."

It sounded as though Chief Sanderson received and understood Kane's radio transmission. The only thing to do now was to wait and keep the body near the boat.

About twenty minutes later Naseer sighted a Harbor Police boat in the distance, headed their direction. He went to the bow and began to wave one of the orange life jackets over his head. The police boat pulled alongside minutes later and the crew immediately began taking photos of the floating corpse. They tossed a net into the water, slowly steered the body onto it, and carefully hoisted it onboard their boat where more photographs followed.

"It's another one," the harbor police boat captain yelled out as he grimaced while carefully maneuvering the semi-rigid, naked, female body with rubber-gloved hands.

"Another one?" Kane questioned.

"This would be the fourth this year. The others were up the Malacca Strait off Penang."

"So, what's happening? Who's doing this?"

"The matter is under investigation."

"She looks Caucasian"

"Blond hair, light skin, probably European or Australian, the others were Asian girls."

"My God," Kane said out loud as he swallowed hard. Both her hands were missing, cut off cleanly at the wrists. And what little remained of a face below the forehead looked like it had been used for major league batting practice. The gaping mouth and jaw area was no more than a pulverized, seawater-draining void. As Kane looked on, the blond, bloodstained tresses spread across her shoulders and drying in the sun with bits of multi-colored seaweed entwined blew lifelike in a sudden gust of warm wind, mocking the otherwise macabre mound of rotting flesh.

The police took their information and said they would be in contact again if more questions came up.

Kane had never been in close proximity to an apparent homicide victim. It was particularly gruesome, but at the same time captivating. Someone had obviously killed her and tried to conceal her identity. The mutilation contradicted any accident or death by drowning. There were no fingers to print and likely no teeth to compare with any dental records. Her knees seemed drawn unnaturally close to her chest. Her head, angling sharply down, touched her chest; her neck appeared broken. Overall, the body had a compressed look. A tucked diving or acrobatic position came to mind.

"Will an autopsy be performed?"

"Usually in these cases, yes, however, the decision on a *post mortem* is made by our inspector and the coroner."

"If a report is generated can you send a copy to me at the US Embassy?"

"I can request that in my report."

It was already approaching 10:00 AM, too late to resume the rest of their planned day and Naseer was in shock, white as a sheet. He could hardly speak. He suddenly lurched from his seat to the far side of the boat and began heaving his guts out. He was definitely too traumatized to continue and Kane could use a stiff shot of something himself, so they headed back so Kane could make his own report.

29

Early the next evening, Omar, was waiting for Kane with the car. Minutes later they passed through upscale neighborhoods to arrive at the US naval attaché's residence on Nassim Road. The hillside property was sizeable and well maintained. The whitewashed stucco house with its tile roof had a majestic turn-of-the-century appearance. A circular driveway aligned with flaming tiki torches led to stairs and a veranda. Kane bounded up the staircase through the heavy scent of night-blooming jasmine. His sudden presence at the top chased two of the staff away from their final preparations to announce his arrival.

The large covered balcony was party-ready. Colorful paper lanterns hung from the ceiling, cocktail bars were stocked on both ends, and food-serving tables arranged in the middle. Each one held a bountiful selection of delicious-looking, hot and cold canapés and other savories. A large ice chest at the far end contained a mound of iced-down beer, wine, and soft drinks. Some comfortable lounge chairs for anyone needing a break and a few strategically hidden mosquito coils behind potted tropical plants completed the setting.

Captain Grusk and Mary soon appeared, welcomed Kane, and inquired about his beverage choice, a Bombay gin and tonic, after which the captain excused himself to activate the tardy bartenders. Right away, Kane renewed a previous conversation on the unusual architecture of the residence. According to Mary the original portion of the house dated back to the early 1900s. Its hilltop location, U-shaped floor plan, and high ceilings made for good air circulation. A number of noteworthy people had called the place their home over the years and included in this group according to cited records was a Japanese music director in charge of an army band during Singapore's occupation in World War II.

A cacophony of car door closings signaled the arrival of other guests. The stream of foreign attaches and their spouses, Singaporean military officers, and attaché officemates began flowing in. Kane prided his recall of names and faces and one of the first couples to offer their official welcome were his most frequent social acquaintances, the British Naval Attaché, Captain and Mrs. Brett.

"I must say hello to the guest of honor," Captain Brett said as he extended his hand outward as did Brenda.

"Good evening, Captain and Brenda; it's always nice to see you two again."

"Dalton, old boy, I heard you made an interesting catch during your fishing expedition yesterday," Captain Brett submitted.

"You must be referring to the body?"

"Indeed, the body."

"What are you talking about, what body?" Brenda demanded.

"Oh, he found a floater in the harbor. I say, Dalton, you must be fated. You've only just arrived and already in your kit are the essential elements of a mystery novel—sweltering Singapore, a Bastille Day party, a beautiful young widow, a boat, and now this. Can't you see?"

Kane nodded in pretend agreement and replied, "Shall I be Holmes, Watson, or Moriarty?"

Captain Brett was about to voice a clever answer, but he halted as other arriving guests began asking questions.

The Indonesian Army Attaché was first. "Dalton, good evening to you, sir, and what's this about finding a body? Who was it?"

"Yes, we found a body in the harbor and the police are investigating. I believe they're conducting an autopsy now."

"How did you find it?" the Philippine Attaché asked.

"We were just cruising the harbor in our boat and stopped to look at some debris and there it was."

"A man or a woman?"

"Woman."

"Oh!" a female bystander shuddered, clearly shaken by the revelation.

"Hold on now. We should be talking about these lovely ladies," Kane suggested while gesturing to the group of attaché wives standing close behind their husbands, and the conversation took a less morbid turn from there.

Later in the evening after food, drinks and conversation, Captain Grusk stepped to center stage and clinked a spoon against his glass to gain everyone's attention.

"Thank you all for coming to officially welcome aboard Lieutenant Commander Dalton Kane. As you all know, we like to have a combined Hail and Farewell for people coming and going, but Charlie and Jill Morrison had to leave suddenly because of a family emergency back in the US. Anyway, I'm sure you've all met our newest attaché addition by now, but in case you haven't, he's the bachelor right over there with the suntan holding up the bar and nipping the gin. And I'm giving you fair warning gentlemen he's a scratch golfer if you haven't heard. So, Dalton, would you care to say a few words?"

"Yes, sir, I would. First, I want to thank the Grusk's for this fine party and thank you all for taking the time to come here this evening, I know you have busy schedules. It's been hectic, but I'm settling in just fine and really enjoying everything so far. You've all been wonderful in accepting me as a part of the corps and I look forward to your continued friendship and working closely with you over the next several years. I've particularly enjoyed learning a little of your language and sampling your interesting and delicious food. Finally, and regardless of what Captain Grusk says I'm not a scratch golfer."

"I heard he's temporarily seconded to the Navy from the PGA tour just to take our money," yelled the New Zealand air force attaché to mock jeers and laughter.

30

The ten-page autopsy report, minus laboratory attachments and photos arrived at the US Embassy two weeks later, addressed to Kane. A separate letter accompanying the report was sent to all foreign embassies and consulates and requested any information that might shed light on the identity of the victim.

Kane perused the contents. The cause, mechanism, time, and manner of death were addressed in detail. The corpse was determined to be a Caucasoid female 25-35 years of age. Hair, skin, bones, cartilage, arteries, and internal organs, including her uterus and ovaries were factors in making the age determination.

There were no identifying birthmarks or tattoos, no fingers to print and compare with missing persons' reports, and no teeth, only tooth fragments making correlation with any dental records impossible. The cause of death could have been attributed to several injuries, but blunt-force trauma to the neck, a broken neck, was cited as the official cause. In the neck region there were three fractured cervical vertebrae as well as a fractured trachea and hyoid bone. The carotid arteries were ruptured along with vein and muscle damage.

Other noted injuries included a contusion from blunt-force trauma on the right temple, a three-inch long simple linear type fracture on the left side of the skull, plus multiple fractures of the mandible, and four ribs with compression-type fractures. Internally, the dissection found a normal, healthy heart and lungs and all organs in the abdomen were of normal size, weight, and without disease. Toxicological testing of the stomach's contents showed the person had recently ingested rice flour bread, peanut paste, and grape jam. *A peanut butter and jelly sandwich?* Kane took note. *Might she have possibly been an American?* Blood tests revealed a high blood alcohol content of 0.08. The coroner ruled out drowning mainly by exclusion based on the presence of the other serious injuries even though there was some saltwater in the lungs.

One comment stood out from the many details in the report. The forensic pathologist performing the autopsy found several organs partially frozen deep inside the body cavity. Therefore, the approximate time of death could not be determined. Finally, based on all the available evidence the coroner classified the manner of death as homicide.

Kane stopped by to discuss the report with Captain Grusk, but he was busy with a visitor, so he took the report up to Eggleston's office.

Eggleston skimmed the document for several minutes then handed it back. "Frozen? For some time, there has been a rumor of a prostitution ring set up to supply girls to certain merchant ships and shipping lines. I know the Singaporean authorities have an ongoing investigation based on the recovery of several drowned girls last year. One theory was that after an unfortunate individual had served her purpose, or didn't perform up to expectations, she was merely jettisoned overboard. Since many Asian girls here can't swim or aren't strong swimmers their drowned bodies eventually wash up on shore. But frozen and mutilation would be a new twist, I think."

"I wasn't aware of such an investigation, but this female wasn't Asian and she wasn't that young, and how many blonde Caucasian prostitutes could there be in Singapore, none maybe?"

"Obviously, you haven't been to Bugis Street. I'll have to take you some evening for orientation and a beer. You can see just about anything and everything if you spend enough time there."

"Okay, but what about the mutilation? It suggests a lot of hate, something personal. Were any of the others found that way?"

"I don't recall anything about mutilation."

"Don't you agree the extent someone went to conceal her identity was extraordinary, particularly for this part of the world? It suggests to me, the perpetrator may have a different background, perhaps not an Asian. I'd be interested in seeing if there are any missing person reports on foreign visitors or US expatriates in the next few weeks."

"Get real, Dalton. A lot of people go missing in this part of the world, some due to foul play and others vanish on purpose; it's not that unusual. Earlier this year there was that missing American yacht you may have heard about in the news. It reportedly departed Hong Kong bound for Singapore, but it never arrived here and there wasn't a trace of it even after an exhaustive international search. However, I recently heard the investigation has been reopened due to some new evidence about a possible insurance scam. The Consul, Ortega, may have more details if you're really interested."

"I suppose it's none of my business, but I would like to know whether any of the others were sliced, diced, and frozen like this one. Personally, I don't think the possibly of it being an American should be ruled out. There about 9,000 American expats living here and at least a couple thousand of them must be women, and the obvious peanut butter and jelly sandwich in her stomach while not exclusively American is pretty much a universal American snack."

"That's true. I'll mention the subject tomorrow during my meeting at ISD and see if they have any comment. So, changing the subject, anything new since the last time we talked?" Eggleston inquired as he reached for the switch to turn on the music to mask their conversation.

"Last time I mentioned I was in receipt of new dinner invitations and went to both the Grusks and Changs. I went back to the Grusks again last night for my welcome aboard party with the attaché corps. The conversation over food and drinks in both households was friendly and wide-ranging. We talked about everything under the sun, from politics and Navy history to Asian art and California wine. I haven't detected anything I would consider suspicious or abnormal in any of them. Mrs. Grusk does like her wine. She might have an occasional glass beyond her limit, but she never loses control of her faculties, and I don't sense it's a sign of tension or another problem. They seem very compatible, good values, good family. As you know, their two sons are married with children and live in the San Diego area and are apparently doing just fine."

"What about Colonel Silver?"

"No invitation yet, but he's busy with the delivery of the new F-5 aircraft and the training and acceptance procedures. I'll keep making myself available though. Has anything come back yet on the leave information and the classified inventory records I provided?"

"Nothing yet, they're still checking the data. It might be some time before they complete the passenger manifests and obtain all the hotel records. What about Chief Sanderson and the Army sergeants, anything new there?"

"No, nothing out of the ordinary. And the copy machine hasn't been used after hours since I've been checking on it; it gets a real workout during the daytime though."

"Besides Colonel Silver, anyone else working long hours?"

"No, only him. As I mentioned before, if I become aware of his plan to stay late, I stay busy in and out of the vault until after he leaves just to see what he's up to. He seldom strays from his desk; he drafts letters and messages and sometimes he's on the telephone for twenty to thirty minutes. Now and then he takes a restroom break and on his morning constitutional he usually takes the newspaper and stays there for fifteen minutes, sometimes longer. I've checked his favorite stall after he's returned— nothing but fumes I hate to say, and nothing inside the tank, under the lid, inside the toilet paper roll. One other thing, do you remember when I mentioned seeing the KGB's dapper man about town, Yuri Lubachev, shortly after I ran into you at the Bastille Day celebration?"

"Yes,"

"I told you we were almost face-to-face, maybe three feet apart, and I said 'hello' in Russian to him, but he didn't reply, but the fellow with him who was acting like a bodyguard did look at me. Who was that other guy? I don't recall seeing his face in our files or in the briefing you gave me."

"It was likely either the deputy *resident* Nicholai Persakov, or a new guy Maxim Egorshin. Egorshin is not on their diplomatic list; he's only identified as staff, but in public he seems to stick close to Lubachev. I'm sure Lubachev knows who you are by now and I imagine they've always been put off a little with the boat operations, so I wouldn't expect him to say hello and buy you a drink."

"True, but they could be accomplishing the same thing in a rented boat or use some surrogate to take photos in the harbor."

"They aren't. Anyway, I would have been alerted, especially if it was occurring on a regular basis."

"Lubachev seems to be quite the ladies' man," Kane asserted.

"He does seem to have rather a long leash, doesn't he?"

"He was cozying up at the bar or dancing cheek to cheek with a bevy of good-looking women and only a few of them were Russian as best I could tell."

"He's a Jekyll and Hyde, the stoic, secretive KGB resident, or the alter ego, the omnipresent, fun-loving cultural attaché. He's groomed, he's urbane, but if you're hinting at sexual indiscretion, I'm not sure he'd go so far even for the motherland. He's got a wife and daughter back in Moscow of whom he's quite fond."

"I sure wouldn't want to try to drink him under the table."

"He can handle it."

"Once when the music stopped, I saw him return to the bar, drain a glass of champagne, and then he slammed two shots of vodka on top of it, one-two-three like there was no tomorrow. Then he returned to the dance floor for a cha-cha and I don't think he missed a step."

"Ha, he's Russian. They drink, they make merry, and there's the diplomatic lifestyle and the freedom. He's built up a tolerance for it all," Eggleston laughed.

Kane was a bloodhound when it came to collecting data. He analyzed it, stored it, and relentlessly filled in the blanks. One remark by Eggleston caught his attention, but it might have been nothing at all. Eggleston's file on Lubachev was certainly more complete and up to date and he surely had more insight about Lubachev's personal life than just about anyone else. But his characterization "quite fond" when referring to Lubachev's relationship with his family back in Moscow seemed to roll so comfortably off his tongue. Kane could conceive of Lubachev being a caring husband and father, but Eggleston's remark nearly implied a cozy level of familiarity beyond the norm for two adversaries.

Kane walked back to the attaché office and directly into the vault. He asked Chief Sanderson to retrieve the file on Lubachev. Information there confirmed Lubachev had a wife and daughter in Moscow, but no other details.

31

Taking deep breaths and sweating freely Kane strained through the last repetitions of curls in the third set of his workout with the 25-pound dumbbells. When he stopped, he thanked God for the fellow, was it Evans or Perkins? No, it was Carrier, yes, Carrier, who invented air-conditioning.

In the kitchenette he peeled a kiwi fruit and a banana and tossed them into the blender on top of a cup of plain yogurt. Chugging down the mixture with an assortment of vitamins he congratulated himself on the concoction rather than room service or pot stickers and fried pork and rice at the nearby New China Moon restaurant.

The weekend yawned before him. The diplomatic corps had an understanding: Weekends were exclusively for personal or family time. Official events on Saturdays or Sundays were only for visiting civilian or military VIPs. A private dinner invitation to Colonel Silver's home was on the schedule for Sunday evening and with that he would have been inside all of the principal attaché's homes at least once, the Grusks and Changs on multiple occasions and still not a hint of Bernard.

Today, Saturday, was all his. Lathering, warm water pounding on his chest, his tenor voice sent *"La Donna e Mobile"* bouncing off the shower tiles as he contemplated the fine two-legged example of semi-Asian art he had encountered at the Bastille Day party, Aurora Booth.

She did tell me to stop by, so why not? He selected his clothing carefully, a monogrammed cotton shirt, linen slacks, and Italian loafers. *Sockless? Nah, too Hollywood.*

The taxi deposited him in the middle of a block of older,

tile-fronted, two-story buildings. The ground floors held shops of every description. Top floors, flats, and most with shutters opened wide and tinny music emanating from a few. Incense from smoldering joss sticks in unseen shrines floated through windows onto the street below. Several windowsills held potted plants and birdcages, one sill hosting a pair of dozing cats in the midday sun. He shuddered, remembering a sleepover years ago at a classmate's house, a house seemingly filled with cats and by midnight his parents had been called and he was getting a very an unpleasant inoculation from Doctor Dad to restore his breathing and reduce the swelling in his eyes.

He spotted the sign. Handsome gold lettering proclaimed: Aurora, Fine European Imports, Custom Tailor for Gentlemen and Ladies. A small hand lettered note taped to the heavy glass entry door said: Closed today at 2:00 PM.

The shop was larger inside than it looked from the outside. A center aisle separated the men and women's apparel. A tall young salesman directly to the rear attended to a sturdy couple sipping dark liquid from small glasses. The salesman gave Kane a nod of acknowledgement and motioned at bolts of suit material and display cases filled with arrays of neckties, handkerchiefs, and other accessories. Kane sauntered over to handle the suit material while listening to the couple discussing the merchandise with the salesman. They spoke Russian in an untainted Moscow accent Kane was able to translate with ease, but such was not always the case. Limited use local dialects could be a translator's nemesis and he sent up a prayer for the Navajo code-talkers.

The salesman excused himself from the couple, saying he would give them a few minutes to consider the purchase. He approached Kane, sizing him up—the haircut, the western clothes, and the Rolex told him he was likely American, but not one of those big, burly American oilmen who occasionally patronized the shop.

"How may I assist you, suh?"

Kane thought quickly, needing to buy time.

"I would like to see some fabric for custom shirts."

"Yes, and may I offer you a drink?" the salesman asked.

"No, thank you."

"Some tea perhaps?"

"Oh, that would be fine."

The salesman disappeared behind a beautifully lacquered Coromandel screen to pour the tea as Kane resumed looking into the display cases and moved closer to the wrangling Russian couple. He overheard the wife tell her husband he would look handsome in the suit and his brothers would be envious. The husband responded grumpily, "For the price I would have to look like a [unintelligible] czar." Kane's Russian failed him there, unfamiliar with the likely negative idiom.

The salesman returned bearing a tray with a steaming cup of tea and a large ringed binder filled with swatches of cloth. He led Kane to an antique gaming table in the corner and then returned to the Russian couple.

Kane selected the chair angled toward the rear of the shop. When he first entered, he caught a distant glimpse of Aurora in the background. Her hair took on a reddish glint under the incandescent lighting. She was spraying perfume on the wrists of two Japanese women, sending faintly exotic bouquets aloft, chattering gaily as she wrapped and bagged several small packages. The women then made their exit, smiling, bowing, and waving goodbye.

Kane made a show of concentrating on the fabric samples as Aurora click-clacked toward him in scandalously high heels. She gave him a polite smile and sailed behind the screen. The Russians still debated over refreshed drinks. Hearing the sounds of her again he looked up to see her juggling a black leather binder with a pen clipped to the cover and a sample shirt draped on a hanger. He stood and pulled out a chair for her while she placed her notebook on the table and carefully arranged the shirt over another chair. She was wearing a pale green raw silk dress with an enormous jade broach pinned near the neckline, dazzling. Kane was wearing a thin line of sweat on his upper lip and hoped for the best.

He need not have worried though because she remembered him. They briefly discussed the extravagances of the French celebration and the antics of some of the guests as the evening enlivened with too much bubbly, laughing and speculating how painful the following day must have been for some of the revelers.

Getting down to business, she pointed out the fine tailoring on the shirt collar and cuffs, and indicated a selection of styles in her binder.

"Have you made any selections from the fabric?"

"Not yet, but your tailor is amazing. The stitching on this shirt is nearly invisible."

"Yes, she has been doing this since she was a girl; it's how she met my father."

Kane blinked in surprise.

Aurora smiled and pointed at the salesman, "That's my brother, Lee, over there."

The Russians departed empty-handed and Lee was returning the suit material to the rack, visibly annoyed at the lack of a sale.

Aurora glanced at her watch and Kane remembered the note on the door. Apologizing, he said he would return another day. She explained the shortened day was due to a planned family gathering. "Grandfather is eighty-seven today; he keeps telling us this will be his last birthday," and with a wicked giggle she added, "and we keep telling him he is just trying to cheer us up!"

Kane stood, fortified himself, and said, "I would very much like to see you again. Will you join me for dinner next weekend?"

"Yes, I would enjoy that. Here's my card, give me a call."

Kane smiled and left. Aurora locked the door and pulled the shade.

The brother, Lee, had been observing the two of them as he occupied himself spraying and wiping countertops, folding and fanning ties and scarves in the cases. His sister's posture told him what she surely would not. She leaned in toward the American as they talked, smiling and gazing into his eyes, and laughing delightedly at comments he made. Lee wondered about the man, what did he do, where did she meet him, and what was so interesting to her? He was itching to ask, but knew she would smack him just as she always had done when he teased and questioned her about her suitors.

32

A long with a variety of support material the attaché office was on distribution for maritime reports. A recent one contained information on a small Soviet Navy task group in the Indian Ocean making its way eastward toward Singapore through the Bay of Bengal. It was likely returning to homeport in the Vladivostok area in the Sea of Japan after a long deployment. Using a nominal transit speed of advance and walking off the distance on a chart with a pair of dividers, Kane calculated the number of hours until the ships' estimated time of arrival at Singapore via the Malacca Strait. Then he called the Aussie Warrant Officer William Ross to alert him of the upcoming collection opportunity.

Several days later Naseer picked the pair up at sunrise at one of the city's boat landings. Ross came onboard toting a large, expensive-looking camera case and Kane was interested to see what new-fangled equipment might be inside. As they motored out to the strait to wait for their quarry, Ross opened the case and began removing its contents: A plastic bowl filled with cooked rice to pair with Naseer's home-cooked curry, a second larger container with fresh green vegetables for a salad, a tall six-pack of Foster's beer, the morning newspaper, and a jar of Vegemite the purported national food of Australia. Kane wondered, *Surely a 35mm camera and telephoto lens was stashed in there somewhere.*

"Amber nectar?" Ross called out as he popped the top on a can of foaming Foster's and held it up for Kane.

"No thanks, I'll pass."

"How about you up there, Captain Naseer?" Ross yelled,

teasing and trying Naseer's Muslim (no alcohol) resolve, "No? Cigarette? No? Okay then, cheers mates."

They moved to a position out of the shipping lanes where they could see up the strait then cut the boat's engines and drifted. Naseer boiled water for tea and broke out hardboiled eggs, a carton of ultra-heat-treated milk, bananas, and a tin of English biscuits. Meanwhile, Kane gave the horizon another scan with the binoculars and re-checked his cameras and film supplies.

With breakfast completed, they sat in the captains' chairs, chatted, shared sections of the newspaper and watched from a distance as the first merchant ships of the day passed north and south in the strait, and in and out of the harbor.

Naseer had exceptional distant vision; he seemed to see just about as well without the binoculars. It was approaching 8:00 AM and he was standing on the bow coiling a line when he called out "They're coming!" and pointed excitedly to the horizon.

Kane grabbed the binoculars and saw four, thin, equally spaced plumes of gray smoke. "I think you're right."

Naseer hurried inside, secured the teakettle and the other cooking gear, assumed his position at the helm, and started the engines.

"Ready—when—you—are" Ross bellowed in between sucking down the remainder of his second beer while simultaneously relieving himself of the first one as he teetered precariously atop the boat's transom.

Naseer shoved the throttle levers forward. The engines roared as they picked up speed toward a good intercept position. "It's definitely them," Kane confirmed as he passed the binoculars over to Ross.

The plan was to stay on the Singapore side of the strait, run parallel with the ships, and take photographs as the group transited into the South China Sea. It was totally overt and legal; no threatening moves, no violations of Rules of the Road or straits transit regulations. The Soviet navy ships were in a column formation, the lead ship, an oiler, followed by two destroyer escorts, and a minesweeper. All were covered with rust from being at sea for such a long time, all were flying the Soviet naval ensign, and the oiler displayed an additional personal flag indicating a Commodore level flag officer was embarked.

This was the first time for Kane to see operational Soviet Navy ships up close in the flesh. Apparently, Morrison had never been inclined to get very close to transiting ships of interest during his tenure, so when Kane told Naseer to ease in nearer to the formation only a slight bit of rudder resulted. Kane finally put his hand on the helm and gave it a good quarter of a turn.

"Hold it steady right about there and give me more speed."

Ross cheered through a sudden douse of saltwater in his face, "Good show, mate!"

It was a hazy bright morning, perfect photographic conditions. The boat climbed over some fairly large bow swells from the lead ship and then maintained the same course and speed for several minutes while camera shutters staccato clicked and rolls of film were exposed. The challenge, depending on the course and sea state, was to brace a knee against the gunwale or hold on to something, anything, to maintain balance while keeping one's self and the camera lens relatively dry. If you could do that while changing cameras, f-stops, and reloading film, some excellent imagery could be obtained.

Russian sailors, many with their shirts removed to soak up the morning sun were on the rails along the port side of the oiler. Some were pointing at Singapore's cosmopolitan skyline, probably wishing they could get some liberty there, while others watched with interest the little white boat keeping pace abeam.

Kane switched to a color movie camera.

Suddenly Ross blurted out, "Bloody hell, what are they throwing at us?"

Kane looked up to see the arm motion and trajectories as well and what for a split second might possibly have been mistaken for a volley of hand grenades was quickly determined to be a well-orchestrated barrage of potatoes, all of the spuds splashing just yards short of their boat.

Ross immediately hoisted a beer in a ridiculing toast while extending the middle finger of his other hand high into the air as further advertisement of his contempt. "Stiff cheddar you bloody arsebadgers!" he yelled at the top of his lungs. "You bastards have no arms!" followed by "Your bowlers can't deliver shit!" which was all somewhat of a semantics lesson in Australian cricket match cursing. Because of the noise and distance, the Russians likely did not hear Ross's comeback, but without a doubt they grasped the visual content of his bravado.

Kane ordered Naseer to ease up on the throttle so they could fall back and photograph the other units in the column. As a final maneuver, they cut across the stern of the trailing mine sweeper and proceeded up the starboard side of the ships, cameras still rolling, until the Russians were through the transit zone where they turned on the knots and slowly pulled away.

"Okay, Naseer, enough, good job" Kane said as he nodded to Ross. Naseer reduced speed and set a course back to the harbor to check the engines and prepare for an early lunch.

"That was outstanding!" shouted a revved-up Ross. "The bloody Russians either took a sudden disliking to us or we caught them at a bad time when they were sucking on trough lollies from their bloody stinking urinals. I've only three coldies left mates, so how about a beer?"

33

Aurora Booth kept yo-yoing in and out of Kane's head. He finally broke down and called her on Thursday to make sure everything was on track for their first date. He was pleased she sounded happy to hear his voice. She re-confirmed Saturday evening and suggested they rendezvous first at her club, the Cricket Club, around 6:00 PM at the bar for a cocktail after she closed-up shop and changed clothes.

Kane knew of the famous old place and was delighted at the invitation. It was only a few minutes from his hotel by taxi. Established in 1852, it was in the older, colonial part of the city near the harbor and it was one of the first sport and social organizations. The parking lot was full when he arrived. He entered through tall dark doors and passed from the foyer into a spacious and chatty bar room. Patrons were either standing at the massive L-shaped ebony bar or sitting at nearby tables. Overhead, an array of ancient ceiling fans barely rotated, appearing to have given up the century-old battle with the muggy air. However, at ground level the bartenders were hustling trying to keep many thirsts quenched.

Kane imagined what the scene must have been like ages ago when the club was "whites only" and catered exclusively to the British privileged class. Well-dressed regulars met there for entertainment and news of the day while partaking of food, drink, and recreation, in those days tennis, badminton, soccer, darts, billiards, cricket, and other games.

He headed toward a single opening at the bar and one of the bartenders, "Vincent", according to his nametag, stopped wiping down the spot and addressed him.

"Good evening to you, sir."

"Good evening, Vincent."

Leaning forward and using a softer voice so as not to cause embarrassment Vincent informed the unfamiliar face, "I beg your pardon, sir, but this is a private club."

"Yes, I know. I'm a guest of one of your members whom I'm meeting in a few minutes, Ms. Aurora Booth."

"Very good, sir. We haven't been honored by her presence in a long time."

Since their scheduled meeting time was imminent Kane inquired whether Vincent recalled the lady's beverage preference.

"Hmm, I believe that would be ... Campari and soda. Yes, that's it. Campari and soda."

"Make it two, Vincent."

Kane seated himself on the edge of the barstool, one foot touching the floor. Moments later he noticed the man to his left swivel around, sit straighter, and suck it in a little, the stock reaction to the approach of an attractive woman. *It must be her* Kane thought, but he resisted immediately turning. As he passed by, Vincent gave a confirming nod and Kane saw Aurora's image approaching in the mirror behind the bar.

He heard her final footsteps, high heels, and a faint scent of exotic perfume wafted by confirming her close proximity. While the nearby voyeurs bettered their viewing angles Kane turned and stepped from his stool. Her hand reached out for his. She looked even more statuesque and radiant than before, finely sculpted nose and lips, and flashing eyes. Kane's jaw slackened, his mouth agape at her beauty.

"You were expecting someone else?" she said in a slightly coquettish way.

"Oh, no, absolutely not and you look terrific, would you care to sit?" he asked as he pointed to a table conveniently emptying in the far corner.

"Certainly."

She started away; her hair trailed to her waist. He tracked her while blindly attempting to collect the drinks from the bar, bumping and nearly spilling them both. The fact she was alluring from every aspect was not lost on Dalton Kane.

They picked up the conversation where they left off in her shop. She alternately talked and listened, attentive and smiling, and he the same.

"I'll stop, but first I must propose a toast."

"To?" she inquired.

"To the magical, mystical powers of the tiny *ikan bilis*. Had I not been crunching a whole mouthful of them at the Bastille Day party when you passed by you might not have spoken and we would never have met."

"To the seductive *ikan bilis*" she responded, touching his glass with hers and adding a cheerful smile. He watched as she tipped the drink to her mouth and ran her tongue slowly across her upper lip as she finished.

"I thought you might enjoy a change of menu this evening. There's a steakhouse in one of the new hotels and they claim to have Angus beef from the US."

"I don't believe I've tasted Angus beef. Is it much different?"

"I'm sure you'll like it and we probably need to head that direction before they give our table away."

"I'm ready. We'll take my car."

Outside, she waved at a newer white Jaguar sedan in the parking area. The auto approached and a familiar-looking driver jumped out and held open the rear door as they both slid in.

"You remember my brother Lee? He volunteered to be our driver tonight."

"Oh yes, very good" Kane acknowledged and Lee replied "Good evening, suh" then quickly re-entered the car and adjusted the rear-view mirror just enough to gaze into the back seat. Moments later they merged into the traffic on Connaught Drive.

"I like your automobile, no wonder he volunteered."

"It is rather grand, especially the burl wood trim. It was my late husband's choice, but the road tax and maintenance on it is very expensive, so I'm considering something else more economical."

The sales office of the new hotel had been offering a good

promotional rate and Kane had referred several of the attaché office's recent visitors there. He had mentioned it to the maître d'hôtel while making the dinner reservation and the favor was returned with one of the better tables, one with a nice view of the city and harbor.

The steaks were excellent, but the portion much too large for her. Following the main course, their small talk turned to discussions of their families, careers, and personal aspirations, and went on comfortably for hour while they nibbled on a Texas-style peach cobbler alamode and sipped espresso coffee.

She had Sunday morning planned with her mother and brother and it was approaching 10:00 PM, so they decided to call it an evening and head for the Raffles to drop Kane off. En route, he contemplated the prospect of stealing a goodnight kiss however awkward it might be with the restrictions of backseat armrest and Lee's beady eyes a fixture in the mirror.

They arrived at the hotel, turning into the circular driveway. A turbaned Sikh doorman stepped forward to meet the car. Kane immediately exited from the opposite side and reached back inside. At first Aurora mistook his gesture as overture for a handshake, but he held on and gently tugged. She slid out. He pulled her closer, placed his arms around her slender waist and told her how much he enjoyed the evening. He did not notice her slipping out of her heels until she had settled to nearly his level.

"There," she whispered.

He kissed her tenderly; she kissed back with greater passion and neither of them spoke until giggling interrupted the embrace. They turned to see a young family on the steps about to enter the hotel with two children pointing fingers in their direction and the mother trying to make the kids stop it.

"I believe it's a sign," Aurora said with a twinkle in her eye.

"Yes" Kane sighed, "I'll save the remainder for next time."

She laughed, "And we'll go dancing next time?"

"Most definitely and soon I hope."

"Yes," she said as her eyes lingered, sending a subtle invitation.

34

The "enemy" held the high ground in well-camouflaged trenches and machine gun emplacements and they opened up with a withering stream of fire, wreaking havoc on the single Singapore army scout vehicle temporarily stopping it in its tracks. A squad of soldiers bounded from the truck and began returning fire with automatic weapons, while their vehicle managed to restart, find reverse gear, and withdraw to cover. In the meantime, the pinned-down Singaporean soldiers used their radio to call for help.

That was the opening scene of the mini war game staged for foreign and local dignitaries including the military attaché corps. It was not the Paris Air Show in scale; however, a fine performance never the less with comfortable stadium-type seating and plenty of action including seemingly limitless pyrotechnics and blank ammunition. The mock battle performed by the combined Singapore military forces was one of the many events taking place on National Day, August 9th, the day commemorating Singapore's independence from Malaysia in 1965. A national ceremony, a large parade, sporting events, spectacular fireworks, and crowds of people wearing the patriotic colors, red and white, filled the streets and venues to see and participate in the festivities.

Full dress military uniforms less the swords were *de rigueur* for the attaché corps and Kane asked Aurora Booth to join him as his guest. Colonel Chang had given his driver the day off for the holiday, so the colonel offered to be the driver to the event. With Ms. Chang in the front passenger's seat and Aurora and Kane tucked in the back seat they headed off to view the battle royal in style, the women wearing stylish frocks for the occasion.

In Singapore like most places, someone in the rear of a car bearing diplomatic license plates is presumably superior in rank and social status to someone behind the steering wheel. This seems to hold particularly true if the driver has Asian features and the male occupant of the back seat is Caucasian.

Arriving at the battlefield venue, Colonel Chang joined the slow-moving queue of VIP cars and eventually arrived at the drop off point. A young Singaporean army officer immediately helped the back-seat occupants out of the car. He turned them over to another escort who lead them along the route to the viewing stands and the section where all the military attaché corps were supposed to sit as a group. In the meantime, back at the car, confusion reigned. Straightaway, Colonel Chang found himself directed to the parking area while he tried in vain to convince the attendants that he, too, was one of the special guests, not merely a driver. It was only after he managed to retrieve his official invitation from the glove box that things started to clear up. Kane was already helping Aurora to their seats when he noticed the Changs were not in the group behind them. He saw Colonel Chang in the distance standing next to the car with his wife. Apparently, about the same time some official must have read the invitation or noticed the insignia on the colonel's shoulders and, realizing the mistake in protocol, was doing his utmost to make amends for it.

Colonel Chang seemed to be smiling through it though, no big deal, but when the Changs finally found their seats Kane could not help but give the colonel a ribbing over the incident. "I kind of liked that relaxing in the back seat with a bird colonel as my driver."

"You'll pay for that commander," Colonel Chang chuckled, as he wagged his finger at Kane. |

The military attaché group looked great in their menagerie of dress uniforms, blues, greens, tans, and whites, along with the spouses' colorful outfits. It looked like opening day of the horse racing season or a polo match. There were smiles, handshakes, and waves all around. They were all anxious to see the big show and more than a few of the men seemed distracted and interested in eyeballing Kane's attractive companion.

The military band struck up stirring martial music and a few minutes later, following Singapore's national anthem, "Majulah Singapura," the "war" began.

The weather was perfect for audience and performers alike, sunny skies and a slight breeze blowing away helped to keep the battlefield clear of smoke and other airborne debris. The nearly two-hour-long schedule-of-events was action-packed with choreographed displays of joint force tactics and weaponry. A noisy "whop-whop-whop" in the distance announced the arrival of the first helicopters and two of them swooped low over the viewing stands as they conducted a simulated rocket attack against enemy positions, while remotely detonated explosives added to the realism. From stage right two light tanks at full throttle roared into view smashing through a barrier of empty oil drums sending them high into the air and then the tanks continued on to squash a second barrier of junked automobiles before halting at their firing positions. Smoke and dust rose to great heights enveloping the battle arena. In the other direction, a hundred yards away, a small convoy of army trucks arrived and began disgorging infantrymen to join in the firefight.

By this time most of the crowd had inserted earplugs or fingers in ears to block out the noise, and the smell of burnt gunpowder was pervasive. Next, in the background a half a mile away in the Johore strait, two Singapore patrol boats took up positions for shore bombardment and began unleashing salvos in support of the ground forces. The "enemy" appeared to be putting up a stiff resistance so a section of Republic of Singapore Air Force jet attack aircraft were called in to join in the fray, conducting simulated strafing and bombing runs. Again, well-timed pyrotechnics hidden on the battlefield made it seem almost real. For a while, not many in the audience noticed a transport aircraft droning back and forth high overhead until it began dropping orange smoke to determine wind direction in the landing zone. Minutes later, a stick of paratroopers dropped-in to help their comrades-in-arms. The tide was slowly beginning to turn and yard-by-yard Singaporean ground forces advanced, casualties appeared light, and battlefield medical support effective. Finally, with a barrage of bombs, mortar rounds, and bullets flying, and the situation appearing lost for the enemy forces the survivors showed hands and a white flag, and a rousing cheer arose from the viewing stands.

During the ebb and flow of the battle Kane took time off to scan the crowd from behind the privacy of his sunglasses. Every member of the foreign attaché corps was present. Many important Singaporean civilian leaders and high-ranking military officers were sitting up front in the best seats and the sections to the left and right of the attachés held other civilian VIPs. Kane looked up and down the rows as far as he could in each direction for recognizable faces. A row behind and about twenty seats to his left he made eye contact with an Asian face, maybe Korean, staring back. Kane raised his hand slightly and wiggled his fingers in friendly acknowledgement, but the other man remained glaring. Kane did not recognize the fellow; he wondered who he might be, and why the face, but he let it pass.

"Dalton, Dalton," Aurora called out trying to get his attention to ask a question.

"Sorry", replied Kane, still perplexed by the stare-down with whoever it was.

In the waning minutes of the performance the wind reversed and a wall of churned-up dust and smoke moved toward the viewing stands. The crowd quickly dispersed and most of them managed to make it to their cars before the thick khaki hue descended over the entire area.

35

In late August, the government of North Vietnam found they had a new problem on their hands. One of their aged cargo ships sold for scrap and much needed cash was in tow to India for dismantling when its contract tugboat experienced an engineering casualty during a freak storm in the South China Sea. At daybreak, the tug and tow limped into Singapore for emergency repairs. The tugboat was half the problem. The freighter in tow had taken on water and needed to be pumped-out and patched-up before it too was again seaworthy enough to continue the voyage.

Heads in Hanoi as high as the Political Bureau level of the Communist party itself might roll for this, but almost certainly officials at the shipyard in Haiphong would take the brunt of the criticism for the poor planning and execution. A hand-selected group of the most loyal workers had been meticulous in removing all physical evidence of this particular ship's use during the war and the final step according to the plan was to make the ship disappear altogether. Upon arrival at the buyer's distant graving dock, a score of acetylene torches would cut the hulk into pieces, furnaces would melt the steel, and any scintilla of physical evidence pointing to the ship's grisly criminal past would be forever obliterated.

Upon hearing of the unscheduled stop, but with no diplomatic representation in Singapore, Vietnamese officials in Hanoi sent a classified cable at highest precedence to KGB Central in Moscow. Representatives there from a special branch of the KGB's First Chief Directorate were certain no others than themselves, a handful of high-level Communist party officials in Hanoi, and a few more, deep inside Fidel Castro's government knew of the highly classified program involving the ship. But they also knew it was a very sensitive subject, so Hanoi's call for help was rapidly elevated. Composed and transmitted in high precedence to the Soviet Embassy in Singapore, a message-directive was received and signed for by the KGB resident, Yuri Lubachev.

Unfortunately for Lubachev, the problem could only be stated in general terms without background because he was not cleared for the sensitive program involving the ship even though it had been terminated several years earlier. The orders left unanswered questions, but even so action was required. Moscow hoped the two units would be quickly repaired and then slip away without further incident. However, if something untoward happened, say, the Americans somehow became involved particularly since their assistant naval attaché cruised the harbor in a boat, Bernard, and others were to be activated. First, Bernard was to report on discussions and decisions the US Embassy planned to take regarding the vessels. Second, Lubachev was to initiate "security measures" to help guarantee the units would depart on their journey as soon as possible. Lubachev was surprised with the audacity of the second part and exactly what action Moscow had in mind for him was not spelled out. As he re-read the order, he concluded it must have been prepared in haste by some bureaucrat unfamiliar with operations in Singapore, and perhaps designed only to protect someone's backside in the Kremlin in case the whole matter became exposed. The risk of course was if any actions were conducted without the utmost skill and caution it could draw unwanted attention to Bernard and perhaps jeopardize his other important work, and Lubachev himself could be held accountable for bungling the whole affair. There was no recourse for Lubachev though, because Moscow's word was final.

"Diamond is a stubborn lout and a fool. I know him, Yuri, and I question his commitment. He will give himself away if something develops and he becomes confrontational, as is his tendency. Our efforts could be ruined, our promotions cancelled, we could be sent back," protested Nicholai, Diamond's controller.

"True, but these are my orders. Signal him; we'll need to talk face to face so he won't 'screw it up' as the Americans say, and ask Grigori to step in here. I need to go over this matter with him as well in case that boat from the US embassy becomes a problem."

For security reasons the KGB never contacted Diamond by telephone because they had to assume the lines at his embassy office and his embassy house, as well as their own phone lines might have taps in place. Only as a last resort in an emergency such as to signal his detection and to execute his escape plan would they ever consider calling him in the clear.

One of several methods to make secret, routine contact to service a dead drop was to exchange covert signals during Diamond's midday exercise routine. Unless pressing business got in the way he always took a walk over the noon hour into the city ostensibly to get exercise and fresh air, but he never failed to stop and have a glass of iced tea with mint and cool off at the same sidewalk café between 12:30 and 1:00 PM before returning to work.

The signals changed from time to time. Now, if Diamond saw one of his Panama hat-wearing-leather-briefcase-toting KGB contacts walk along the sidewalk opposite the café and step off the curb, right foot first, dead drop "A" needed servicing; left foot first meant the site had not been loaded. Likewise, if Diamond sat sipping his drink and reading the paper or watching the pedestrian traffic go by with his right leg crossed over his left, he had placed something in dead drop "B" and the KGB needed to retrieve it; left over right meant he had made no deposit.

Late that night Diamond went out for a walk and a short distance from his house he retrieved a cryptic note from the dead drop, a tiny, magnetized box clinging to a metal brace on the underside of a city bus stop bench. The alphanumeric message contained six characters, "81012C". The first digit represented the day of the week and he was to subtract one from whatever number appeared there—in this case, 8 minus 1 was 7, meaning Saturday, the seventh day. The second and third digits were random, and always changed; they were only there to add confusion in case some outside party discovered the message. The fourth and fifth digits represented a 24-hour military clock and he was to add three to whatever digits were there, so 12 plus 3 was 15 or 1500 hours. And the final character, a letter, identified one of six different meeting places from a list he had committed to memory. Translated, the note instructed him to meet the next day, Saturday, at 3:00 PM at the sauna and massage facility in the alley at the rear of the Jade Garden hotel. As Diamond walked back to his house, he chewed the note until it was pulp and swallowed it.

36

Eggleston and Kane continued their efforts though nothing had surfaced and pressure was building. Likewise, after thorough analysis back at Langley there was disappointment in not finding discrepancies in the attaché office's classified inventory files or the destruction report documentation. And so far, the vacation and leave records proved a dead end as well. Lastly, the attaché office's travel records remained un-correlated with known movements of foreign agent operatives in Southeast Asia and there was no new, exploitable communications intelligence.

Several groups at the CIA, FBI, and NSA continued their vigilance, waiting, watching, and listening for any scrap of information that might help crack the case. Teams at Langley and Fort Meade remained active for weeks, now months since the inception of the operation, but it had grown quiet, too quiet. Initial interest and excitement had waned and more than one apprehensive analyst called evidence of Bernard's continuance and even his existence into question. For a few, several fragments of information did not seem to fit and there were new questions about MI5's defector. His *bona fides* had yet to be established; information he provided on an unrelated matter was uncorroborated and ultimately proved to be incorrect, so uncertainty about him had crept in. Was the defector credible or part of a plot of deception? Was some of his material merely disinformation leaked by the KGB and designed to expend and divert US intelligence resources? Was the overall analysis accurate or had too many incongruous dots been connected in haste?

Janis Crowell directed a review. A two-day meeting convened to re-examine everything germane to the case. Facts, assumptions, conflicting data, historical comparisons, and opinions were all laid-out, dissected, and analyzed. Several finger-pointing arguments were intense, inversely proportional to the quality and quantity of evidential material brought to the table. In the end, though, consensus remained the same. Bernard probably existed and he or she likely continued work inside the embassy.

One perhaps significant piece of information surfaced during a review of the defector's debriefing file. While reportedly eavesdropping on a telephone conversation between a possible KGB official and a GRU Colonel in Moscow, the defector had heard Bernard's name mentioned in association with the Russian word, *problema*. However, the defector was not able to establish the context. Was the problem with Bernard, his handler, the operational environment, or what exactly, or was the defector telling the truth?

The Eggleston-Kane team had inherent advantages and disadvantages. In some ways the two-person effort on-site made counter-detection by the KGB more difficult. Conversely, there were only so many hours in a day and just so much two people could accomplish without drawing undue attention to work outside their normal spheres of activity.

It was also more difficult to prove a negative, but after almost three months of closely monitoring his co-workers and with virtually nothing incriminating or even suspicious to show for it, Kane felt the attaché office was clean and he made his feelings known to Eggleston. Kane also saw signs Eggleston was stressing out, so he offered to lend additional assistance to Eggleston beyond his own attaché office efforts. Eggleston responded he would take Kane's offer under consideration.

From the beginning, Crowell perceived the possible downside of trying to work the case with too few assets inside the embassy. However, her calculation was tempered with Kane in place since there was strong opinion put forth early on that Bernard was in the attaché office. It was becoming clearer now to Crowell, though, that the restrictive approach onsite might need revisiting.

In the meantime, the CIA's desire to clear Ambassador

Lipka resulted in her being read-in to the operation. A complete re-scrubbing of her life history revealed nothing new or derogatory except for a real estate-related lawsuit settled out of court some twenty years earlier. So, during a regularly scheduled trip back to Washington she attended an additional meeting at CIA headquarters. Following a polygraph examination, she was indoctrinated into the effort, no active role, just to keep her eyes and ears open and report anything suspicious to Eggleston.

A short time later, one of Eggleston's assistants was also cleared. Tasked with additional after hour's surveillance of suspects, he also helped with preparations to move into a more pro-active phase with taps on telephone lines and installation of other covert surveillance devices.

At the CIA, Crowell approved Eggleston's request for an expanded role for Kane, with some restrictions.

37

Upon receiving approval from Crowell for Kane's offer of help, Eggleston invited him to his office late one afternoon. He opened with several new, but insignificant details in the case and then shifted to a review of suspects. For more than an hour the two of them huddled over a legal pad with names and notes and a stack of personnel folders as Beethoven's piano concertos played in the background.

"Let's see if your observations, intuition, and prejudices jibe with mine. Give me some feedback as I go through these, if you disagree or have anything to add."

"Sure, but I don't have the familiarity with the entire staff that you have."

"I know, that's okay. There's nothing new from any source, nothing in-house yet, and the pieces we do have are diverse. There's the sketchy communications, the questionable defector input, and what may have been a slip of the tongue by a Russian diplomat during a Law of the Sea conference in Brussels concerning national boundaries and super tanker transits of international straits. In fact, that's what drew initial interest. The Russian stance was far too insightful, almost as though they had read point by point our position paper regarding proposed changes to the rules for the Malacca Strait."

"Who saw the point paper here?" Kane asked.

"Many people saw it. I developed the initial draft and then it was routed to the various other offices for information and comment. The DCM saw it, your office, Economics, Coast Guard, DEA, USAID, and others, and finally Ambassador Lipka signed it and sent it off to Washington. More than twenty people initialed the routing sheet and I assume others read it, but didn't initial. I still have the original routing slip if you want to see it."

Eggleston continued. "We don't know Bernard's motivation. We do believe this person probably has access to classified information though because the position paper was marked Secret. That by itself might eliminate the pool of Singaporean national employees with no clearances, so then we have remaining some fifty or so Americans holding a Secret or Top-Secret clearance. How Bernard gained access to the document is another question, through his own position and clearance, or possibly a surrogate friend or co-worker who had access and purposely or inadvertently allowed Bernard to see it."

"So, with that, I'll begin at the top, Ambassador Lipka. She's read-in now as you know, so I've eliminated her from suspicion for purposes of this discussion," Eggleston said as he crossed through her name with his pencil. "Any problem with that?"

"No, my gut says Bernard is not the ambassador, but other than my infrequent escort duties I don't really have much face time with her, not nearly as much as you have, so I'll defer to your judgment."

"I began with Lipka, so I'll continue to her secretary, Judith Feldman. Nothing suspicious there, but as the ambassador's secretary she's in position to know a little and sometimes a lot about everything going on around here. She's single, in her early thirties, attractive, a sweetheart personality, and a textbook target for the KGB. She appears to be a hundred percent dedicated to Lipka, though, and has the ambassador's full confidence. Lipka laid it on the line for her back at the agency, said she trusts Judith Feldman as much as her husband. Regardless, and I'm being totally objective here, she's a suspect for the time being."

"Anything special planned for her?"

"My eyes are open. I've planted several phony documents for bait, so we'll see what happens, and she'll be receiving another upgrade to her office telephone."

The lead on Eggleston's pencil broke with a pop as he checked the next name on his list. "Historically, statistically, Bernard is male, and DCM Bass fills many of the profile criteria.

He has access to virtually everything the ambassador sees and hears, all the clearances, participates in the important meetings, travels regularly on official business throughout the region and to Washington. That provides him with opportunity and cover for clandestine contact. On the other hand, he's a horse's ass, a lightning rod, someone who incredibly made it up the ladder to where he is today. I've been tempted to punch his lights out on more than one occasion and torch that silly-ass toupee of his. I honestly don't know how Ambassador Lipka puts up with the guy. Nevertheless, it seems to be his genuine personality and that's my other problem with him. I'm not sure he has the subtlety to pull something like this off. If he's Bernard, he deserves a fucking Oscar. Your thoughts Mr. Intelligence Officer?"

"No one in my office gets along with him and since my initial meeting I've managed to stay out of his way. I agree based on what you've said, though, he should be a suspect."

Eggleston continued. "For some reason, as you're well aware, he also seems to have a real problem with military people even though he has a son who was in the Navy. Bass, though, is on my list because of position, access, and travel, asshole notwithstanding. I've put occasional after-hours surveillance on him, and he's covered like a blanket on all travel outside of the country."

"In my office, my group, only Mike Drum has been cleared and he's the one tasked with most of the surveillance duties. The others you may not have met because they're in and out. I'd like to think they'll all come out clean in the weeks ahead though since everything and everyone is being scrutinized."

"Everyone in the Economics section has at least a Secret clearance, but no one there handles classified materials on a daily basis. Some of their work is important and interesting if you are an economist, but for the most part it's not the kind of stuff spies get heroic medals for. There's only one person in the whole bunch I consider a possibility and it's purely because he's a misfit and a troublemaker, and that's Steve Diamond. You've met him, I presume?"

"I have."

"He has difficulty speaking or even saying hello and there's never more than minimal eye contact with me although I see him regularly in the hallways engaged with the younger women employees."

"Perhaps he's intimidated by your position."

"I don't think so. He's married, but he's got a real eye for the young ladies. There's a lot of material on him: Greek ancestry, inner city kid, minor run-ins with the law, father unknown, mother a prostitute, welfare case, and more including appointments two to three times a week at a massage parlor not far near here. With all the baggage he somehow graduated from high school and college and subsequently married into a wealthy family. To date his performance as a State Department employee has been abysmal at best. Here he's already been reprimanded several times for his emotional outbursts and profanity against fellow employees. He's on my list because he's disgruntled, conniving, seemingly on edge, and perhaps too smart in the wrong ways. It's a gut feeling for me. You haven't found him a little abrasive and strange?"

"No, not really. We've talked a couple of times in passing and he seemed friendly enough, not as you've characterized him. He wants to play golf too. He did ask me if I had met any local women, though, and he recently bought me a Singapore sling at the Raffles Hotel during preparations for a seminar. We chatted at the bar, but it was nothing. While we're in economics what do you think about that guy Peterman, the section head down there?"

"Samuel H. Peterman, no, no way, that feckless twit couldn't be a spy. If he were older, I'd argue the Peter Principle was named after him. Spying would be way, way too difficult for him to handle, trust me on that one."

"Then I have Kazmar and Jones in the radio shack, they're workaholics; you hardly ever see either one. Have you met them?"

"Kazmar, yes, a memorable dead mullet handshake and I have seen Jones, I think, in the cafeteria from time to time."

"The two of them have the clearances; they see every message coming and going. They're workaholics as I said and neither one is very sociable except for showing up for events at the ambassador's residence. Kazmar's married. His wife's in Texas, a teacher. She's back here for a visit during school holidays once or twice a year. When you look at both of these guys all you see is red, white, and blue and I can't believe Bernard could be one of them; however, because of position and access, they both have to be in the finals for the time being along with Bass and the others."

"Probably so."

"Then there's the good Consul, Manny Ortega. As you know, the consular stuff is mostly notary, passport, and visa processing, some birth certificates, and visiting incarcerated Americans to see they've been treated properly. Ortega, however, does spend time every day updating Ambassador Lipka and DCM Bass, and on weekends, he's usually on the tennis court or the golf course with the ambassador's husband and sometimes her. That puts him in position to see and hear things he's not cleared for. And as Consul, he does have access to a lot of other people-related information on American expats and locals. Want to know who from MINDEF is traveling to some office in the Pentagon next week? He knows. But the unique thing about Ortega is he's one of the most distinguished and personable individuals you'll meet outside of the ambassador. He's a charmer, can make you feel like what you're saying is the most important thing he's heard all day and that's powerful with some people. You have to like the guy, but he's a master at extracting information with his seeming impartiality and purported influence with the ambassador; he could talk you out of your first born and more if he were inclined to do so."

"So, he's...?"

"No, just another name on my list. Then I have the GSO, Davidson Peeler. The thing about Peeler is he's cleared SECRET, but doesn't really have access to any spy-worthy materials. He does have physical access to virtually all spaces, equipment, and residences including the ambassador's place. For example, he and a Singaporean air-conditioning crew were at the ambassador's residence most of last week working on the new installation. If Bernard's a technically skilled person, and there's no evidence of that to this point, the GSO position could be perfect cover for the installation of clandestine devices. However, you'd probably need a well-trained team supporting a sophisticated install and I have no indication of that so far.

"I've eliminated all the Foreign Service National (FSN) employees, all the Singaporeans from the equation. Many of the FSNs are long-timers and are in fact the institutional memory around here. They perform administrative and logistical functions, all the non-sensitive work, receptionists, switchboard operators, drivers, your boat driver, admin personnel, and others, as you know. In the first place, the government of Singapore has already vetted them. Now I don't doubt some of the cafeteria crew or the drivers hear classified conversations from time to time, but it doesn't correlate with the level of what we have going on here, they don't have clearances, and I don't feel Bernard is one of them. More likely, I could see a local doing his or her patriotic duty for the government of Singapore, but I don't see a Singaporean as Bernard."

"Me either. How about the Marine Detachment, you've eliminated them, right?"

"I think so" Eggleston replied, waiting to hear more from Kane.

"I concur" Kane replied. The Marine guards have after-hours access to almost every space in the building and could bypass or defeat the alarm and surveillance systems if they wanted to, but beyond physical security duties, their access to and knowledge of classified discussions and materials is limited. I've also gotten to know the Gunny and most of the other Marines pretty well. A couple of them are seeing Singaporean employees, but no other foreign women are being dated according to the Gunny, and he's always looking out for honey traps. Outwardly, and according to the Gunny, they're a tight group, and I feel pretty comfortable Bernard's not among them."

"I've crossed off the remainder of your office too, the principal attaches, enlisted personnel, and the civilian spouse" Eggleston offered.

"I agree."

They pressed on and Eggleston continued striking names from the list, eliminating the two-man Coast Guard Detachment,

USAID office personnel, and the small DEA office. He flipped back to the front and scanned the entire list again, more than half of the names were lined out, and shortly three quarters of the names were eliminated.

Finally, at the end, Eggleston asked, "Anyone we haven't covered?"

"That's everyone I can think of."

"Crowell is on top of this and she's looking as deep and broad as she can. A few discrepancies have emerged, the usual screw-ups on dates and places in personnel history files, and it looks like there may even be a fraudulent M.A. degree, Fisher, in Economics. He arrived just before you did, though, so he's not Bernard."

"I could go deeper, like the household domestics, but I think not. Feldman, Bass, Kazmar, Jones, Diamond, Ortega, and Peeler, those seven, they're at the top of my list."

"What about the ambassador's driver?"

"No, I can't see any of the drivers. Bernard has to be someone with access, someone cunning, and someone secretly disgruntled. None of the drivers come anywhere near meeting those criteria.

"What's next then?"

"Well, you wanted to get more involved, so now you are. Which one of these outstanding individuals do you want to add to your dance card?"

Kane hesitated. "Let me begin with Steve Diamond. So, what are the parameters of my interaction with him?"

"Here in his government workplace, you have a freer hand, conversation, eyeball surveillance, collection; his desk, files, gym locker, they're all fair game. Outside, different rules; his house and car for example, they're off base for now unless you're invited inside. I'll give you some time to cozy up to him and then let me know if you feel there's a need to wire his place. It would be relatively easy since I understand his wife's away a lot. Out on the street, restaurant, golf course, you can meet, dine, hang out, and act like a regular human being, but any deeper incursions I must know beforehand. Remember whom we're dealing with here. I'll keep Feldman, Bass, Ortega, and the guys in communications on my roster because of my regular contact with them. Peeler, we'll keep on the shelf unless something happens to draw our attention back in his direction."

"That sounds good to me."

"Now don't go get in over your head with Diamond. If you think you're onto something I have to know pronto. And don't ignore your officemates just because of him."

At that, Eggleston reached for and unzipped an executive-sized notebook, a constant companion on his desktop. Besides a pen and notepaper pad, it cradled a black pistol. "I've been in this business a long time and you never know" he said as Kane's eyes were directed to it.

"As I mentioned, Diamond and I have talked golf, so there's some basis for me to reconnect with him. I was also thinking about having a party; haven't had one yet, but it looks like I'll be getting the embassy bungalow that's being remodeled. I could invite your list of suspects along with the requisite Singaporean military officials, and foreign attaché guest list. It could prove interesting. If Bernard's an invitee, he or she might not want to miss the opportunity to mingle with such a group."

They agreed on a day in early September. "I'll give Janie Tan the list and have her start on the invitations. I think I'll have her call the Petroleum Club and get the name of the oil guy running that catering business on weekends, the Crawdad Suckers. If it really looks like I may have my place before then, they could set up in the backyard for a shrimp boil or something else Cajun."

38

More heat, more sweat, more whispering. Inside the sauna the KGB wasted no time in detailing Diamond's new task involving the damaged North Vietnamese cargo ship in the harbor.

Afterward, when they were showered, cooled down, and dressed, Nicolai introduced a new subject. He reminded Diamond to pay closer attention to the prioritized list of collection objectives and stop wasting film on the *lopata* approach as he hesitatingly called it while temporarily drawing a blank on the English word "shovel." To make his point he produced a single printed photograph processed from a recent roll of film from the dead drop, a slightly blurred picture of the embassy's cafeteria menu for the third week of August. Diamond guiltily acknowledged his slip-up, but felt stung by the criticism because his treachery was often committed in haste, sometimes in mere seconds, and occasional honest mistakes can happen when you are in a hurry.

"You stupid fool, Nicholas. The Koreans would appreciate my efforts, is that what you're asking for? Is it? And next time no goddamn sauna. Don't you think it's hot as hell here already?" Diamond snapped.

"My name is Nicolai."

"Then speak up, you dumb Cossack."

"Keep your voice down. Just follow our agreement and instructions and everything will be okay. Can you do that, can you?" Nicolai pressed, pointing an accusative finger at Diamond.

"If you think..."

"Look, Mr. Diamond, while you're busy fucking that secretary just try to do something good for us, okay?"

"Don't YOU worry about it," Diamond replied, glaring, the muscles in his cheek twitching, the color in his face turning sauna pink again.

"And what about the cameras and film? Did you find better places to hide them?"

"Of course," Diamond growled. "The film is in the false-bottomed tea tins and I've found better locations for the cameras in my garage and office. Any other complaints from Moscow today?"

So far, Diamond had not been unable to gain access to the daily, classified message folder the CIA shared exclusively with Ambassador Lipka and DCM Bass. One of the CIA staffers always waited and retrieved the folder as soon as it had been read. Information from that source remained one of Diamond's top collection priorities.

To reaffirm Moscow's sincerity and end the meeting on a positive note, Nicholai produced a business size envelope containing $2,500 dollars cash in various denominations. "This you will like." Then he handed Diamond a folded note on executive stationary, and a Moscow bank statement showing regular deposits on Diamond's behalf in a growing escrow account now totaling over $65,000 dollars. Diamond knew the bank account could be a sham because the KGB could forge anything and really the money did not matter that much because his motivation was not financial. He only wanted to get back at them, those stupid bastards at State and the embassy, and the thrill of doing it right under everyone's noses turned him on even more. The note Diamond opened, handwritten in English, expressed sincere gratitude and a "special thanks" for his continuing work, and the KGB's Director in Moscow had signed it. The high-level blandishment was a total surprise. Diamond was flattered, but tried not to show it, not remembering the last time anyone so important had ever thanked him quite like that.

The KGB trio then extended dutiful handshakes before filing out in cautious intervals. Diamond remained standing alone, staring into space, eyes tear-filled.

39

"Big problem!" yelled Naseer as he jerked both throttle levers back and shut down the boat's engines after he noticed the port engine's oil pressure gauge pegged at zero.

"What's wrong?" Kane asked, looking up from the shipping list.

Naseer tapped the gauge, "Oil pressure nil."

"Oh, great" Kane exclaimed with both surprise and disgust as he turned to see how far they had come from the pier. A multi-colored oil slick floated on the waves as far back as he could see.

Naseer left his seat at the helm, opened the engine compartment, and jumped down inside to investigate. It was not long before he reported the problem, "Bad oil filter leak on port engine."

"How did that happen? You just got the boat back Friday afternoon from the shipyard and it checked out okay, right?"

"All good" replied a puzzled Naseer.

They were off Sentosa Island, almost into the Western anchorage. "We can get back on one engine, can't we?"

Major doubt was apparent on Naseer's voice when he replied, "Big problem." Kane would find out just how big because the boat had very poor steerage on one engine, you could not steer it straight, so fighting the current and weaving back through all the merchant ships to Clifford Pier would indeed be a problem.

As they discussed their dilemma, the current slowly took them further away and Kane also found the radio was having one of its moments, not transmitting. His growing concern was drifting too far out into the shipping lane where merchant ship traffic was a threat to run over them. He needed to take quick action, but unfortunately, once again, there were no Harbor Police boats around for assistance.

Kane joined Naseer in the engine compartment where he had just finished wiping clean the exterior of the oil filter. In doing so a dent was discovered along the rim where the filter's rubber gasket made contact with the engine block. The filter appeared slightly cross-threaded as well. Try as he might Naseer could not turn the filter in either direction. When the oil got hot and thin, the gap in the gasket at the dent allowed the oil to leak past—that was the problem. Fortunately, the bilge pump worked because the situation might have turned catastrophic with hot oil sloshing on a blistering hot engine manifold. A fire would have started for sure.

Naseer kept spare oil onboard and Kane came up with an idea. "What if you drive and I'll stay below. I'll start by adding the new oil and catch the leaking oil in one of the plastic buckets. As soon as I have a bucketful, I'll yell for you to stop. Then I'll pour the hot oil back into the engine and you can start up again and we'll do it over and over until we get back to the pier. What do you think?"

"Okay, we try."

Kane added oil. Naseer started up the engines and they motored along for several minutes before hot, thinning oil began dripping, then running from the filter into the bucket. A few yards farther along their route the flow increased, the plastic bucket grew warmer then hot, "Ouch! Hold it! STOP!" Kane set the overflowing bucket down, removed the filler cap, inserted the funnel, and returned the first bucket of hot oil back into the engine. Not long after that he poured in a second, a third, and a fourth bucket, as hot oil continued to stream past the filter. "Engine room to bridge, how are we doing up there, Naseer?"

"Good."

"How close are we to Clifford pier?"

"Maybe half way now."

"Half way! I've been down here for most of an hour!"

Nearly another hour later they reached the pier. Kane

emerged from the engine compartment wiping oily sweat from his face. He looked like the proverbial grease monkey, smeared and soaked with motor oil from head to toe.

Try as he might, Naseer could not suppress a smile as he handed Kane a clean towel. "You look like mechanic apprentice."

"Thanks a lot. If this ever happens again, I'll be the helmsman and you'll be the oiler, Kane answered back, pretending to be mad, but understanding how out of character and pitiful he must have looked.

"Can you make it back to our buoy by yourself? If you can, I'll call the shipyard as soon as I get back to the embassy and have them tow you to the shipyard. I'd like a little word with their shop foreman and manager as well."

"I can get back to the buoy okay."

"Are you positive you checked everything on the boat before you accepted it Friday?"

"Everything good, work order finished, engines start good, idle check, engine compartment, everything okay from shipyard to buoy, no oil leak, no problem, everything good."

But Kane wasn't convinced. "Have there ever been signs of anyone sneaking onboard or anything ever missing from the boat?"

"No."

40

Kane began collecting information on Diamond as often as possible, discretely noting his patterns of activity, situational behavior, and topics of conversation, the same level of detail as he had been gleaning from his officemates. An immediate item of interest was Diamond's daily exercise routine. He was the only civilian who regularly exercised outside the embassy over the noon hour.

Again, Kane went down to the Consular office shortly before noon and browsed the various Government Printing Office-produced brochures and application forms. He mixed with patrons and pretended to be searching for information, but all the while keeping his eye out for Diamond; the plate glass door afforded him a clear view into the embassy's front lobby.

Diamond was punctual, arriving again just before noon. He adjusted his orange and black Baltimore Orioles baseball cap, cleaned his sunglasses, and then departed on what seemed to be a ritual jaunt. Necktie removed, he wore a white short-sleeved shirt, light gray suit trousers, and tennis shoes. Stopping for a moment to twist, stretch, and look skyward, he took a few deep breaths and then strode off. The spring in his step and his skylarking at the traffic and sidewalk pedestrians suggested he enjoyed the brief respite from his workplace.

Kane gave Diamond credit for the physical exertion, but a walk seemed curiously out of character considering his relatively young age, boasted athleticism, and type-1 personality.

After learning basic foot surveillance techniques at the attaché course, Kane developed a knack for it. He knew covert observation on foot by a single individual could be difficult if not impossible against a wary person or team of professionals; counter detection was likely. If Diamond was Bernard, he might pass through checkpoints, be "deloused", warned along the way by KGB lookouts, and his mission aborted. For that reason, Kane never trailed too closely. And he made a concerted effort to vary his own patterns, leaving before or after Diamond from the front or rear of the embassy, jumping ahead a few blocks in a taxi, or heading off in the opposite direction just to keep it random. However, once he was able to establish Diamond walked the same basic route every time out, Kane's note taking increased in detail.

It was the sixth outing. Diamond's pace was usually a moderate to brisk 3.0 to 3.5 mph, so Kane gave him a little less than a minute head start on his course toward the heart of the city. Kane exited the embassy, caught a taxi, and circled around a few blocks before being dropped-off. He crossed over to the opposite side of the street and accelerated his pace in order to maintain visual contact. As he walked, he adjusted his Panama hat, unbuttoned the top of his safari suit, and from a package of French Gitane cigarettes, placed one in his mouth, unlit for the time being. Along with the sunglasses and camera he hoped a stray glance might mistake him for a European tourist from one of the several cruise ships in port. Pedestrian traffic was heavy and Kane was already a little too far behind for comfort and feared losing sight of Diamond on the crowded sidewalks. However, contact was maintained thanks to the ball cap, which seemed to pop into view just at the last instant when Kane feared he had lost him.

Block after block they progressed in cat and mouse tandem until Kane felt it was time to stop. He looked into the angled window of a furniture store where he could see the reflections of the people overtaking him. He remembered the admonition from the instructor at the attaché course: *Don't ever try this in a window filled with items you normally wouldn't stop to gaze into, for instance, ladies' lingerie; you'll give yourself away.* Kane observed the reflections in the store's window for a few seconds. None of the passing pedestrians gave him an uneasy feeling, but he needed to be cautious so he swung around with the camera

hanging at waist level and casually squeezed off several expo-
sures of sidewalk passersby. If nothing else it was good practice.
On the other hand, the photos might prove interesting and he
intended to pass the imagery along to Eggleston for review.

The next day Kane had a boat run in the morning and business at MINDEF which kept him engaged until mid-afternoon.
But two days later, he was on Diamond again. Kane left at 11:30
AM by the embassy's back door, hailed a taxi, and had it drop him
off a block ahead of the location he last saw Diamond two days
prior. Upon exiting the cab, he went inside a large department
store and into shops on the second, third and fourth floors via
the escalator. He always paused to take notice of who was around
him on each floor. He checked his watch. If Diamond maintained
his normal pace he would be walking by on the opposite side of
the street in the next minute or so. Kane went down the escalator to the main floor and stood in front of a restaurant where
he viewed the glass display case filled with tasty looking plastic
replicas of menu items. He glanced over his shoulder once, twice,
and then like clockwork Diamond strode by on the other side of
the street. In the next block Diamond stopped at a small sidewalk
café.

Kane quickly slipped into a small shop catty-corner across the
street from Diamond's front row table position. Kane watched a
beverage order arrive and saw Diamond browsing a section of a
newspaper left behind by a previous customer.

Later, returning to his office, Kane retrieved a folder from his
personal safe and made a number of check marks and cryptic
notes next to key words in a day-coded column of the encyclope-
dic activity matrix he had created.

The next time out Kane took a camera with a telephoto lens
and went directly to the little hardware store across the street from
the café. Inside he took a concealed position to the rear and spent
time handling merchandise without drawing too much attention.
Everything looked pretty much the same across the street, but he
snapped several discrete photos for comparison. The scene was
the same the next few outings as well, in fact, everything seemed
almost precisely the same, Diamond's pace, the route, the stop,
the beverage, a newspaper, and the photos confirmed it.

However, the next time the scene changed. Diamond had a visitor. A man approached who seemed to surprise Diamond and then he seated himself at the table. Kane thought the new arrival looked familiar, his height and gait, but when he finally saw his face, he was surprised. It was DCM Bass. He did not stay long or partake of any food or beverage, but he did converse with Diamond for a few minutes before he left, hailed a taxi, and headed back in the direction of the embassy.

Was that a chance encounter or a prearranged meeting?

41

It was the last day of August when Kane received the telephone call from the GSO, Davidson Peeler, confirming the earlier informal offer of the newly renovated embassy bungalow for his permanent residence. After a brief review of its amenities including two air-conditioned bedrooms, bathroom, small kitchen, living room, single car garage with attached amah's quarters, plus patios front and rear in one of the best older neighborhoods in the city, Kane did not hesitate, "Yes sir, thank you, I'll take it."

Residence at the world-famous Raffles Hotel was a once in a lifetime opportunity. It was Old World charm, but a little pricey and not all that conducive to the attaché business. Kane would miss occasional dining in the Tiffin Room, the excellent room service and the svelte Alitalia airlines flight attendants who mustered poolside for cocktails and a bikini dip almost every afternoon. He had considered the lease of a flat near Eggleston's place too, but the embassy's little house was by far the best deal.

They were putting on the final touches of paint and trim and it would be ready for his occupancy in less than a week. The GSO said he would be in contact with a moving company to make arrangements for the delivery of Kane's household goods shipment as well. With a sigh of accomplishment Kane hung up the telephone and went down to the cafeteria to check the bulletin board. The embassy provided major appliances wired for Singapore's higher voltage, but smaller appliances from the US needed a transformer. He wrote down a few telephone numbers including the consul's, who just happened to be advertising two transformers. Kane called Ortega and they struck a deal. He could pick up the items in Ortega's office at the close of business, 4:00 PM.

Kane told Captain Grusk the good news and then he informed Janie Tan. Everything was now on track for the party at his new digs. The remainder of the day was uneventful. There was no boat run scheduled, so he and Chief Sanderson researched and produced two Intelligence Information Reports based on a series of defense-related articles in the Straits Times newspaper. A third report was produced from information provided by a confidential source with occasional access to restricted countries and ports in the region. Additionally, Kane took care of several telephone inquiries from foreign embassies referred to him by Captain Grusk, and he finally got around to completing the lengthy questionnaire from DIA about his experience as a student in the Defense Attaché School course.

Kane left his desk at 3:50 PM to retrieve the transformers. Arriving in the lobby, he stopped briefly to chat with the Marine guard and then headed to the consul's office. As he reached for the door, it had already begun to open so he courteously stepped aside to let a small, dark, and surprisingly dirty little man exit. Normally, people who conduct business at the embassy clean up for the occasion, but not in this case, not this fellow, and because of his appearance he drew Kane's attention.

Upon entering the Consular office, Kane went straight to the business counter where the staff was busily completing their last paperwork of the day and securing files and office equipment. One of the young Singaporean clerks acknowledged his presence as she glanced at a small piece of paper she had just retrieved off the counter.

"I'm sorry, Commander Kane, but I believe we're already closed for the day."

"That's okay, it's personal business. I'm here to pick up transformers from Mr. Ortega."

"I'll get him, oops," she said as she turned and almost ran into Ortega who had exited his office upon hearing Kane's voice. She handed him the note from the counter and Ortega accepted it in stride.

"What's this?"

"I'm not sure, a man just placed it on the counter."

Ortega looked at the note and with raised excitement in his voice he asked, "How long ago did you get this? Where did he go? Where did he get this?"

Temporarily shaken by the rapid-fire questioning, the young woman began to respond. "He...he went out just as Lieutenant Commander Kane was coming in. He said he found it on a ship, he put it on the counter, and left. I didn't know it was important."

"What's the problem?" Kane asked.

"This," said Ortega as he handed over the note and hustled out the door.

Kane looked at the soiled brown scrap of paper. It was more or less oval-shaped, about 3 inches by 4 inches. He read it over several times not quite believing what he saw. In scratchy, faded block print the three lines read:

PRISON SHIP, TORTURE, CUBANS, SEND TO STATE DEPT, WASH, DC, USA

CDR EMIL "YOGI" BEARE 10 DEC 75

Kane hurried into the lobby where Ortega was just about to leave to search for the man, "The guard isn't sure which direction he went."

"I can give you a bit of description," which Kane did, and then they both darted outside in opposite directions. But the dirty little man had disappeared in the teeming pedestrian and vehicular traffic; he could have hopped on a bus, taxi, or even a bicycle, he was long gone. Kane returned after his brief search and the Marine guard informed him Ortega had gone up to the ambassador's office.

Kane went up to tell Captain Grusk what had transpired, but he found everyone except Colonel Chang had already departed for the day. Kane told Chang about the incident and then he made a few quick notes before calling Grusk's residence.

Captain Grusk arrived home just as his telephone rang, "Okay, thanks for the report, Dalton, but don't stray too far from a telephone. I have a feeling the ambassador may call a meeting to discuss this and you'll need to be a part of it for sure."

Grusk was right. By the time Kane got back to the Raffles there was a message for him to call Captain Grusk. "As I suspected, the ambassador wants to have a meeting about this tomorrow at 9:00 AM in the conference room and she wants both of us there. I recommend you come prepared to talk about the fellow who delivered the note as best you can. We may engage in some broader search for this person and possibly for the ship if the whole thing looks credible. If you have any additional thoughts about the matter let me know before the meeting begins."

Kane stayed in his room and ordered food from the room service menu. He reviewed his notes and contemplated the dirty little man, the note left on the counter, and the alleged POW ship for most of the evening.

42

They assembled inside the ambassador's conference room early Saturday morning for the hastily called meeting. Present were Ortega, Bass, Eggleston, Grusk, and Kane. While awaiting the arrival of the ambassador they all talked about the note, but Bass being his usual boorish self did not engage in any direct conversation with either Grusk or Kane.

The ambassador and her secretary entered the room and everyone took their seats. Ms. Feldman placed a tray of bakery sweets and a freshly brewed pot of coffee on the table, which generated a "Thank you, Judith" from everyone.

The ambassador sat in her usual position in the large chair at the head of the table, flanked by the Ortega and Bass on one side, and Eggleston, Grusk, and Kane opposite. As coffee cups filled, Ambassador Lipka began to speak.

"I'm sorry to draw you away from your families, golf, or whatever your plans were at this early hour today, but something interesting and perhaps very important has come to our attention and I'm sure you've already heard about it. Judith has copies of the note and she'll pass it around for those of you who haven't seen it. For everyone's information I want to have Manny begin and tell exactly what happened yesterday and then Lieutenant Commander Kane, but first I want you to know I called Under Secretary Shannon in Washington yesterday and told him about this. He was extremely interested to say the least, enough to call back twice. We've subsequently packaged the note and it's in a pouch on its way back to Washington as I speak. Name verification is already underway at the Pentagon and the FBI will conduct forensic analysis of the note as soon as they have it. I expect feedback on the name from DoD sometime today. If it turns out there is a Commander Emil Beare, and he's missing or believed captive, Secretary Shannon wants an all-out effort to look for the person who delivered the note, find the ship, and do everything else possible to find Commander Beare or more evidence of his existence. And that's why I called you here this morning, to develop a plan of action. I need your input because Shannon wants to see what we have by tomorrow. Any questions so far? ... No? ... Judith, you're taking notes?"

Ortega provided his recollection of what happened, including verbatim what the administrative clerk told him the little man had said when he left the note on the counter. But that was all he had, not much really.

Then it was Kane's turn and he stood to speak. He confirmed Ortega's account and added a detailed description as his audience listened intently. Using gestures and carefully chosen words, he tried to bring his image of the dirty little man to life, his looks, movement, and even possible insight into his occupational background. He described the fellow as being approximately 5'1" tall with neatly trimmed black, oily, hair matted down in a pattern in several places. He was very thin and deeply tanned. His left hand, the one he placed on the handle to push the door open had black grime embedded under and around his fingernails. He wore a dirty, holey, white t-shirt with a faded, unintelligible circular logo on left breast pocket and a pair of baggy, blue British military style shorts, partially covering knobby knees and bowed legs. On his feet were black rubber flip-flops and there was a white chalky substance on his feet extending up his legs beyond his ankles. "He must have waded through or brushed against some foreign substance leaving the residue" Kane speculated. "And the imprint on his hair. It looked to me as though he might wear some kind of head cover or safety helmet. He did not speak or make eye contact as he shuffled past, clearly uncomfortable amongst strangers in white shirts and neckties. However, to his credit, he was savvy enough to know the significance of the note's content and deliver it to the embassy, unless the whole thing's a fraud."

"Okay, very good, Dalton. Please make sure Judith has all

that. Anyone, questions?" Ambassador Lipka asked.

Bass spoke up. "I have one. So, Lieutenant Commander Kane, tell me again just how long you observed this person?"

"For several seconds as I held the door and he passed by."

"Come now, do you really expect us to believe you recalled this level of detail, the dirt under the fingernails of someone who merely passed you by? Pleeease!"

"Yes, that's correct."

Looking around the table for confirmation, Bass made no effort to restrain his cynicism with a smirk and frown, and to solidify his point he followed-up with another provocation designed to blow a hole in Kane's presentation. "So, Lieutenant Commander Kane, just how observant are you? What kind of shoes am I wearing?"

Kane anticipated a confrontation with the DCM at some point based on their first encounter, but he was not expecting it to happen in a forum with Ambassador Lipka present. He was torn between just standing there or going on offense and putting Bass in his place, which itself was not without risk.

Their gazes locked on to each other—neither blinked. At the same time Kane's mind was going a mile a minute, but then he had a sudden, compelling urge to act. However, an instant response would not have the desired effect so he hesitated in delivering his comeback. A moment later though, as Bass began to break a sardonic victory smile the timing was perfect and Kane pounced, "I believe they're Nike brand tennis shoes, sir."

Ortega shot a confirmatory sideways glance at the floor toward Bass's feet, while Kane continued. He actually disliked what he was about to do next, but he did it anyway. "Last Thursday when I saw you in the cafeteria, you were wearing black oxfords, ten eyelets, and a collegiate necktie, Michigan State I believe. If you also question how I determined the little man's height, it was quite simple. I recalled where the approximate top of his head was as he passed through the doorway. The Consular office business hours are painted on it and his head appeared about even with the top line, 'Open Monday through Friday.' I got a tape and measured, sixty-one inches from the floor."

Except for the ticking second hand on the wall clock there was not a sound or movement in the room. Bass's jaw jutted, his breath held, and eyelids tightened as he looked across the table. Kane was hoping for some support from his side, however, Captain Grusk managed only to inhale and execute a very un-captain-like squirm. Eggleston jumped in, cleared his throat with a loud, phony theatrical cough, and boosted himself in his seat, barely restraining a laugh, which had worked its way up from his chest. "Well then, Jonathon, I think Lieutenant Commander Kane just told you where to stick ..."

Saving what might have come next, Ambassador Lipka interjected, "Okay, gentlemen, enough, let's get back on track."

"May I continue?" Kane asked.

"Go ahead."

"Let me add this for your consideration, since we're tasked with a search. There are normally several hundred ships in Singapore's various anchorages and shipyards and many come and go on a daily basis. Therefore, unless we focus our search, I believe the effort will have a very low probability of success because time may not on our side, we are relatively few in number, and unfortunately we haven't a lot to work with."

"I totally agree," Lipka added.

"If we assume the little man who delivered the note found it at his place of work then I think we need to look closer for clues to help narrow our investigation. The picture I have of him is a common laborer, a man making his living with the strength of his hands and back more so than his intellect. He's probably not part of the skilled workforce, so I think we should eliminate the various engineering and technical support shops in the shipyards as well as the ships and personnel at the container port facility for now."

The ambassador continued endorsing Kane's remarks with silent nodding so he continued. "He may work outside a lot, perhaps as a stevedore, based on his dark tan, but equally important, I think, he's small in stature. Small is best suited for some of the dirtiest and most dangerous maintenance and repair jobs on a ship. Small can climb through the narrowest of access hatches into voids, half decks, and shaft alleys in the deepest, darkest areas. Small cleans noxious bilges, the insides of fuel tanks, and maintains or repairs equipment in the tightest of spaces. My hunch is the person we're looking for, if he was the initial person to discover the note at all, may have been working deep inside a ship when he found it. Therefore, as a first priority, I believe we should concentrate on ships we can identify as undergoing repair or overhaul work below deck. A ship having its hull repainted, topside electronics changed, or deckhouse refurbishment accomplished we should bypass until after we have eliminated the others."

"It sounds like a reasonable approach to me,"Grusk piped up. "Unless someone has a better idea Commander Kane could search the repair anchorages from the boat and the rest of my staff and I could split up and cover the shipyards, concentrating on Keppel, Jurong, and Sembawang, the big ones first. I think we could make good progress in a couple of days. However, if and when we find a ship meeting the criteria, we may want to be careful what we say."

Lipka continued to steer the discussion. "First, I agree with the idea. Objections anyone? No? You're absolutely right about what we say too, and I'm glad you brought it up. Secretary Shannon provided some guidance. He directed we couldn't mention Commander Beare's name or use prisoner of war terminology when talking to anyone. I know it's a handicap, but all we are allowed to do is ask if anyone has heard about a note possibly from an American being recently discovered onboard a ship. You can't mention the note's content. I know it's a long shot, but if such a note was found the finder might have mentioned it to his friends or his foreman, at least it's what we're hoping. Secretary Shannon's concern is if the note is somehow found to be valid, we don't want to alert the other side so they could begin damage control action and remove evidence. Shannon did agree to my suggestion that I talk to the Minister of Defensce about this and I have an appointment on Monday to tell him everything and ask for his help if we encounter resistance with any of the shipyards. A reward for information may be authorized too and I expect to hear more from Shannon about that later."

"What about the press?" Eggleston asked. "If they get wind of this, it'll be everywhere."

"Shannon was adamant, no leaks," Lipka said. I'll mention that to the minister too. As this unfolds there will likely be an official press release, but not now. In addition, Manny, you need to get back to those people in your office when this happened and tell them they can't discuss it with anyone. Jonathan, we may want to have them sign some type of non-disclosure statement, and start thinking about a future press release too."

Bass nodded. "I'll draft up something and coordinate it with Manny."

"Of course," Grusk added, "if there is such a ship the captain or master or whoever is in charge might not want to admit such a note was found on his ship."

"That's true," Lipka agreed, "and with the reference to Cubans, are we definitely looking for a North Vietnamese ship?"

Everyone looked at Kane.

Kane shrugged. "Well, I believe so, but I doubt the ship would bear any telltale signs of such use, so its function could be changed and I certainly don't think it would be holding any prisoners here, now, in Singapore. There's also the possibility the ship is no longer owned by the Vietnamese so it could be flying some other country's flag. As to the reference to Cubans, well, perhaps Mr. Eggleston has some insight on that."

Eggleston did. "I've already requested information and I'll let you know what I receive. There is a steady stream of sympathetic foreign delegations in and out of Hanoi and I know the Cubans have provided moral support to the North Vietnamese regime as well as material assistance."

Bass cooled down a little and asked a civil question. "I've never heard of a POW ship. Has anyone? And why a prison ship instead of a normal prison on land? They must have dozens of them."

Kane answered. "It's not unprecedented for ships to transport prisoners. "In fact, during World War II, US Navy submarines torpedoed and sank several Japanese ships transporting American prisoners, and some POW lives were lost because of it. However, after looking at this note, the way it's phrased and, of course, the reference to torture, I have the feeling its author was referring to residency, more so than mere confinement during transit. You're correct on your last point though, they do have many prisons ashore. So, if there is such a ship, it might represent a special type of incarceration for a particular type of prisoner. A ship would obviously be a very secure place as far as anyone on the outside or overhead knowing what was going on inside. It wouldn't have the typical terrestrial POW camp facilities and components, perimeter fences, guard towers, and latrine pits. It would also be an easy place, underway at sea for example, to dispose of any damning evidence."

"Such as?" Bass asked.

"Human remains," was Kane's response.

Lipka asked, "Any other insight?"

"I held the note," said Kane. It's a scrap of lightweight cardboard, similar to cereal box material. I'm left-handed and I can assure you whoever wrote the note is a lefty as well. I think the forensic people will probably come up with the same conclusion and it might be helpful in confirmation of the possible author, particularly if there is a left-handed Commander Beare. The block printing as you can see is rather scratchy, blunt short strokes, and somewhat smeared. It suggests a soft writing material and unconventional writing tool, perhaps charcoal on the end of spent wooden match or some other improvised writing instrument cleverly acquired in captivity. Moreover, I would contend someone familiar with the US military wrote the note because of its brevity; the way Commander is abbreviated CDR, and the day, month, year date sequence. Overall, it's rather neatly laid out, letters evenly spaced, and the lines are parallel perhaps pointing to the writer being in relatively good mental and physical shape when he composed it."

"Insightful." Said Lipka.

Bass played devil's advocate. "But it could it be a hoax too."

"It could be, but..." Kane began.

"If it's a hoax, who's behind it?" Bass asked.

"The usual suspects," Eggleston replied. "But I can't see a motive unless they just wanted to spin us up and have us dedicate a lot of time and effort on a wild goose chase while they stand by laughing. It's just as likely it could be from some random angry person and we just happened to be the next on their hit list; however, I don't have that feeling either. I tend to agree with Commander Kane's characterization. I think we may be on to something and I can certainly spare a body or two to help with the search effort."

Grusk broke in. "Dirk, let's talk about who you have after the meeting."

"What bothers me, though,"Eggleston said," is if this supposed individual was a Navy pilot, why was the note was addressed to the State Department instead of the Department of Defense, the Department of the Navy, or even the White House? And you'd have thought he might have included his squadron name or number."

"That's perplexing to me as well." Kane added, "I could think of some explanations, but none is compelling and at this point only the author knows why he didn't address it like that."

"Judith," Lipka sighed, "I hope you wrote all this down. Beginning Monday, I'd like to have a daily status report from the attaché office before 6:00 PM to see how we're doing."

"Remember," Kane said, "we're looking for a ship in port on or before yesterday, the day the note was delivered. Also, all the shipyards are pretty well closed down tomorrow, so we might want to begin our full court press about 8:00 AM Monday morning."

Lipka stood and leaned on the table. "We'll start Monday, everyone in agreement? Okay, thank you, and if any of you come up with something new on this, I want to be the first to know."

As they were getting up to leave there was a knock on the door and the ambassador's secretary, standing nearby, opened it. It was a message for Ambassador Lipka.

She read the first few lines to herself. "Now, this is perfect timing. This is from Secretary Shannon. Let's see ... DoD has confirmed the name. Commander Emil Beare was shot down in his A-4 Skyhawk attack aircraft by enemy antiaircraft artillery fire near Than Hoa, Socialist Republic of Vietnam on 14 June 1974. His wingman reported a good ejection and parachute and there was brief communication with him on the ground. Follow-on search and rescue attempts were unsuccessful. That's it, gentlemen, we've got our work cut out for us."

It was a risky move by Kane the new guy, the junior attaché, the unproven Intelligence Officer standing up to Bass and convincing the ambassador and the others to follow his plan. Not that any of them had better ideas though. The whole thing was a long shot based on the number of ships in port, the small size of their search party, and the constraints placed on the effort by Washington. Kane recognized it and most of the others privately doubted a positive outcome as well.

43

Early Monday morning, Captain Grusk's team rendezvoused at Keppel Shipyard with Major Wee from the Attaché Liaison Office, who presented the shipyard manager with a hastily drawn up letter from MINDEF. The letter to all Singaporean shipyards requested full cooperation with US Embassy personnel in answering questions about finding the note.

It was a cooperative and methodical effort in Keppel beginning with a list of all foremen and their work assignments and certain ones of them were summoned. The interviews began by Grusk asking if they had seen or heard any recent talk of a note being found on their ship or any ship. There was some initial anticipation of possible success. A couple of the interviewees responded they were "unsure" or "maybe", or perhaps they did not understand the question. Grusk accompanied several foremen to their ships and spoke directly with personnel working onboard. One worker actually said he had seen a note in a void. After an hour's delay in getting permission to see for himself, Grusk found the "note" to be graffiti, likely written years earlier during the ship's construction. In the end, none of the leads at Keppel panned out.

The shipyard also provided a separate list of all ships having below deck repairs or maintenance accomplished. The idea was to talk directly with one of these ships' representatives, Master, First Mate, or some other knowledgeable representative and ask the questions. Unfortunately, many people were not available; they had gone ashore and their return was not known. Others were reluctant to talk to foreigners, and still others seemed to want to avoid contact because they spoke very little English.

Of the officials willing to talk to Captain Grusk, none had any information of interest to offer.

It took a full day to complete Keppel shipyard, but Captain Grusk was undeterred and had learned from the experience. The next day they planned to move up the coast and split up into several groups to take care of Jurong shipyard and the smaller shipyards along the south and west side of the island, and then head to the northeast side. They still had hopes of stumbling onto something.

44

Kane and Naseer were underway in continuation of their search for the POW ship from the previous day—into the Eastern anchorage, then Keppel Harbor, and around Sentosa Island into the Western anchorage from the north.

They then headed toward one of the repair anchorages delineated on the chart. Ships there were under repair or awaiting pier side repair space to free up at Sembawang or Jurong, or one of the smaller shipyards up the coast.

A smaller-sized merchant ship caught Kane's eye because of its aged profile. He studied it with the binoculars as they dodged around ships at anchor and headed for it. The ship had a straight, vertical bow, the oldest style, and a counter stern. It appeared to be a general cargo vessel approximately 350 feet in length with a deckhouse and funnel amidships, and single masts fore and aft; at least a 1950's vintage, maybe older, and perhaps a coal burner as well. Kane motioned Naseer to slow down and then he took several distant, full frame photographs of the vessel. As they drew nearer, he could see the ship was in very poor materiel condition. Entombed in rust and moored to a buoy it lacked the usual features of an operational unit. There was no name or number on the bow, no anchor in the portside hawse pipe, no lifeboat in the davits, no radar, nor any communications antennas, or national ensigns or flags of any sort. As best as Kane could tell from his low viewing angle the ship appeared stripped of all its cargo-handling gear. It looked like a totally derelict hulk except for a small motorboat tied to the rung of a Jacob's ladder rigged over the ship's port side.

Kane made a hand signal for a slow circle around the ship.

He wanted to pass close astern to view any possible homeport place name. Some faint letters were detected, but difficult to make out, masked by age-old layers of paint, rust, and welding scars. A barely discernable "ong" letter combination was curious. It might have read Chittagong or Haiphong in a former time. He continued to take photographs as they proceeded up the equally deteriorated starboard side.

Upon completion of the standard eight-point photography Kane decided to hail whoever might be onboard and ask about the note. When they arrived again off the port beam Naseer stopped the engines and Kane lifted the bullhorn to his mouth, about to speak, then stopped. When they first approached the ship, he counted eight portholes open on the second level of the superstructure, but now only seven were open. Portholes on ships in quiet anchorages do not close by themselves. Someone onboard evidently coveted his or her privacy. They sat and listened for a few minutes for any sounds of work emanating from the ship, but there was no noise, nothing except the lapping of small waves against the hull of their boat.

"Hello, hello, anyone onboard?" blared Kane's electronic voice thru the bullhorn, but there was no reply, no sign of life from the ship.

Kane wondered if more of a nautical sounding call might produce results. "Ahoy there, anyone onboard?" It reminded him of an old pirate movie and he said it again louder. "A-HOY THERE!"

He decided to check the motorboat. With a seaman's eye, Naseer gauged the current, pulled up parallel, then quickly reversed engines and backed down, pinning the boat gently against the ship. The small craft held a pair of oars, a nearly empty gas can, a knotted starter rope, and a small outboard motor fastened to the transom. A soggy pack of Russian cigarettes sloshing in several inches of water also caught Kane's attention. He reached under the cowling of the motor and touched the cylinder head and spark plug area, cold.

Returning to a position off the ship's port beam, they watched and listened for a while longer. When Kane stopped drumming, he told Naseer of his plan. He would be going onboard to roust out whoever might be there and ask the questions. It was not the usual protocol; normally you do not board someone else's ship uninvited. However, he rationalized it was hardly a ship. It was without identification and it looked headed to a graving dock or readied to be sunk as an artificial reef. More importantly, he was looking for evidence of an American POW.

Naseer was to stand off in their boat far enough away to monitor Kane's movements onboard the ship. Unless Kane finished up quickly at least once every thirty minutes he would appear on the port side so Naseer could see him. If he was out of sight for more than thirty minutes Naseer was to leave immediately and bring back help. Under no circumstances was Naseer to let any strangers on their boat while Kane was on the ship, nor was Naseer to come onboard the ship to look for Kane. Concerned and stammering, Naseer repeated the plan. They synchronized watches. Kane placed his camera around his neck and clipped a Navy gooseneck flashlight onto his belt. Naseer remained uneasy. He made a very slow approach to the ship, hoping someone might appear on deck at the last second and Kane would cancel the plan. As they came alongside, Kane stepped up on the gunwale and grabbed hold of the Jacob's ladder. Slowly, hand over hand, he went up then clambered over the ship's railing and fell from sight. A second later he reappeared and flashed an "OK" sign to a very relieved Naseer.

"Hello, anyone onboard?" Kane yelled out as he stood and surveyed the main deck. He waited, but heard nothing in return.

He commenced his walkabout going forward. The ship was stripped of all cargo handling gear. Its winches were gone and what little topside equipment remained was rusty beyond repair, except for a good-sized gasoline-powered pump with several water hoses attached. The covers on the two big cargo holds forward were in place, but both had multiple puncture holes in them, definitely not watertight. A thick hawser apparently used for towing lay coiled and ready for use near the bow. Kane turned and proceeded down the starboard side temporarily out of sight behind the ship's superstructure.

He continued to call out as he walked, but to no avail. The aft deck looked much like the forward deck, vacant and rust covered. He headed to the port side, waved to Naseer, and received immediate acknowledgement.

Next, Kane stopped at the main deck entrance to the superstructure and signaled his intent to go inside. The door was closed. He opened it and called out before entering. This main athwart passageway was in shambles and smelled old and musty. He propped the door open with a piece of metal to let some natural light in, an effort to conserve the batteries of his flashlight. All the passageway light fixtures were gone. Some doors to offices and staterooms were broken to pieces but most were totally missing from their hinges. Glass, plastic, paper, and miscellaneous other debris covered the deck. He stepped carefully over the piles of rubble and looked inside the first room. Judging by its size, it was probably some senior person's stateroom. Everything of possible salvage value was gone. Several exposed pipes protruded from the bulkhead where a washbasin had been. He proceeded down the passageway to the next room and switched on the flashlight. The beam startled two, gray, four-legged stowaways, which scurried into the trash. Further along there was a small head; however, the washbasins, shower stalls, and toilet fixtures were missing. The space definitely smelled like an outhouse though and the stillness and heat intensified the stench. Kane choked on the rancid air, which prompted him to retrieve his handkerchief and place it over his mouth and nose. His flashlight illuminated a pile of human feces on deck, a near miss of the apparent target hole. Scatological analysis was beyond Kane's realm of expertise, but the pile was abuzz with a fixated squadron of flies and looked to be fresh.

What was perhaps a small galley was next along the way, but it too was trashed and empty. Kane could see where acetylene torches had been used to cut away the metal fixtures. His watch showed twenty minutes had elapsed so he picked up the pace, looking in the remainder of the rooms along the passageway then exiting on the starboard side where he took a huge breath and called out again. He walked aft and around to the port side of the superstructure where Naseer could see him and he saw Naseer with the binoculars glued to his position.

Kane signaled his next objective, the second level of the superstructure, and then he took the external ladder upward. Overall, the spaces looked like the first level, totally stripped. All the navigation equipment on the bridge was gone except for the ship's helm. Kane tried to turn it, but it didn't move.

At the very top level of the superstructure was an open-air signal bridge. On deck and attached to a rope halyard he saw a black diamond-shaped piece of canvas several feet long, which he recognized it as the International Rules day shape for a ship in tow. There was also a small wooden bench nearby and day old or so orange peelings and cigarette butts strewn about.

Returning to the main deck level, Kane signaled he was headed below. Inside the superstructure, he took the first ladder down one deck. This area had the remains of a small galley and mess area with nearby head facilities, and the smell of tobacco smoke.

Kane deduced whoever was onboard the ship must be knowledgeable of its layout, moving stealthily, keeping their distance, evading or trailing, and remaining unseen by Naseer as well. Although the thought was unnerving, he pressed on.

His flashlight was still strong so he went inside and down one deck to a door on the main passageway. A metal plaque above it in English and French read, "Engine Room." He stepped cautiously through the door onto a metal-grated landing where he stood adjusting to the darkness as the door swung closed behind him. The space was catacomb quiet inside of Stygian blackness—even his flashlight's beam seemed narrowed as it pierced the obscurity. He shined it up, down, and around as he called out. The ship's main propulsion plant loomed the next deck down. The layout was totally rusty and appeared to be diesel. He went carefully a few steps down, facing outward from the ladder, so he could scan the entire engine room. While stepping back up his foot slipped on a rung and he turned facing the ladder to keep his balance. In doing so he clanked his light against the handrail. It blinked once but remained lit, but it was time to go, time to get out of there. However, on his next step up his light flashed across a large set of double metal doors behind and below his level on the ladder, the same level as the engine room. *How strange? There shouldn't be doors on the forward bulkhead of the engine room because directly on the other side would be a cargo hold. The layout did not make sense.*

With fifteen minutes remaining and driven by inquisitiveness, he worked his way down to the bottom of the ladder and around to the doors for a closer look. A short chain with a padlock was lying on deck. The heavy door creaked as little by little it opened. Inside the space his light reflected off a liquid surface, probably water based on the lack of a distinctive fuel oil or chemical smell. Looking for something to check the depth of it he grabbed a nearby length of angle iron and stuck it in— six inches deep. The space itself was maybe fifteen feet by fifteen feet and contained two pieces of furniture: A broken chair turned upside down and a desk, from its slant missing both legs on one end. He considered turning back at that juncture, but another heavy-looking door on the far side of the room was more intriguing. Its large and well-worn handle now marked with his flashlight beam, beckoned. If he did it, it needed to be quick because he was running out of time.

He stepped into the water and a cool bottom layer, mushy and slippery, clouded up as he made cautious footsteps toward the far door. With each stride, he inserted the piece of metal and swept it from side to side like a blind man crossing a street. He reached the door, pulled the handle, and it opened. Inside, the space was also flooded, but it was much larger and partially lit by rays of sunlight coming through the holes in the cargo hatch covers high above him. He stepped carefully inside. It was quite vast, from the engine room forward to probably the bow, and from close to the ship's keel up to the main deck. He could see from the extensive black scoring on the bulkheads that cutting torches had removed several intermediate decks all the way up to the main deck.

A very unwelcome sound to the rear cut short his puzzlement. The metallic squeak startled him, and he swung his flashlight around in the direction of the entry door to the first room and saw that it was closing.

"Wait, hold on, wait a minute!" He lurched back into the first room, and splashed toward the door, as it slammed shut.

He grabbed the handle, but it wouldn't budge.

"Hey, whoever you are, let me out of here! I'm an American from the US Embassy!" He struck the steel door twice with the metal rod, and then put his ear to it. A moment later he recoiled from a deafening BOOM! BOOM! –Two taunting strikes from his hostile tormentor on the other side of the door.

"Open the goddamn door!" Kane listened, but heard only muffled laughter, then silence.

Kane's mind was reeling as he moved toward the desk, intending to climb upon it. He stepped on something and nearly twisted his ankle, but scrambled onto the desk.

He turned his flashlight off then on again for a second to check his watch. If Naseer followed his instructions he should be heading back for help by now. If everything went as planned, help should be back in two to three hours. It was a major "if", but a bigger one was what he could do to defend himself if the door suddenly flew open and things got ugly. He had the angle iron and the camera had a flash, so with any luck he might be able to temporarily blind any assailant with the flash and make a good dent in somebody's head. Was there any other escape route? He needed to stay out of the foul water because it might be caustic and dangerous. These were some of the things racing through his mind as he sat on the desk in the darkness at the ready.

His brain was still going a mile a minute when he checked the time again—thirty minutes had elapsed. He planned to begin tapping out an S.O.S. on the bulkhead at the two-hour mark. As he sat there thinking about the whole episode, the note, the search, the ship, its unusual configuration, the ship's hostile occupant, and his own captivity, it suddenly all came into focus. This had to be the ship they were looking for. He knew it and tightened his grip on the metal bar. The bar itself may well have been from a cell and the adjacent multi-level space may have been a cellblock before it was dismantled. He clicked the light on again and looked at the bar, and he knew he was right. The light also illuminated his trouser legs and shoes. They were starting to turn a chalky gray, just like the legs of the little man delivering the note in the embassy. This was the ship.

He had to escape; he could be in grave danger.

At the two-hour mark his tapping began. He tapped and listened, waited ten minutes and began all over again. Back on the desk, he sat silently in the dark a few minutes longer and then began dragging the piece of metal back and forth through the muck close to the desk, "fishing" in the spot where he had slipped.

Afterwards, he left the desk to inspect the boundaries of his confinement. In the adjacent room his flashlight illuminated an open porthole high upon the bulkhead. Getting through the porthole would be problematic if not impossible, but getting closer was the immediate task. He struggled to drag the broken desk and chair into the space and stacked and stabilized the structure. Then he climbed upon it high enough to where he could feel the bottom arc of the porthole. No jagged edges, but no idea what might be on the other side. It was his only viable escape route though, so he didn't hesitate to go for it.

He stripped down to his boxer shorts and took postures trying to visualize how he could contort his shoulders and compress his rib cage enough to make it through. He was certain he could get one arm and head in, but then what? An item that might prove helpful, in addition to a finger of grease taken off a door hinge, and several handfuls of slippery muck from the deck, was a small tube of lotion he carried for sun protection. He lubricated the entire left side of his ribcage with the muck and greased his neck, right shoulder, and the outside of his right arm. Then he stood on the wobbly chair, leapt, and grabbed the bottom of the porthole. He thrust his left arm with the flashlight and the object retrieved from near the desk through first, then his head with the lotion clasped in his teeth. The other side of the porthole was connected to a large air duct. Hanging by his armpit, he took a couple of deep breaths, exhaled as completely as he could while pressing hard against the far side of the bulkhead with his left arm to help force himself through, while the rest of him bucked and flailed in midair for unattainable traction. On his first try he progressed maybe an inch or so. *Damn!* He couldn't take a deep breath now because his lungs were compressed, but he knew from Navy survival training a successful outcome was as much mental as physical—*never give up—mind over matter--never give up—never give up!* Seconds later he made a second wild, writhing, squirming effort with comparable, trifling results. Sweating profusely and gasping for breath with the porthole seemingly ratcheting tighter and tighter around his chest with each passing moment, he began to feel trapped and claustrophobic.

Suddenly, a hand seized one of his ankles and began to tug him back. Kane recoiled in shock. He drew both of his legs up tight and mule-kicked as hard as he could, making violent contact with someone behind him. Whether it was divine intervention or superhuman effort, he incredibly popped through the porthole like a cork from a wine bottle on his next gallant rib-crushing, pushing, and straining attempt, and dropped a couple of feet into the air duct where he laid in semi-consciousness.

A tinny "Hello-hello" from an American-sounding voice passed through the vent an hour or so later. Awakened, Kane yelled back, weakly, "It's me, Dalton. I'm in some sort of vent system below deck off the engine room."

"Okay, okay, this is Captain Grusk and Colonel Chang. Start banging, we'll find you. We've got the Harbor Police with us too."

"Be careful, there's at least one unfriendly onboard."

Everyone was delighted with the outcome and no one more so than Naseer, and Kane, sore ribs and all, thanked him abundantly for carrying out the plan.

Of course, a thorough search of the ship did not produce Kane's captor nor was the motorboat alongside the ship when Captain Grusk and the police arrived.

Following radio communications with headquarters, the Harbor Police stationed a patrol boat near the ship. No one, including the ship's owners, would be allowed to board until reports were filed, and the whole matter sorted out.

Back at the embassy, Ambassador Lipka, DCM Bass, COS Eggleston, Captain Grusk, and Colonel Chang gathered in the ambassador's conference room to hear Kane's intriguing tale. Ms. Feldman took copious notes. Nearing the end of his delivery, Kane stood, patted his pocket, and produced the object he had almost forgotten about in all the excitement. He held it up before the group. "I found this in the water near the desk. It's a ring of stubby, brass-looking keys and I'm wondering if they could be jailor's keys? They probably should go back somewhere for analysis."

"I'll take that for action," Eggleston responded.

The text of Kane's debriefing was included in a lengthy message back to the State Department, DIA, CIA, and several Navy addressees. A week later the old hulk of a ship was purchased from the salvage company by the US government. Released by the government of Singapore, it was then towed under escort of a US Navy destroyer to the Naval Base at Subic Bay, Philippines, where a team of US forensic analysts and intelligence professionals descended upon it.

Meanwhile, in Washington, officials at the DoD and State Department prepared a briefing for the White House, as well as other possible follow-on presentations; the United Nations was rumored. Kane continued to respond to telephone inquiries from US officials and Ambassador Lipka advised at some point it might be necessary for him to go to back to Washington for more debriefings. However, he was never called and the investigation droned on for weeks with no compelling evidence turned up from the ship. A short article appeared on one of the inside pages of the Washington Post but there was never enough evidence to confront the government in Hanoi head-on and, of course, they were already in complete denial. The company towing the old ship into Singapore also rejected the idea it was their motorboat tied to the Jacob's ladder. The tugboat crew all had good alibis too. Most of them were in jail for drunkenness and lewd behavior in a hotel bar at the time of Kane's confinement.

The embassy advertised a reward in the Straits Times newspaper and television, but the dirty little mystery man was not identified and never came forward, and nothing else related to the incident materialized even though the note and the keys remained the strongest circumstantial evidence. CIA analysis of the keys found them to be similar to ones used in the French penal system in the early 1900's. And since France was involved in what is now Vietnam from the late 1940's to the early 1950's the keys being of French origin made some sense.

Moscow and Hanoi were initially silent after hearing what had transpired, and then cables from the KGB's First Chief Directorate began to fly. Lubachev feared the next one might be notification of his reservation for a one-way ticket back to KGB Headquarters in Moscow.

45

A week later, Aurora was busy with the day's final customer, but she promptly excused herself when she saw Kane entering the shop.

"You've been away?" she inquired, showing concern at not receiving his usual mid-day telephone call.

"Sorry, but I was incommunicado touring military facilities with the attaché corps most of the day. So how about an impromptu dinner tonight? I know its short notice, but I could use your company and a good glass of something in a quiet place."

"I'd love to. I was about to close anyway. I shall not be long."

"Take your time."

She rejoined him a few minutes later, and he complimented her on the new merchandise arrangement and trendy displays in the shop.

"Yes, my niche has always been continental as you know. My clientele are mainly European expatriates, embassy personnel, and tourists, like the Japanese ladies you saw here. They love those Bruno Magli shoes like the ones you wear, so I try to stock the short and wide sizes just for them. I plan to go to Europe again next spring to see the fashion shows. I'll buy a few things and try to keep up with the latest trends. Want to come along?"

"Ha, I'd love to, but I'll have to take a rain check on that. Do you ever have any customers from my embassy?"

"Yes, your ambassador for one. She ordered a dozen custom tailored dress shirts a few months ago for her husband and some other people come in occasionally although I'd need to look up their names from my files."

"I saw a Russian couple the first time I was here. Do you make many sales with them?

"No, the visiting Russians mainly browse; most don't seem to have much money to spend."

"What about clientele from the Soviet Embassy?"

"A few. In fact, this morning something happened as one of my seamstresses repaired an item. This man, this Russian, he speaks English well and comes in now and then, but he's rude. He purchased a suit from me almost a year ago and recently the right sleeve on the suit coat began to detach a little from the shoulder so he brought it in and demanded I repair it at no charge even though you could see it had been stretched and was well worn. I finally agreed to do it because he was making such a row in front of my other customers."

"Do you remember his name?"

"His name is Lubachev and he works at their embassy."

"Yuri Lubachev?"

"I believe so, do you know him?"

"Yes, in a way I do. So, what was unusual today?"

"Come, I'll show you." Kane followed Aurora to a room in the rear with the sewing machines, bolts of cloth, and multiple racks of clothes where the several seamstresses labored. She reached into the pocket of a dark blue suit coat and said "this" as she turned and held out a stars and stripes bowtie.

Kane was speechless. It was one of his ties; one he had given away at the 4th of July party at the ambassador's residence. "It was in his suit?"

"Yes, I was watching to see how extensive the repairs might be when my seamstress turned it inside out to look at the lining and the tie dropped out of the inside breast pocket."

"When is he coming back for it?"

"I told him it would be ready tomorrow afternoon. Why?"

"Could I borrow the bowtie if I promised to have it back to you before then?"

"Yes, of course, but ..."

"It's a long story and perhaps it would be better if I didn't tell you any more."

"It must be a military secret."

"You're right."

"Okay, well then, I'm hungry and ready to close."

"Let's try Indian food tonight."

The evening was a struggle for Kane. There was no one else he would rather be looking at across the table. On the other hand, he had an item burning a hole in his pocket that might prove significant in unmasking Bernard. As he tried to keep the dinner dialogue interesting, he mentally listed the thirty bow-ties he had given away. *Which person had provided this tie to the KGB? Bowtie number one I gave to Captain Grusk, number two to the Malaysian Attaché number three to the Indonesian Attaché, number four to ...*

They ate and talked about travel, fashion, and leisure time interests including movies.

The buffet was excellent. They nibbled, talked, and had fresh fruit for dessert.

"I really must be going. I have early appointments with salesmen tomorrow, so can I drop you off at your place?"

"Oh sure, and I apologize for my mind being elsewhere tonight."

"It must be the bowtie."

"Yes, but we need to do this again soon."

"My treat next time," she concluded.

46

Kane dialed Eggleston's number, but he didn't answer. He tried again a few minutes later and the telephone was picked-up on the first ring, "Eggleston."

"Dirk, Dalton here, we need to talk right away, can I come up?"

"Sure. I just got back so give me five minutes to clear up some things."

Kane arrived clutching a small envelope.

"What's the urgency?"

"How about some background music?" Kane requested as he handed over the surprise.

"Can do and what's this...ah, one of your little bowties."

"And take a wild guess where it turned up?"

"I haven't the slightest idea."

"How about in one of Yuri Lubachev's suits."

"What?" Eggleston exclaimed. "Tell me more."

"Yes, and needless to say, I never gave him one. I handed out twenty-nine ties at the 4th of July party to you, people in my office, the attaché corps, and MINDEF, and I kept one for myself, which is identical to this one."

Then he told Eggleston the background about Aurora, her shop, the suit repairs, and the necessity to have the bowtie returned to her before noon the following day.

"I don't suppose you remember everyone you gave a tie to, do you?"

"I knew you'd ask. I'm racking my brain. I recall most, but I'm still working the chronology of the party to complete the list. I thought it might be worth a try to lift a fingerprint off the metal clip on the back of the tie."

"Definitely," Eggleston acknowledged as he reached for the telephone. "I'm calling Singapore's ISD. I'll see if their forensic lab can give us a quick turnaround; they owe me."

"Just make sure they know I need the tie returned no later than about 11:00 AM tomorrow, okay?" Kane added.

The telephone contact was successful and Eggleston left for the ISD. "I'll try to be back early tomorrow and I'll call you as soon as I return."

Under strong light and magnification, the bowtie, unfortunately, yielded almost nothing. The small metal clasp on the backside was dusted, but no latent fingerprints were revealed. Several friction ridges from a print were present but not enough of a pattern for identification or classification, not enough to help in revealing who might have handled it.

Eggleston and Kane met again the next day and Eggleston broke the bad news. "No good prints and no stains on the tie. However, there was a single hair recovered, a white cat hair. The forensic analyst said the cell structure and thickness of the central medulla of the hair confirmed it was from a cat. The write-up and the hair itself are in the separate envelope. It's probably not going to help us much since we don't know about contamination possibilities. Does Ms. Booth or any of her employees have cats? I don't know if Lubachev has one."

"I don't know either" Kane responded.

"Well, give me a call when you puzzle out all the recipients. It might be something we can pursue."

"I will, and thanks for the quick work. Got to go."

Later, back in his office, Kane retrieved the list of bowtie recipients from his desk and traced his finger along the underlined names and check marks. In the attaché office, he had handed out ties to Captain Grusk, Colonels Silver and Chang, Chief Sanderson, and Naseer, and saved one for himself, six out of thirty. Elsewhere within the embassy staff he had given ties to Eggleston, Ambassador Lipka, Diamond, Ortega, and Peeler, five more ties. In the foreign attaché corps, he dispensed ties to the two French attachés, the two Indonesian attaches, and the Philippine, Thai, Malaysian, Australian, and New Zealand attaches, nine more ties. From MINDEF he provided ties to the Liaison Officer, Major Wee, the Chief of the General Staff, General Yuan, MINDEF Training Officer, Colonel Singh, the Commander of the Singapore Navy, Colonel Ng, two missile patrol boat Captains, Lim and Zong, and the two F-5 squadron Commanders, Chong and Yip. The final two ties went to the Aussie, Warrant Officer Ross, and the Royal Navy Attaché, Captain Brett. That was it, thirty ties.

Which of those ties had ended up in Lubachev's pocket? Kane pondered the tie recipients within the embassy. *Could one of them have just lost their tie and Lubachev or one of his cronies stumbled onto it? No way. And the cat hair?*

He began crossing through the names, the ones he had already underlined and checked off, eliminating one and then another. When he finished, he had crossed out all the names in his office and at MINDEF. There remained five people. Then he crossed off Dirk Eggleston and Ambassador Lipka; remaining were Steve Diamond, Manny Ortega, and Davidson Peeler.

Kane thought about it then reached for the telephone and dialed. "Hey, Steve, Dalton here. You've been avoiding me, when are we going to play some golf?"

47

"Lubachev is dead."

The telephone call from Eggleston at 7:25 AM interrupted Kane's first coffee and his examination of the morning newspaper. "What? Say that again."

"I said scratch one KGB officer, Comrade Yuri Lubachev is no longer with us and it looks like it might be a homicide."

"When did this happen?"

"I received the call late last night. Someone found him around 8:00 PM in the uninhabited jungle area in the center of the island where that World War II archeological dig is ongoing. His body was reportedly pinned under his car near the end of a dirt lane. According to my source it looked like he might have been changing a tire and the car fell off the jack, crushing his head. However, the police are calling the situation suspicious. They've cordoned off the entire area for the time being. There are additional tire tracks and footprints nearby and the police are trying to sort it all out. A gaggle of Russians from their embassy is on scene and asking questions. This will undoubtedly be a huge flap and there's a little more to it I need to discuss with you. Can you stop by?"

"Sure, when?"

"Right now, if you're available."

Eggleston pressed the "play" button for music as Kane entered his office.

"Have a seat. Here's the situation. I was making some progress with Lubachev, you know, some discreet contact with him over the past few months. Recently I made a pitch and there appeared to be a good chance he was coming over to our side. I wanted to keep him in place though, double him, but he wasn't having any of that. It was too risky; he said he was no Penkovsky. His concern was the safety of his wife and daughter in Moscow. They were part of the deal and we had reached agreement on a plan. I assured him his wife and daughter would be taken care of, the timing, the documentation, and all the transportation arrangements necessary to get them out. Things were in motion, and we were all set to rendezvous tomorrow at noon. He would be hidden in the ambassador's limo and ride to Tengah air base. There we were booked on a special flight to the Philippines and then on to Hawaii to begin the debriefing process and reunite him with his family the next day. He promised to bring along a treasure; said I'd be impressed."

"This trove of treasure would have included Bernard's identity I assume?" Kane asked.

"I have to believe so as well as other important information."

"So, do you think it's possible Bernard found out and..."

"I think it's entirely possible. I need to know where everyone in your office was last night. Do they all have alibis?"

"What time did this take place?"

"I don't think it's been established yet, but I'll let you know as soon as I know."

"I can personally vouch for the Grusks, Changs, and Silvers for most of the evening. All of us were at the New Zealand attaché's place from about 7:00 PM until late. The Grusks departed around 10:30 PM and the Changs, Silvers, and I all left the party shortly before 11:00 PM. The whereabouts of the rest of my officemates will take a little time to establish, but I'll begin making conversation right away."

"Let me know immediately if you come up with anything out of line."

"I can envision the car falling off a jack and hands, feet, or legs being in peril but not someone's head. Was he robbed?" Kane asked.

"I don't know and unless there was some road hazard wrapped around the axle and he was under the car trying to get it free I can't see how it would happen either. I'll get the full report soon enough though."

"Who else knew about the plan to fly him out tomorrow?"

"Here at the embassy only Ambassador Lipka, but she didn't have any specifics."

"Still, could the plan have been somehow leaked by her?"

"It's possible, but I doubt it"

"Someone else in her office then, like maybe Judith Feldman?"

"I made the request for the limo privately and directly to Ambassador Lipka only a week ago after a dinner party for that congressional delegation that passed through."

"Perhaps she made some kind of a reminder to herself?"

"She knew it was sensitive information."

"Who was the limo driver?"

"There were only to be three of us, Lubachev, myself, and Michael, my guy, as the driver. Mike had no pre-knowledge of the real mission with the limo, only that I needed a car and driver to pick up some materials at ISD headquarters around noontime."

"So, what do you think?" Kane asked.

"If it's a homicide, I can't rule out Bernard for the time being. It would be unusual for Lubachev to be in such a place without a bodyguard somewhere nearby. I would think it's against their operational rules for him to be out by himself in such a remote place after dark except for a clandestine meeting. I don't know of any enemies in Singapore who might want him dead either. I'm pretty sure if the Russians had found out about his plans to defect, they would have taken care of business differently, out of sight, on their turf, not where someone would find his body right away."

"So, you think Bernard offed him?"

"For now, he's the number one suspect in my book unless there's something else going on I don't know about. The KGB won't take this lightly if it's a homicide. If Bernard is the perpetrator, he may already be dead unless he's somehow convinced them Lubachev had his bags packed for Disneyland. We've probably never been closer to finding Bernard than right now and the next few hours may be critical. Call me if anyone in your office doesn't show up for work this morning."

48

The waiter had cleared the table and coffee was on its way. In the candlelight, Kane took pleasure in savoring the last drop of his champagne as he watched Aurora extend her arm outward again to admire the sparkle of the large, gold, four seasons design bracelet, a surprise birthday present. As she rotated her arm from side to side, he noticed a glistening in her eyes.

"Is everything okay?" he asked as he passed his handkerchief across.

"Yes, it's so beautiful."

"I'm really glad you like it; it looks good on you," he responded, holding back a little emotion in his own voice.

The conversation stalled yet their eyes continued to communicate as her warm bare foot moved slowly up inside his trouser leg.

He would have taken her to his new place, but she insisted on going to hers. She poured cognac, put on some Errol Garner jazz, and excused herself. When she reappeared, her lovely black mane was flowing and she wore only the bracelet, a smile, and a filmy negligee that left nothing to his imagination.

He set the drink aside and they embraced, tenderly at first, but then with mutual passion. He lifted her in his arms and attempted to ask directions to the bedroom, but she had suction on his tongue. She shared his objective though and motioned him in the right direction.

Along the way he managed to walk out of his shoes with little difficulty while she unbuttoned the top of his shirt. In the moonlight he laid her on the bed and shed his clothes quickly.

A rooster crowed about daybreak. Kane was awakened and

listened to Aurora's slumber. He couldn't resist running his fingers lightly along the silky-smooth contour of her ribs and up and across the curvature of her hip.

"Don't stop," she cooed.

"Good morning."

She turned, kissed him, and pulled him closer, their bodies melding together. "Tell me, Lieutenant Commander Dalton Kane, US Navy, you don't have to go to work today."

"Sorry, name, rank, and serial number—okay, okay I don't have to work today," he laughed.

"Ha, I know you do" she said as she propped herself on an elbow. "Are you okay? Your eyes look a bit ruddy and puffy."

"You're kidding, I've just spent the night with the most desirable woman on the planet, but they do feel funny now that you mentioned it. You have a cat, don't you, Kane asked curiously, recalling the cat hair found on the bowtie in Lubachev's coat pocket at Aurora's shop.

"Yes, but he's not here now, he comes and goes."

"I knew it. I'm allergic to cats." *I'll have to let Eggleston know in order to clear up the question about the possible origin of cat hair.*

"Can you stay for breakfast?"

They parted company after she prepared tea and crumpets with orange marmalade and fresh fruit. He went back to his place, showered, changed, and rushed off to work, already a little late. She was all he could think about.

Returning to the bedroom to tidy things up, Aurora paused to cuddle a pillow and daydream about the romance. She always wondered whether she would find another man she could love and trust, and share her life. Everything about this man, this American naval officer, she liked, his intellect, kindness, and humor, and she hoped his feelings were growing as deep for her. As she reflected on their relationship one thing came to mind, which might be of concern to him, her height relative to his. On the other hand, he was out of proportion in an utterly different dimension, but delightfully so.

49

At 2:00 AM Singapore was asleep, but not Steve Diamond. He sat wide-awake in his car behind an abandoned two-story building on an uninhabited kilometer of secondary road beyond the city to the northeast. A light breeze rustled the tops of the palm grove while he waited, watched, and listened. It was always possible the police might check a place like this for hoodlums and illegal activity although everything seemed okay for the time being and the tardy Russians should be arriving any minute. They had signaled their desire to meet, another risky get-together, and Diamond had even more reason to be nervous this time because he knew exactly why they wanted to see him. He was prepared though, he hoped.

As the distant glow of headlights from a solitary vehicle drew closer Diamond's pulse revved to over a hundred. Moments later the automobile rolled into view at the end of the clearing and drifted past. The same car returned, unhurried, entered the parking area and proceeded to a spot on the far side opposite Diamond's car, well positioned for a quick getaway. Its lights doused, an infrared night-vision scope panned back and forth around the entire locale paying special attention to windows and doorways and confirming Diamond's identity. A cigarette lighter flashed twice and Diamond responded with his signal. He stepped out and approached the other car. Its right rear door swung open and a burly man with wire-rimmed glasses and dark clothes stepped out and allowed him to enter. He squeezed inside between the two thuggish-looking men, recognizing only Nicholai in the front passenger seat.

The bald, ox-faced man to Diamond's left maintained a

blank forward stare as he took breaths through a mouth that reeked of decayed teeth marinated in cheap vodka. Resting on his stomach, clutched in his left hand, a dark pistol with a silencer pointed at Diamond's chest. Unseen on the other side, the man with the wire-rimmed glasses rolled a spring-loaded syringe back and forth in the palm of his right hand, poised to plunge the lethal dose of chemicals into Diamond's neck, sending him to an instant oblivion. The callous enforcers awaited only their command.

A hidden microphone captured every spoken word. "Are you carrying any weapons tonight, Mr. Diamond," Nicholai asked as the ogre with the fire breath continued to pat Diamond down, and concluded with a menacing clutch of Diamond's scrotum.

"No, no, nothing" Diamond responded as he squirmed, his voice edgy.

"So, how are you this evening, Mr. Diamond? You don't sound well," said Nicholai, flicking his lighter in Diamond's face for a second to get a better look.

"Oh, I'm okay. Look, I can tell ..."

"Shut up Mr. Diamond. I'll tell you when I want to hear more," Nicholai shouted, as the goons restrained Diamond's arms and pressed them firmly to the seat.

"Have you seen Mr. Lubachev recently, Mr. Diamond? Did you make it to the meeting place yesterday?"

A resigned "Yes" slipped from Diamond's lips. "And I wanted to call you right away, but I thought it wiser not to. I knew we'd need to talk about this very soon."

"Was he alive or dead when you last saw him, Mr. Diamond?"

Silent seconds passed before Diamond responded. "Yes..."

"Mr. Diamond, please pay attention and speak up."

"Yes, I killed him!" snapped Diamond and he felt the gun pressed hard against his ribs in reaction to his outburst.

"I thought you were an intelligent man, Mr. Diamond."

"I..."

"Why did you kill him, Mr. Diamond?"

"He was going to defect."

"Oh, and how do you know that Mr. Diamond?"

"I saw evidence on the ambassador's desk calendar. There was a note on it, I have it with me."

"And what does it say, Mr. Diamond?"

Diamond tried to reach for his pocket and was slugged in the gut. "Ugg-hh!" he cried out as he bent forward and twisted in pain.

"Softly, Dimitry!" Nicholai ordered and reiterated the command in Russian.

"Keep your hands out of your pockets, Mr. Diamond, you're upsetting Dimitry. What does the note say, Mr. Diamond?"

"It, it's short. It says 'Limo with Eggs to TAB'. They call Tengah Air Base, TAB, and noon was circled, and it was in Ambassador Lipka's handwriting."

"What eggs?"

"That's Eggleston, they call him "Eggs", but it's not his real name; it's a nickname, and he has his own government car as you know so he doesn't need the ambassador's limo. They were going to use the limo to transport Lubachev to Tengah, it's safer, armored, no one would dare stop it with the flag and diplomatic plates and no one else drives the ambassador's limo except the ambassador's driver, Nani, and he had the day off and there was no event, nothing scheduled for the ambassador at Tengah either. If there was any cargo to be picked up or delivered, they would have used one of the government vans and..."

"Slowly, Mr. Diamond, speak slowly."

"I also found out there was a US Navy C-130 transport aircraft scheduled from Tengah to the Naval Air Station at Cubi Point, Philippines. I called operations at Tengah and asked if there was any space available seating for US Embassy personnel on the flight. The Navy representative I spoke to said no. I persisted. He checked with the duty officer and reaffirmed no other seats were to be released other than the two passengers already confirmed on the manifest, a Mr. D. Eggleston and a Mr. H. Lowell. There is no H. Lowell. I've never heard of such a person and the name isn't on any of our current visitor lists or in the Singapore telephone book. And there's no reason for Eggleston to book a military flight; he always flies Pan Am business class wherever he travels."

"Anything else, Mr. Diamond?"

"Eggleston, he's acting strange. He works late nearly every day. He always has lunch in his office now. Something is going on, I can feel it. When I confronted Mr. Lubachev with this information, he looked shocked and said I was on drugs. We argued and got out of his car. He wanted to fight, tried to kill me, bit my ear as we struggled. Can you see it? Think about it, Nicholai, why would he do that? His actions convinced me I was right so I fought back, hit him on the head with a rock, and hurt him bad. I jacked up his car and let it fall on him to look like an accident and I left the area, but then I returned a short time later to let the air out of his tire so it looked right, and that's when I heard some kids approaching, so I fled. He was leaving you, I'm sure of it; you should search his office and quarters ..."

"Why didn't you tell me your suspicions before this, Mr. Diamond?"

"I didn't know who to tell, who to trust."

"You're lying, Mr. Diamond."

"No, I'm not!"

"Did you find it easy to kill my friend, Mr. Diamond?"

"No, I was defending myself! You have to believe me. I wouldn't be here tonight if I thought you wouldn't believe me."

"You had no other choice, Mr. Diamond."

Nicholai, now silent, looked deeply into Diamond's shadowy face while Diamond's eyes wandered nervously from side to side. A decision on Diamond's fate was imminent because the Russians needed to depart the area soon. Nicholai's stare shifted briefly to the gunman, the needleman, and back to Diamond. "You know we're investigating this very thoroughly and for your sake I hope you have been truthful with me. In the meantime, don't do anything foolish and leave the note with me. You'll write a detailed confession and I want it by next Wednesday. And take care of that ear, you look terrible."

"Everything I told you is true on my mother's grave, I swear."

"And the hardware Mr. Lubachev was going to hand over to you, Mr. Diamond, where is it now?"

"I took it when I left him and I've already begun the installation process."

"Then leave immediately and go home, Mr. Diamond. Try to get some sleep, you need it."

"I will. Thank you."

50

The weather forecast for the evening was partially cloudy, no rain, and temperature in the mid 80s. A small group of Louisiana oilmen home-based in Singapore were part-time caterers and called themselves The Crawdad Suckers. They pulled into Kane's driveway around 4:00 PM and began setting up equipment for the cookout. Zydeco music was part of the package and the lively beat added to the atmosphere and put some zing into the steps of the setup crew. Kane had taken the afternoon off to prepare for the event and Aurora planned to join up after closing her shop.

The menu was authentic Cajun: Boudin blanc, frog legs, crawdads, red beans and rice, jambalaya, and collards, plus sweet Chicory coffee, and warm sugar-dusted beignets for dessert. Kane knew most of the foreign guests, except for perhaps some of the French, had not experienced this cuisine. Kane was busy instructing the bartenders where to set up and where to get more ice in case the reserves ran out when Aurora arrived. He gave her a hug and a quick peck on the cheek.

The invitations specified 7:00 PM and a trickle of guests began to show up right on time. Thirty-five of the forty invitees had responded positively to the RSVP. The main interest to both Eggleston and Kane, of course, was how many people from Eggleston's list of suspects would materialize. Except for Kazmar and Jones in the communications shack, both declining due to work schedules, five others on the list including DCM Bass all replied in the positive. Eggleston was certain Bass would not show up though, so he initiated a wager with Kane for a bottle of scotch.

As the crowd grew in numbers two groups formed, half around the bar in the yard near the buffet tables and the other in the center of the living room, close to the other bar. Everything seemed to be going smoothly with greetings and introductions and the chef reported the food would be ready on time.

Besides Aurora, one of several woman drawing a great deal of male attention was Nikka, the good-looking, extroverted, administrator from the Finnish Consulate who Kane had danced with at the Bastille Day party. Kane had also invited several bachelor officers from the Singapore Navy, plus a last-minute add-on, a visiting liaison officer from the Seventh Fleet flagship, USS *Oklahoma City*. In no time at all, the men discovered Nikka was unescorted. While holding refreshed drinks in both hands and encircled by competing male hormones, she caught Kane's eye and winked her satisfaction.

Steve Diamond was one of the early arrivals. Kane introduced him to a few Singaporean military officers and Aurora and then following minimal conversation he abruptly pivoted away to the inside bar. Diamond stayed there most of the evening as he nursed fruit drinks, chewed on ice cubes, and gazed idly into the crowd. Eavesdropping on or striking up a dialogue with strangers, particularly diplomats or high-ranking military officials regardless of what the Russians wanted him to do was not in Diamond's comfort zone.

When the food was signaled ready Kane escorted Major Wee and several others from the Singapore Navy to the buffet line. He offered plates and utensils, described the first few dishes, and encouraged them to proceed. It was enough of a prod to get all of the guests headed toward the food.

Aurora and Kane stepped to the rear of the line as it dwindled. He began describing dishes to her, adding samples to her plate, and loading-up his own; the crawdads looked particularly fine. Then, as they neared the end of the serving line a lone figure walked up the driveway out of the darkness. It was DCM Bass.

Kane quickly set his plate aside and rushed forward to greet him. "DCM Bass, I'm so glad you could make it this evening."

"I thought I'd stop by to see how the remodeling turned out, we spent so much money on this place. And I've never really tasted Cajun food."

"The house is perfect. I'll give you a tour later, but first let's start with some nourishment and an introduction or two. There are still some seats available inside and one or two outside. Do you have a beverage preference?"

"I could use a quality margarita on a night like this. I don't suppose your bartenders have the ingredients for one of those, do they?"

"I'm sure we have some good tequila; on the rocks or blended?"

"Rocks and salt."

Grusk, Chang, and Silver were stupefied at the sight of Bass and Captain Grusk wasted no time in leaving his seat to buttonhole Kane at the bar. "How in the hell did you pull this off?"

"I wish I knew"

Compliments on the food started to flow right away, even from first-timers, so Kane asked the cooks to step forward and take a bow.

Bass took the vacant seat at a table next to the Consul, Manny Ortega and they immediately engaged in conversation. The GSO, Davidson Peeler, and his wife finished the main course and were heading back to check on the desserts.

With a couple of gin and tonics taking hold and the bayou music turned up, Kane took off on a two-stepping spin with Aurora in his arms. The move was infectious. First, his good friend the French assistant naval attaché, Philipe, and his wife got up and followed suit and then Captain and Mrs. Brett, the Grusks, the Changs, and others. As they cut in and out through the mostly Asian bystanders, the Acadian accordion and harmonica wailed, and couples moved, skipped, and circled from the living room to the porch, to the driveway and back again.

The New Zealand Attaché cut in, briefly switching partners with Kane just as the music ended with a cheer. Kane then proceeded to the inside bar to check on things.

Diamond was still holding up the bar and talking to the Australian naval attaché, but he stopped to make a comment to Kane. "Foxy, she's real foxy, Dalton. Where did you find that piece of ass?"

"Excuse me? When did you say your wife was returning?" Kane replied.

"Who the hell knows and why would you care?" Diamond answered with disdain as he downed the last of his drink.

Sensing discord between the Americans, the Aussie turned the conversation to wine; he was holding a glass of champagne in his hand. "Did you know this year's grape harvest in 'Stralia has been sold entirely to the Frogs?"

"I didn't know that, I'll have to give Philipe a hard time," Kane replied. "I think I found several good bottles of a 1973 vintage Perrier-Jouet champagne in town last week. The tasting report said it has fine color and sparkle, fragrant and charming aroma. What do you say we sample it?" Kane offered.

When Kane returned with the bottle Diamond was gone, but Kane continued his conversation with the Aussie. He was having difficulty with the cork when Philipe stepped in and asked for the bottle. "Let me help you with zees. Have you your sword?"

"It's in my bedroom closet."

"Get eet and I will show you how a real Frenchman does eet."

Minutes later Kane returned, sword in hand.

Nearby guests stopped conversing at the sight of the sword and soon more people crowded into the living room to see what was about to happen.

Bowing to the spectators with the fanfare of a Las Vegas magician, Philipe extracted the sword from its scabbard, touched the blade, feigned a cut, and then held both the sword and the champagne bottle out at arm's length. Slowly, he retracted his right arm with the sword back across his left shoulder and held it there.

"Pleez, make more room," Philipe asked in a serious tone.

With a swift sweeping motion, he ran the blade down the length of his left arm to the bottle. It made a sharp "clink" on contact and the severed bottleneck flew into the air with only an initial gush of the bubbly spilling on his arm.

"Bravo! Bravo!" the audience cheered.

From across the room Aurora raised an eyebrow to Kane as if to say, *Okay, let's see you do it.*

Kane shook his head *no way* and then he made a similar motion, but without the sword and ducked his thumb out of sight at the last instant along with a frightful look, as though his thumb had been severed.

Aurora laughed.

Eggleston had pretty much made the rounds of everyone he wanted to talk to and headed back to the bar to order water, having reached his limit of alcohol consumption for the evening.

After chatting with a few other foreign guests, Bass re-engaged with Manny Ortega and they both strolled down the driveway away from the crowd in order to converse in private. Ortega stood with his hands in his pockets most of the time, nodding his head and listening, while Bass, animated in several instances, waved his arms in the air and gestured in Ortega's direction, making his points. Kane wished he were close enough to hear the conversation.

The caterers finished cleaning up, returned the equipment to the trucks and pulled the plug on the music around 10:00 PM. All the guests began saying their goodbyes and cleared out about the same time. After congratulating Kane on the party, one of the Singapore Navy's missile patrol boat captains inquired if he would be interested in joining him on his boat as an observer for the forthcoming exercise with the US Navy."

"Absolutely" Kane responded with enthusiasm.

Kane could no longer resist, so he strolled over to Bass and Ortega who were still talking. Kane interjected, "I didn't mean to neglect you two gentlemen, but attaché business first."

"Dalton you're a gracious host. The food was absolutely superb and your friend Aurora is quite charming" Ortega responded.

"You left out the margaritas, Manny" Bass stated from behind a slightly inebriated grin.

"We were discussing lifestyles of the gay and lesbian kind," Ortega added.

"Oh, I'm sorry I interrupted. I try to keep an open mind about that" Kane replied.

"It's too bad your Pentagon doesn't see things that way," Bass said, his face filled with a dour frown.

"The DCM and I have similar situations we're trying to come to grips with, that is, his son and my daughter. The social stigma has impacted their professional careers much more than we and they ever anticipated," Ortega offered.

At that moment Kane understood the possible root of Bass's misgivings about the US military and he searched for some comment to address the subject.

"Deputy Bass, I..."

"John's the name, John," Bass reiterated while tossing down the last of his drink along with a face full of ice cubes, "Damn."

"John, my father's a doctor in Florida. If your son has a resume, I could send it along to him and he could route it around to his associates. A fresh start in a different location with some new contacts might be helpful and the medical profession is booming down there in south Florida with all those retirees."

"I'll think about it...good party though" Bass answered somewhat begrudgingly, the compliment almost too difficult for him to deliver.

The following day Eggleston and Kane met to compare notes. The alcohol-induced revelation from DCM Bass about his son was interesting and it was elaborated on in Eggleston's report to Janice Crowell. Diamond's detachment, hardly conversing with anyone at the party even after Eggleston and Kane made overtures to him was not a complete surprise; he was one strange fellow. Manny Ortega had been his usual extroverted self, but nothing interesting was gleaned from eavesdropped conversations between him and other guests. Both Davidson Peeler and his wife seemed more interested in the menu and the caterers than just about anything, and Judith Feldman was a last-minute cancellation. Overall, except for Bass's comments, the outcome was about what Eggleston expected.

51

To the casual observer everything about the office in the newer high-rise building directly across the street from the US Embassy appeared normal and legitimate. The directory near the cluster of fancy elevators in the lobby and lettering on the frosted glass and mahogany door on the fifth-floor hallway read Equatorial Steamship & Trading Company, Ltd., Room 510. Monday through Friday and Saturday mornings the office was open for business. Two and sometimes three day-worker in business suits with brief cases arrived about 7:00 AM and departed late in the afternoon, the same general work schedule as other commercial enterprises in the city. One additional man always arrived in the afternoon and stayed overnight for security.

Inside Room 510 things were different. The hallway door was at all times locked. Interior lighting was maintained at normal levels, but window blinds except for one on the end remained closed regardless of the time of day or weather. Furnishings were Spartan and peculiar for a business with such a grandiose title and address. There was a double size air mattress on the floor along with four folding chairs and a table holding a radio receiver, a tape recorder, and antenna wires.

KGB operatives manned the clandestine listening post. While they waited for activity to start, they chain-smoked cigarettes, read the *Pravda* newspaper, and made more than necessary trips to the toilet to break up the monotony.

One of them leaned forward, pressed his hand against his headset and listened. He hurriedly wrote down the time, took a final drag on his cigarette and placed it in the ashtray. Then he pushed the play button on the tape deck. As the reels began to spin his partner set aside his reading material and inserted his own earpiece.

"Good morning everyone. So, let's begin with Manny today and go around the table this way," Ambassador Lipka motioned after she had settled into her chair with her coffee and notebook for the Monday morning staff meeting.

"Good morning, ma'am, I hope you had a good weekend. First, these are the compiled stats from last week as of Friday. We processed fifty-five visas, ten passports, twelve student visas, and one birth certificate. For the week, it was a hundred ninety-eight visitor visas, a ten percent increase over the previous week. Second, the new travel advisories were posted for the Mideast ..." and so on the speaker, Manny Ortega, ran through his notes.

"Thank you, Manny, that's good. Davidson, what do you have?"

"Nothing significant to report this morning, ma'am, but how did your new air-conditioning system work this weekend?"

"We loved it and tell your people they did a super job. Okay, Dirk."

"There are several messages from Langley I highlighted and posted to your read board. You should look at them this morning if you can. Secondly, I'll be going to see Mr. ..."

Broad grins spread across the Russians' faces as if they had won the Singapore lotto; the listening device was still working. The ambassador's voice and those seated nearby her were loud and clear. The ingenious piece of spyware, a miniscule FM microphone-transmitter looked almost exactly like one of the wheel assemblies on the ambassador's executive chair. It only took KGB technicians a few weeks to modify and test one once Diamond provided photos and the chair manufacturer's name so a replacement wheel from the parts list could be obtained. In order to conserve battery power, the transmitter had a pressure-activated switch turning on only when the ambassador's chair was occupied. Such a feature made detection of the device problematic during electronic sweeps of the embassy. Once Diamond got the antenna wire installed and oriented properly, the KGB was in business.

The listeners strained to hear other voices, briefly weaker and indistinct, as the conversation travelled to the far end of the conference table, then back.

"What do you have this morning, Jim?" Ambassador Lipka inquired of Captain Grusk.

"It was a productive week ma'am. Colonel Chang reports the additional quota for Singapore at the Army's Command and Staff College has been approved and they'll be sending someone back next year. The new contract for the M-16's is still winding its way through the Pentagon and we hope to have some more specific status later today or tomorrow. Colonel Silver says the F-5 pilot training is going very well in Arizona. The only trouble is some of the Singaporeans pilots are missing momma's home cooking. The new engine maintenance syllabus has reportedly completed review at MINDEF with only minor changes and it should be signed-off this week. Lieutenant Commander Kane has been out in the boat a lot and we received some nice feedback from DIA and the Navy on some of his latest work. Let's see, I attended the change of command for Captain Lim and he asked for some additional information on the Soviet Navy's coastal minesweeping capabilities. I'm checking with DIA to see what's available and can be released. I'll have my updated visitor list to Judith later this morning. We are expecting some Navy VIPs from the Pentagon in about two weeks, but I don't have any specifics on the visit just yet. That's all I have at the moment."

"Thank you, anyone else? Okay, folks, that's all," Ambassador Lipka said, ending the meeting at forty-five minutes duration.

52

Kane had good intentions, but he had only managed to hit a bucket of golf balls at a public driving range and stroke a few putts on his carpet before the outing with Captain Grusk and the attaché golf association. There were some good golfers in the group and Kane's ballooning score on the back nine showed his game needed attention. But with the rigors of his work and seeing Aurora Booth on the side as often as he could there was just not enough time to tune up his golf game.

However, following several iterations of telephone tag with Steve Diamond they finally synchronized their schedules and got together for a round. They joined up at the Singapore Island Country Club (SICC). The course was one of the stops on the Asian tour and many of Singapore's elite, including the prime minister with his entourage of armed bodyguards was among its members. Diamond was not a member, but he had "connections" for tee times whenever he needed one, or so he claimed.

Next in queue at the caddie shack were two young Filipino lads, Miguel and Max, clad in SICC monogrammed tee shirts and shorts; both were barefoot. It turned out Max and Diamond were golfing acquaintances with Max having caddied for Diamond on several previous outings.

On the way to the first tee, Diamond suggested a wager, "Based on your bogus handicap I'll give you three strokes a side and we'll make it friendly, say, fifty dollar Nassau, match play."

"No, no way, that's too rich for my blood and I'm really not up on my game yet, no practice time with the new sticks."

"No guts, no glory, Navy, so how about ten dollars and press whenever you want. You can surely afford that, can't you?"

"Press only when you're two holes down and we're playing by the rules of golf."

"Of course," Diamond sneered, as he cleaned and adjusted his sunglasses.

"What happened to your ear?" Kane asked, referring to a loosely fitting bandage on Diamond's right ear.

"Damn cat."

The caddies extracted drivers from the golf bags, wiped them clean and handed them over to the competitors who loosened up with a few practice swings. In the background Kane could hear Miguel and Max in a sidebar in their native Tagalog language. They gestured at the contestants, their bets obviously resting on the outcome of the match.

Right away Diamond showed good distance off the tee, not always in the middle of the fairway, but playable. Kane was not quite as long, but his chip shots and some luck with the putter was keeping him alive. An impossible twenty-footer snaked its way into the cup and won the last hole for him.

Soon they were fully warmed-up, actually hot, so they stopped at the first refreshment stand where young SICC girls offered iced towels and freshly squeezed fruit juice to revitalize the competition.

When they reached the first par three, 182 yards, Kane asked for his mashie. Miguel handed over the five-iron without hesitation and Kane was impressed. He teed up the ball and took what was intended to be his normal swing, but something went haywire and a giant divot flew into the air as the ball, barely touched with the iron, skittered away like a hardboiled egg. It travelled only a few yards then stopped dead center in the ladies' tee box.

Diamond danced a little jig in the background and turned away, hardly able to contain himself at Kane's misfortune. His own tee shot was a good one, coming to rest on the green about twelve feet from the pin.

Kane tried to blank-out his previous swing while he resolutely re-gripped the same club and addressed the ball for his second shot. Following a little waggle, he had a much better turn. The ball left the sweet spot of the clubface with a distinctive report, which eloquently informed him he had hit a nice one. It soared high with a slight draw toward the target and landed a few feet short, but directly in line with the pin and rolled onto the green ... and rolled... and progressed in slow motion until it looked to balance on the lip of the cup. They all stood stock-still and watched. Then a final blade of grass gave way and the ball disappeared into the cup with the last erg of its kinetic energy.

"Nice shot, mister!" shouted Miguel as he leaped into the air and gestured toward Max.

"You've got to be shitting me!" Diamond screamed. On the eighth tee, Diamond hooked his ball sharply to the left into a group of trees, but instead of playing a more conservative second shot he might have had a chance to make, he went for it, trying one even the professionals would not attempt. He chose his three-wood, intent on threading it between trees and getting it all the way to the green, a shot he might make maybe one out of a dozen times. Kane thought he would have been better off with a safety shot, lying up short of the green with a more lofted club, playing it back onto the fairway through the largest gap between the trees. Diamond's high-risk gamble was un-rewarded. His ball hit a tree almost dead center and bounced back to within about twenty yards of where he stood. He turned and gave Kane a look and Kane knew he had him exactly where he wanted him. Diamond took a double bogey on that hole and the match stood even at four each.

At the ninth, both tee shots ended up in the rough to the left. Kane followed his caddy to the location of his ball and Miguel pulled out the five-iron again. Kane checked the depth of the rough, medium height. "Yes, that should do it."

Diamond and his caddy were still looking for his ball. Kane thought it landed farther and more left, close to out-of-bounds. After Kane took his shot, he and Miguel set out to help search for Diamond's ball. More than five minutes had expired, the ball was still lost, and the foursome stuck behind them was anxious to tee off.

"Here" yelled Diamond's caddy. They all looked to an adjacent knoll recently canvassed by Kane and saw a ball sitting up nicely on a tuft of grass.

"Good eye, Max," Diamond yelled as he trotted toward the fraudulent discovery. Miguel and Kane looked at each other in disbelief.

"He cheat, mister," Miguel whispered as he dropped a ball and grasped it with his toes showing the technique to seize and tee up a ball in stride without anyone noticing.

Diamond's second shot was well struck, but to the right this time, just missing a greenside bunker and eventually stopping in short rough on a tricky, downhill lie. Kane's shot ended just short of the green in a good level position to chip it close.

Diamond analyzed his shot, a tough one to execute correctly. Kane could see the tension building as Diamond took his stance. He needed to get the ball up and with enough backspin to stop it before it rolled over the green. He swung too quickly at a bad angle, miss-hit it, and the ball blew across the green and off the far side. Kane watched stone-faced, but said *Cha-ching* to himself.

"Fuck this," Diamond yelled, "I can't play shit today." Flipping his club high into the air he reached for his billfold, extracted a handful of cash, and tossed the wad on the green in Kane's direction as he walked away.

"Hey, we're not finished, but thanks, we'll play again soon," Kane yelled back as he winked at Miguel.

Diamond did not turn, but waved a contemptuous acknowledgement as he continued toward the clubhouse with Max in trail.

It was a good round for Kane. He completed the back nine, shot an eighty for the eighteen and gave Miguel a handsome tip. He kept the scorecard with the intention of explaining "the shot" to Captain Grusk and sending the scorecard back home to his dad.

The match actually worked out better than Kane had expected. When you're around someone, you develop insight into character, sensitivities, and tendencies, and Kane had begun to find out more about Diamond. He looked forward to a rematch or some situation in the near future where Diamond might be provoked into saying or doing something careless, or let something incriminating slip; that is, if he was Bernard.

53

It was a quiet Sunday afternoon in the embassy. A Marine guard and Kane were its only occupants. Down on the first floor the young corporal had just completed his internal check of the building and returned to the security control booth where he tested the alarm systems and the camera monitoring circuits. All systems were green, operational. Then he inventoried the weapons and made the appropriate entries in the logbook before settling back in his chair. It would be several hours until his next lap around the inside of the building. Deep from within a drawer filled with emergency action instructions, telephone recall lists, and standard operating procedures, he extracted an old, well-thumbed magazine. He held it up by its spine and shook it until the Playmate of the Month centerfold exposed herself for the umpteenth time.

Knowledge, visualization, the right tools, plus a sensitive touch are what it takes to surreptitiously open most common locks. Kane resumed stretching and massaging his hands as he stood with his back to the wall in the dimly lit portion of the hallway outside Diamond's outer office. It was time to get to work. He pulled each finger once more to relax the joints and then he extracted the small leather case from his pocket.

He knew Diamond's outer office door to be locked, but he had determined from a previous reconnoitering it was not alarmed. Nor was there any security camera coverage on this end the hallway, and access to the third floor via the staircase made this part of the operation all too easy. Always with an escape plan in mind, he was familiar with the hum of the elevator and sure he could make a dash from the hall to the staircase quickly enough not to be seen.

The door lock was a common pin tumbler type, most likely a 5-pin. Kane knelt with a penlight clasped in his teeth, slipped the pick into the keyway of the lock with its hooked end up, and moved it to the rear. Carefully touching the last tumbler and raising it slightly he inserted the tension wrench. While applying gentle clockwise pressure he slowly raised the tumbler with the pick and felt and heard an almost inaudible click. Then maintaining pressure on the wrench, he moved to the fourth tumbler raised it carefully until he obtained a similar result and continued on to the others. At the last, closest tumbler, he carefully lifted it too. The decisive moment was at hand, slowly he turned the wrench, the cylinder rotated, the lock opened.

He went directly to the door with Diamond's name on it. Inside, the usual office accouterments, papers scattered across the desktop, and full "IN" and "HOLD" boxes. He rifled through the papers and the unlocked desk drawers—nothing of interest there. A hasp and padlock secured the lower left drawer so he got down on his knees for a closer look. It was a Master combination lock, the kind typically used on gym lockers. When those little locks are new and unworn, they can be difficult to open with conventional methods and he didn't have time to dally so he decided to try a shortcut. A wooden elephant bookend from Diamond's bookcase might do the trick. He held the lock and compressed the shackle and then struck the side of the lock along its centerline with the bookend while simultaneously releasing the shackle. The blow was supposed to jolt the internal locking dog enough to compress its spring and release. He tried again. It required perfect timing to release the shackle at just the right instant. He hoped he might get lucky before damaging the bookend too much. One more time, a harder blow—the shackle popped open.

Inside, a handful of green hanging files pushed to the rear, otherwise, a disappointingly empty drawer. Whatever had been stored in the vacant space up front was now missing. The first thin file contained a carbon copy of a round trip airline ticket for Diamond from Singapore to Kuala Lumpur and return. The other files were labeled, but completely empty. Pulling them forward one-by-one Kane was surprised to see a stash of multi-colored ladies' panties, at least six of them, behind the last file. *Huh?* He started to close the drawer but his light picked up a glint of something else on the bottom of the drawer. He stuck his head further inside for a closer look and pressed his finger on the object it to pick it up. It was a small piece of undeveloped photographic film about an inch long and a quarter of an inch wide with five intact sprocket holes along one side. He placed the film scrap in his shirt pocket, locked everything up, and quietly made his way back to his office.

54

Mid-morning the next day as Kane was returning to his desk his telephone rang. "Defense Attaché Office, Lieutenant Commander Kane speaking. Hello... who is this?"

"My name is not important," a voice whispered at last.

"Speak up, I can hardly hear you. Yes, okay, have we met?"

"Oh no, no, but a friend told me of you. He said we are of the same mind."

"Well, that's good, so what can I do for you today?" Kane asked as he tried to identify the speaker's nationality, likely from somewhere in the Middle East.

"Oh, nothing, no, no, but I can be of service to you. You see I am in possession of a document America would be interested in having."

"What kind of document are you talking about?"

"It would be unwise for me to say, but I can have it delivered to you soon. What would be a good time?"

"Let's see...I can be at the front entrance of the embassy at 1:00 PM today"

"The rear of the embassy would be better."

"Okay, 1:00 PM at the rear door."

"Please be on time because my driver cannot linger."

"Okay, I understand, and may I contact you if I have questions about this document?"

The phone line was dead; the caller had hung up.

Kane made some notes, jotted down the time, and then mentioned the telephone call to Chief Sanderson. It was standard procedure to discuss strange telephone calls with someone else in the office. There was the risk it could be a setup, a terrorist attack was a possibility, but at the moment there was no official heightened threat alert in affect for Singapore or the region.

At 12:50, Kane went down to alert the Marine guard and to see if the front and rear security cameras were working, which they were.

At 12:58 a white Mercedes sedan with Singapore plates and blackout window tinting pulled into the rear parking area and stopped near the rear entrance. No one got out of the car.

Kane waited inside a few seconds, assessed the situation, then exited and approached the vehicle. As he started to knock on the front driver-side window it rolled down. A dark-skinned driver in a black suit, necktie, and sunglasses handed over a large manila envelope without uttering a word. The package had the length, width, and girth of a large Yellow Pages telephone book from a major US city. It was entirely unmarked, no protruding wires or greasy stains, no metal components felt within, and no smell, just the weight and approximate flexibility of a package of printer paper.

Kane examined the package externally one more time just inside the rear entrance to the embassy and again at his desk before he opened it. He surveyed the contents and called for Chief Sanderson. "Hey Chief, come and look at this."

"What is it?" Sanderson inquired.

"It appears to be schedules, materials and hardware lists, and cost estimates for a major construction project, underground, and these look like the blueprints for it. Check out these dollar amounts. Not too many countries can afford a price tag like that."

"Wow! How did you get this? Are you going to show it to Mr. Eggleston?"

"Yes, and Captain Grusk, too, before we package it up, but you can start typing the report right away. It looks like my investment in all those cocktail parties is beginning to pay off. I only hope my liver can keep up the pace."

55

Kane received the reply from DIA he was waiting for regarding the film scrap analysis. He had forwarded the piece found in Diamond's desk drawer along with his questions and the answers were returned in a classified letter: "A snip test of the unprocessed sliver of film you sent confirmed it is 35 mm Kodak TRI-X pan, ASA 400. It measures 25.4mm long by 7mm wide, and contains five sprocket holes and one partial sprocket hole along one side. The side opposite the sprocket holes is clean and straight and appears cut from a roll using a sharp blade or die process. A frame reference number 'OA' is visible on the margin of the fourth and fifth sprocket holes, an indication this piece of film is from the extreme lead end of the film roll."

The second paragraph was more riveting. "Those are the facts and here's the deduction and speculation for what it's worth. If you doubled the width of this piece of film residue, i.e., equal 7mm sides of the roll you would have 14mm. Subtract 14mm from 35mm and you have 21mm and 21mm happens to be the width of film used in the KGB's F-21miniature camera. If I were to go out on a limb about this, I would say it could possibly be residue from the film splitter device used to reduce a roll of 35mm film to 21mm width for that camera. Then again, it might be a coincidental tear from a roll and I'm totally wrong. Let me know if I can be of further assistance. Very Respectfully, Robert."

Kane went up to show Eggleston the response, plus it was an opportunity to recap his recent observations of Diamond as well.

"This is the same piece of film you showed me before?" Eggleston asked.

"Yes, the same tiny piece and I received the reply to my inquiry about it just today from DIA."

"That was a quick turnaround."

"I have a friend. He says there's a possibility the piece is associated with the KGB's F-21 miniature camera and..." Kane went on to give Eggleston all the details about the film scrap and then he updated Eggleston on Diamond's activities.

"His exercise routine, it's precise, set-piece. You'll have to join me some time and see what I mean. I can almost tell you in advance his exact route and next step before he takes it. He's doing it for a reason, for an appointment or something else he doesn't want to miss."

"Do you think you've been burned, he's on to you maybe? It's just a performance?"

"It's possible I guess, but I've been careful."

"So, he's on a timed route making checkpoints and perhaps conducting a brush pass of materials along the way or a rendez-vous with someone?"

"If he is, he's very good and I keep missing it. The stop at the café is absolutely the same too as far as I can tell, but he talks with no one."

"You say he always sits in the row of tables nearest the sidewalk?"

"Yes, but once they were full and he had to sit to the rear."

"He seats himself in front to be seen or see someone?"

"That the most plausible reason. The next time I think I'll position myself somewhere on his side of the street and take a few photos of the pedestrian traffic across the way while he's at the café. Maybe someone interesting will turn up in that imagery."

"You're turning into a real sleuth, Dalton, but be careful, and nice work on the film. I need to pass it and the report back to Crowell. I haven't come up with anything as provocative yet, but based on this I'm thinking about pulling Michael off sur-veillance of the DCM and putting him on Diamond from time to time to see if he's up to anything after hours."

"Let's do it."

"Why don't you get together with Mike sometime tomorrow

and relate what you know about Diamond's routines before I cut him loose."

"Sure, I don't have anything pressing early in the morning if Mike's available. Also, Diamond's after me with a vengeance to play golf again, he's sore about our last outing; the guy has a real temper. I almost forgot to mention the bow tie. I figure it has to be Diamond's, maybe Peeler's, or possibly Ortega's. I know it's circumstantial, but now with the film it's beginning to point toward the mad Greek, Steve Diamond, don't you think?"

"It's titillating, Dalton, but it's way too early to be putting him in handcuffs."

56

The office telephone rang. "Steve Diamond speaking."

"Your laundry is ready for pickup," announced the voice on the other end of the line.

"Uh, okay, what time do you close?"

"We close at 4:00 PM."

"I'll be there."

The laundry pickup notification was an imperative request from the KGB for an impromptu meeting. Diamond quickly locked his desk and left for the open-air market several blocks from the embassy. Arriving there, he spent an inordinate amount of time handling fruit while another male customer sauntered close by and spoke in muffled undertones.

"The jackfruit is ripe," the stranger offered.

"I prefer the carambola" Diamond responded.

"The attaché, Lieutenant Commander Kane."

"Yes?" Diamond questioned.

"He may be following you."

"Here?" Diamond recoiled with a look around the market.

"No, no, not here, but twice he's been in the vicinity of the café at times when you were there. This noon hour he was within a block of you when we lost him on the street. It may be coincidence, but we can find no reason for him to be in the area at the same time you are. Have you ever seen him while you're walking?"

"No."

"Has he ever mentioned seeing you on your walk?"

"No, but I told you DCM Bass stopped by the café once."

"Yes, we know. Beginning tomorrow, we're changing your

refreshment to location 'F'. It's in the other direction about the same distance, but not as much sidewalk traffic to get in the way and that will be helpful. Everything else will remain the same. We will see if the attaché makes any changes. Try the passion fruit, it looks ripe."

Diamond paid for his fruit and began to return to the embassy unmindful of the plastic bag swinging from his hand; his head was elsewhere. *Kane's following me? Kane, what could he know?* As he continued along the sidewalk, he made direct eye contact and analyzed approaching strangers as he whispered, "Goddamn, Goddamn, Goddamn."

57

As Kane stepped out of the office for a quick pit stop in the men's room, he glanced at Janie Tan and did a double take. Her skin was the color of richly burnished teak. "Yikes, I didn't notice that tan earlier and I won't even ask what you did this weekend."

She laughed. "My father had a fit. He said I looked like a common laborer. Good thing he didn't see my bikini lines or he would have tossed me out into the street."

"So where did you go?"

"We went to Shah's Beach near Malacca. It's nice but you have to watch out for sand fleas, they bite a lot."

"Then count me out for that place."

"And you'll never guess who I saw there," she added.

"Oh? Hit me."

"Don't think I haven't been tempted!" she laughed.

"Well?"

"I saw Judith Feldman and she had a male companion," Janie said while she needlessly reshuffled papers on her desk.

Kane looked at his wristwatch and made a speed it up motion with his other hand.

Janie stopped and spoke in a whisper. "She was with Steve Diamond and they were lovey-dovey as you say."

Kane's eyes bulged. "No shi... no kidding? Are you sure it was him?"

"Oh, please, how could any woman not recognize him?" she replied, panting lustily.

"Quick, more details" he demanded.

"They were having lunch on the porch of a small cottage

near the beach, holding hands and kissing. It looked quite romantic."

"Who would have guessed? Well, I'm going to run down to the cafeteria for a donut, want one?"

"No thanks, my bikini is already showing off a part of me I don't want to see."

Kane sailed out. But instead of heading down to the cafeteria he raced up the stairs to Eggleston's office and the secretary, noting his urgency, waved him in. Closing Eggleston's door, he repeated what Janie Tan had just told him.

Eggleston dropped what he was doing and pushed back in his chair, "This might be the break we've been waiting for."

58

Judith Feldman opened yet another roll of antacids; it must have been the salad. She had retched every day since Saturday and it was not looking good now. She sprang from her desk and fled to the restroom, hitting the lavatory just in time. Two other secretaries were at the sinks, washing hands, running combs through hair. "Hey, are you okay in there?" one asked.

Judith came out slowly, bent over the sink, and splashed water on her face, "Food stall" she responded weakly.

"Ew-w-w" the others chorused.

"I've done that," said one.

"Yuck, same for me" said the other. "Well, I hope you feel better soon."

Ambassador Lipka noted Judith's ashen face, "A big weekend I take it?"

"A bit too big. I went to Malacca with a friend and broke the first two rules."

"Oh, no," chuckled the ambassador.

Judith nodded, holding up an index finger, "raw veg" and then the next finger, "ice in my tea."

Ambassador Lipka frowned, "I really must speak to you about your depraved lifestyle" and then she shook her finger at Judith in mother-daughter mode. "You do insist on living on the edge."

Judith laughed aloud at the ambassador's little joke. *You haven't the faintest idea* she thought to herself.

"Do we have any coffee left?" the ambassador inquired from the kitchenette.

"Not much; I'll make a fresh pot" Judith answered.

"No, no stay right where you are. I can do it—just yell out the quantities." The ambassador piddled, chatted about her weekend, and also made a pot of tea for Judith as the coffee brewed. Handing Judith the tea, the ambassador inquired if she wanted to try a small lunch.

"I might be able to handle it. I just ate another antacid and packet of soda crackers I found in my desk drawer and I feel better now."

"Good girl, that's the way to do it, baby steps," and the ambassador strolled back into her office with her mug of coffee.

Judith sipped her tea and felt a stab of depression. What would she do when Ambassador Lipka retired? There was only about a year left of her career and Judith dreaded her departure. They had worked together for a number of years and she and her loving husband had become a major part of Judith's existence. She had grown dependent on her counsel and words of wisdom. *Baby steps*, sensible advice in almost any situation. Judith's mind drifted to her tiny nephew, watching him take a tumble, getting up, and then trying again. Suddenly she caught her breath; her hand knocked pens and papers aside to view her desk calendar. Gasping "Oh my God, oh my God," she counted the days, flipped back a month, and counted more. Covering her face with her hands, she dropped her head and closed her eyes. How could she have been so stupid, so careless? She must seek confirmation with a doctor, quickly. Flipping through the Rolodex, she found Dr. Quon's number and dialed. The receptionist said the doctor's schedule was fully booked, and the waiting room packed with walk-ins. Judith could see one of the associates if she chose, no, she knew him well and trusted his discretion so she would wait until he was available.

"Friday afternoon at 1:00 PM is the best we can do" the receptionist answered.

"That will be fine." Judith thanked her, hung up, and made a note. She was aghast at her own ignorance and fearful of waiting so long to see the doctor. She was able to keep down a light lunch at her desk, but concentration was out of the question. It was an afternoon of tension and she was relieved when the day ended.

Tuesday morning there was more nausea and dizziness even though she had slept deeply for more than nine hours. Crackers, tea, and antacids seemed to have helped.

She jumped as the phone on her desk rang, "Ambassador Lipka's office."

"Seth Barron here, hello, Seth Barron here calling long distance from Scottsdale, Arizona. Can you hear me okay? Can you hear me? I want to talk to the American ambassador."

Everyone had to pass through the "Feldman filter", no exceptions. "I'm sorry sir, she's away from her office now, but I'm Judith Feldman, her secretary. Is there any way I may help you?"

"No, I need to talk to the ambassador. I've been trying to get a hold of my daughter, but her husband won't cooperate," voiced the angry father.

"Sir, I will ask the ambassador to call you. Is she personally acquainted with your daughter and son-in-law?"

"She ought to be, the guy works there, his name's Diamond, Steve Diamond and my daughter's name is Constance."

Judith's stomach heaved. *What in the hell is this all about?* "Let me have your number and I will have the ambassador call you as soon as she returns."

The instant she hung up, Judith called Steve Diamond. "It's me," she spoke softly, "A mister Seth Barron just called from Arizona to speak to Ambassador Lipka and I thought you'd want to know."

"Shit, are you kidding, that crazy bastard!" Diamond exclaimed as he slammed down his telephone.

Judith was still regaining her composure when Ambassador Lipka walked in. She reported the telephone call from Mr. Barron without comment, closed the ambassador's door, and crossed back to her desk.

Soon one telephone line button lit up, then another one, "Yes, ma'am?"

"Call Mr. Diamond and have him come up."

"ASAP?"

"Give me a few minutes; I'm doing a little research," Ambassador Lipka answered.

Diamond entered, fidgeting and distracted, seeming not to notice Judith, but as always, her heart stopped when her eyes met his. Today, he was resplendent in a designer suit, highly buffed shoes, every strand of gorgeous hair in place; she wanted to eat him alive. Straining to remain in the real world, she pressed the intercom button, "Mr. Diamond is here."

"Send him in."

Judith was disappointed, but not surprised by Steve Diamond's behavior. The unpredictable nuances of his personality had not escaped her attention and from time to time his eyes took on the peculiar cast of a feral predator, however, today he was the prey and he knew it. She remembered the first night he had come to her flat. He had already told her about his separation from Constance and asked if he might spend the evening; he would "bring something special to munch on." She agreed, made a lovely plum torte and (just in case) put lavender scented satin sheets on her bed, and chilled a bottle of champagne. Half expecting a deli bag or Chinese carryout, she was delighted to see a lovely basket swinging from his arm. It held prosciutto, goat cheese, Kalamata olives, a large ripe Roma tomato, sourdough rolls, and exotic tropical fruits. He had also tossed in a tiny bottle of raki picked up at the Plaka in Athens. Both of them downed a thimbleful of it with coffee after dessert, and then concurred, laughing and wheezing, it tasted like a combination of jet fuel and paint thinner.

The evening ended as both had known it would, he meeting all of her fantasies without breaking a sweat, quite a feat in that climate.

His fantasies were much the same, and she shivered. They had been seeing each other for a couple of weeks and enjoying each other's attributes, inside and outside the embassy on a regular basis. It was a quiet morning. The ambassador, DCM, and an impeccably polished retinue of Marine guards had motorcaded to the airport to greet the US vice president and several cabinet members. They would be busy for three days, and Judith had welcomed the opportunity to tackle the mountains of paperwork accumulating on the ambassador's desk. She had just begun when she heard someone in the reception area.

Peeking around the door she saw Diamond smiling back. He closed the door, locked it, and crossed the room in long strides. Enveloping her in his arms, he began whispering in her ear, "I couldn't stop thinking about you, your beautiful body, your sweet smell, last weekend." He swept her up with ease, carried her to the ambassador's capacious sofa, quickly and deftly removed every article of her clothing and took care of business with speed and energy. He then helped retrieve her clothes.

She scurried into Ambassador Lipka's bathroom feeling as if she had been hit by a tornado, clothing in a jumbled heap, needing a complete makeup re-do. She looked in the mirror at tousled curls and smeared lipstick, and rooted around in the cabinet for a washcloth and a comb. Finally, fully clothed, she emerged to find Diamond straightening his necktie. He smiled, patted her derriere, picked up his notebook, and left.

He kept track of the ambassador's schedule, made similar visits, and kept taking her panties. She would sit at her desk in a daze afterwards, "*Whatever it takes,*" she thought, he, addictive, she, hopelessly besotted.

The ambassador went over the conversation she had with Constance's father. Diamond calmly replied that his wife made frequent trips to Europe on her never-ending quest for antiques. Sometimes she was away for weeks, sometimes incommunicado for days. He explained she had called him only five days earlier and he had reminded her to call her parents who were by the way, "elderly and quite absent-minded." In the end, Ambassador Lipka seemed satisfied with the explanation and Diamond left her office.

The ambassador appeared by Judith's desk, "Feeling better now?" and she put her hand on Judith's shoulder.

Judith smiled and looked up, "A little and I have an appointment with Dr. Quon on Friday at 1:00 PM. I've asked Linda to fill in for me, I hope you don't mind."

"I'm glad you are going. You need to see about this. By the way, what was your impression of Mr. Barron?"

Judith pondered for a moment. "I only had a brief chat. He seemed gruff and accustomed to being obeyed."

"I felt that as well. I'm off to meet my husband for lunch,

back by 2:00 PM, bye."

Ms. Feldman tried to reach Steve Diamond in the afternoon, but he had taken the remainder of the day off. It was just as well. She was obsessed with fear about her condition and a slip of the tongue might cause him to take off like a rocket.

59

Arriving home, Diamond went directly into the living room and hurled his briefcase at the sofa. He stood there, arms ramrod straight with fists, eyes closed, gorged veins pulsing in his temples. *They're getting closer, time to fly.* He took a deep breath, opened his eyes, and reached for an antique blue and white porcelain vase, one of Constance's favorites, on a nearby table. He held the vase at arm's length and addressed it as though a living person, wailing in an almost effeminate voice, "No, Ambassador Lipka, I don't want to talk to Constance." Then he let it slip to the floor and break into countless pieces and stomped the larger shards in a rage.

In his bedroom, he removed two pre-packed suitcases from the closet shelf and took them to the back door. He returned into the living room to gather up his briefcase and on to the kitchen. From a cabinet he extracted a can of cat food, opened it, placed the contents in a dish, and watched the cat eat in silence for a few minutes longer before he locked up and left.

He failed to show up for work the next morning and as luck would have it his supervisor, Peterman, and most of his office-mates were busy at an all-day seminar in a downtown hotel. So, it was not until the following morning, two days after his departure that concern for his whereabouts had grown. Repeated telephone calls to his residence went unanswered, and an office mate who had been dispatched there reported his car missing, the house locked, and curtains drawn.

Peterman subsequently informed Ambassador Lipka that Diamond was absent and incommunicado and he, Peterman, intended to go to Diamond's house with the GSO to determine

Diamond's health and welfare. As necessary, they would open the house with a duplicate key to see if Diamond might be sick or incapacitated. Ambassador Lipka agreed it was the appropriate action under the circumstances, but she requested Peterman stand fast for a minute while she checked on something.

Ambassador Lipka rested her hand on the telephone; an uneasy feeling had crept over her. She picked up and dialed, "Dirk..."

Lipka provided Eggleston with what she knew about the situation with Steve and Constance Diamond, the telephone communications from Seth Baron, Constance's father, and the plan for Peterman and the GSO to enter Diamond's residence.

"Stall them for a while. I'd like to have a look around there by myself before too many people trample the place," Eggleston replied.

"I'll hold them off until 3:30."

Thirty minutes later Eggleston pulled onto Diamond's street and parked in front of the house. As he walked up the driveway, he looked around for anything unusual or out of place, any clue to help him understand what was going on and how recently Diamond may have been there. He knocked on the front door and waited. With no response he made his way around the house behind the bushes trying each window for one that might be unlocked. Returning a second time to the back door he knocked again and hearing nothing inside he gained entry with the help of some pocket tools.

As he took a step inside the back porch, he placed his hand on the gun in his waistband holster, loosened it, and called out. "Hello there! This is Dirk Eggleston from the US Embassy. Is anyone home? Steve Diamond, can you hear me?" Only the cat came forward. "Anyone here?" Eggleston made his way down the hallway, putting on a pair of thin white cotton gloves as he went.

In what appeared to be the master bedroom the king size bed was unmade. One pillow was on the floor, and the sheet and tossed lightweight blanket arrangement gave an impression of single occupancy. Nearby, a chest of drawers and from a low angle Eggleston could see a fine layer of dust on it. Inside, women's items, under garments, panty hose, and socks, neatly arranged. Lipsticks, makeup, face cream, nail files, tweezers; the usual cosmetics filled a nearby dressing table drawer. A small jewelry box was open and empty. From a brush he removed a few long blond hairs and placed them in an envelope from his pocket. A second chest of drawers was completely empty. He looked under the bed and then went to the walk-in closet. Both sides were crammed with woman's hanging clothes and dozens of foreign-labeled shoeboxes. A high shelf held expensive-looking pink leather suitcases and smaller travel bags. He pondered, *She's returned from her trip?* A sturdy looking medium-sized floor safe with its door ajar was empty except for a single document cover sheet stamped SECRET and a package of a dozen or so rolls of 35mm Kodak film.

In the bathroom shower stall the bottom of the bar of soap was moist. There was no noticeable evaporation of the water in the toilet, the water level even with the faint ring inside the bowl. *Not gone long.* The shelves of the medicine cabinet were clear of men's toiletries; only a jar of face cream, hand lotion, and a pink toothbrush remained. A disposable razor and several tubes of lipstick were scattered on the floor.

The second bedroom had an unmade single size bed and Eggleston collected a few dark hair samples off the pillow. The small closet was partially full of men's hanging clothes and a single pair of shoes on the floor, but nothing on the vacant overhead shelf. Eggleston stood on a chair to view the shelf space and saw a dust outline and skid marks suggesting luggage had recently been removed. *He's gone, she's not, and it looks like they weren't sleeping together.*

The living room floor was littered with pieces of a broken vase, but nothing else was there to shed any light on Diamond's vanishing act. In the kitchen, the cat stopped by to weave its way through Eggleston's legs.

The trashcan under the kitchen sink was full; an empty can of cat food balanced on the top of the heap. The remaining morsels inside the can were still relatively moist and bug free and the cat's water dish was more than half-full. The milk in the refrigerator smelled fresh and the bananas on the counter were not overly ripe.

Mail tossed on the dining room table had recent postmarks, including several opened personal letters addressed to Constance from the same return address in Scottsdale, Arizona.

With questions remaining, but time running out, Eggleston headed toward the back door to check the garage. As he returned to the porch, he took an un-planned look inside the full-sized freezer. The gaping space in the middle seemed an odd arrangement and the pool of bloody ice on the bottom stopped him in his tracks.

Kane had spent most of the day since dawn in the boat and returned to the embassy late in the afternoon.

"Lieutenant Commander Kane, that was a longer than usual boat ride. Just look at all the calls you missed: Major Wee, Jackie from the French Embassy, Mr. Eggleston, and these others. Mr. Eggleston wants you to call him back ASAP. Should I ring him up right away for you?" Janie Tan asked.

"Can't, I'm in a hurry. I'll take care of it in a minute."

"Call Dirk Eggleston right away, apparently it's urgent" Chief Sanderson called out as Kane entered the vault to deposit the camera equipment and report the interesting sighting in the harbor.

Minutes later, still a little out of breath, Kane began to return the calls, "Dirk, Dalton, I just got back, what's up?"

"Don't sit down, your golfing buddy Steve Diamond is missing and the GSO is headed out to his place with a key to open it up. You need to break away right now and ride out there with me because there's something I want you to see. Meet me in the parking lot and be thinking about that female floater you found in the harbor."

60

Still nauseous on Wednesday, Judith Feldman rose early try-ing to think of a way to control it. Perhaps she could get over it before she left for the embassy. Tea, crackers, antacids, and do not hurry—It worked.

Ambassador Lipka was meeting another congressional delegation at the airport. She left at noon telling Judith to take the rest of the day off and Judith did so with gratitude.

Thursday morning Lipka arrived a little later than usual and went straight to the kitchenette to get her cup of coffee. She stopped at Ms. Feldman's desk and studied her face. "You look better today, that afternoon nap must have helped."

Judith took Ambassador Lipka's hand and held it in hers, "What will I do when you're gone?"

"You'll be absolutely fine, I intend to make sure of it," the ambassador said as she bent and hugged Judith's shoulders.

A movement in their peripheral vision brought their focus to the doorway where Eggleston waited, and both wondered, without caring, how long he had been there.

Ambassador Lipka spoke, "Don't just stand there, Dirk, come in and grab a cup of coffee."

When they entered the ambassador's office Eggleston closed the door and spoke quietly about Judith Feldman's weekend with Steve Diamond. Lipka processed the infor-mation in stunned silence and utter disbelief. "And there's more" Eggleston went on. He told her about the conditions inside Diamond's house, the blood in the freezer, and unhesi-tatingly aired his suspicions regarding the disappearance of Constance Diamond and even the possible connection with the KGB resident, Yuri Lubachev's, death.

Lipka pressed her thin lips together in thought. "I need to warn Judith."

Eggleston shook his head. "No, you can't do that, not unless we bring her in on it. Do you trust her?"

Lipka's face was somber, "With my life."

Eggleston, ill at ease, gazed out the window and after a brief pause he asked, "Anything I should know about the two of you?"

The ambassador stared at him coldly and replied, "That's not funny, Dirk. I just don't want anything to happen to her."

Eggleston apologized. "I'm sorry if I crossed the line, but I had to know. Blackmail attempts at your level have become so common place they're one of our biggest headaches."

Lipka stood, signaling the conversation was over. "I'll give Judith an abbreviated version," she said, "and you know as well as I do this will all be in the headlines in a few days."

As Eggleston departed, Lipka pressed a button on her telephone, "Judith, could you come in here for a few minutes?"

"I'll be right with you, ma'am."

Judith sat in the chair by the ambassador's desk; pen and note pad at the ready but they were taken from her. "You'll not need these and I'd like to ask you a couple of questions if you don't mind." She seemed reluctant to continue, but finally said; "I understand you were in Malacca with Steve Diamond last weekend."

"Yes, we have been seeing each other. He didn't want it to get out yet, but he told me quite a while ago he and his wife had split up. We didn't think we'd be seen in Malacca; I guess we were wrong" Judith responded, open and matter-of-fact.

"How long have you been seeing him?"

"A little over two months now."

"And when was the last time you saw him?"

"Tuesday morning when he came in to see you about the call from Mr. Barron."

"Has he phoned you since then?"

Judith cocked her head, a little puzzled and annoyed, "Ma'am, this is so unlike you. I have never known you to express interest in matters I consider private. May I ask why?"

"You certainly may and I owe you an apology." Ambassador Lipka started at the beginning with sketchy outlines of suspicion and espionage and Constance's disappearance, then noted Steve's mysterious absence and the condition of his house.

Judith was not buying any of it. "There has to be a reasonable explanation for all of these things. I don't think he's that kind of person."

The ambassador went on and when she mentioned the presence of Constance Diamond's personal effects and few of her husband's, and described the bloody freezer, Judith swayed in her chair and slipped heavily to the floor. With difficulty, Lipka lifted and laid her on her couch, then went to the bathroom for cold water and a washcloth. Placing the cool cloth on Judith's forehead, she slapped her wrists and called her name. Judith slowly opened her eyes, having difficulty focusing at first. Then Lipka pulled a chair over to the side of the couch and sat, asking Judith to take a sip of water.

"I haven't finished and unfortunately it gets more complicated. I'm afraid you may be in grave danger because the body Lieutenant Commander Kane found floating in the harbor not long ago just might possibly be that of Constance Diamond."

Judith clamped her hand over her mouth, sprang up and flew to the bathroom, vomiting violently. When she returned the ambassador was at the telephone. "My driver will take you to Dr. Quon. I told his nurse it was an emergency."

61

D r. Quon waited, sympathetic and patient, as Judith struggled to stop the flow of tears. She had begun to experience painful and frightening cramps and flinched as the doctor began his examination.

"I'm going to give you something for the pain before I continue." He spoke to the nurse in their shared dialect and Judith awoke later in a hospital room with Dr. Quon standing by her bed.

"We did our best Ms. Feldman, but I regret we were unable to save the baby." He patted her hand, "You are thirty-three now?"

"Yes."

"No other pregnancies?"

"No."

"You are probably aware the risks increase with age so if you and your partner plan to have a family, it might prove difficult, but not impossible. I would advise changes in your diet and routine, adequate rest, and mild exercise." He went over her health history and closed with advice to fill and use the prescription for birth control pills he would include in her discharge instructions. He started toward the door and then returned.

"Ambassador Lipka called to inquire about your condition. I told her you had eaten something contaminated and we would keep you here for 24 hours. At her request, I have ordered a 'No Visitors' sign posted on your door and have instructed the nurses to enforce it." He opened the bedside table drawer and handed her a small box of tissues. The tears had started again.

"I'll be in tomorrow around noon," he said.

She thanked him, aware the pregnancy, while not necessarily a career ender, would certainly leave her credibility irretrievably compromised. *No one must know—no one, ever.*

The nurse came in with a tiny syringe and injected Judith, took vital signs, made notes, and left. Judith soon felt better than she had in days, in weeks, and she lapsed into deep dreamy thoughts. *This was all Dirk Eggleston's doing—he trusted no one—a spy under every rock—his own mother probably a suspect. Steve's behavior could easily be explained as well as his disappearance. The whole thing was ridiculous. He no longer needed a sprawling bungalow and had relocated to a flat in the city; he'd show up at the GSO's tomorrow and give them the word he vacated the embassy's place. His car was missing, so what? That heap was always in the shop. Blood in the freezer; he probably unplugged it thinking it was empty, food thawed, and he chucked it all out. And the body in the harbor could be anyone. She smiled, thinking of her lover and he smiled back, his eyes twinkling, his teeth a dazzling glow, and he opened his arms to her.*

62

In the middle of nowhere on a road north of Johore Bahru, Malaysia, a cloud of steam burst through the grill and fogged the windshield of Diamond's old Bentley. It had to be the radiator hose so he pulled over and stopped. As he stood there with the hood propped up, cussing his predicament, a chartered tour bus, one of only a few vehicles on the road rumbled by on its way from Singapore en route to the casino in the Genting Highlands.

Someone on the bus must have noticed his plight and took pity because a few minutes later the bus returned, stopped, and the tour guide approached to offer Diamond a welcomed lift. His suitcases were stowed and then he took the last available seat in the rear, adjacent to the sloshing, stinking toilet compartment and across the aisle from an elderly American couple. They seemed intent on making conversation with the new arrival, but Diamond was in no mood to talk to anyone.

"So, young man, where are you from, where are you going, and what happened to your poor car?"

"I have a headache."

"Oh dear, I have aspirins. Harold, get the aspirins."

Diamond jumped to his feet and yelled, "No, leave me alone!" which startled the nearby passengers.

Black clouds of diesel exhaust billowed into the air as the bus resumed its trek along the roadway, dodging occasional pedestrians and ox drawn carts, and snaking left and right every hundred yards or so to miss another Volkswagen-sized pothole. They continued onward for several hours through miles of rubber plantations and past occasional kampongs where happy-looking children at play ran to the roadside to wave to the mostly pale-faced foreigners.

To avoid conversation, Diamond feigned napping, and during a rest stop he remained slumped down and partially hidden in his seat. The next and final leg of the journey to the casino, according to conversations he overheard, was a departure from the main road onto a scenic, winding secondary road through deep jungle with tortuous turns eventually reaching upwards of 6,000 feet to the destination. As the bus began to reload, Diamond had a change of plans. Abandoning all courtesies, he rudely shoved his way past milling seniors to the front of the bus and inquired of the driver and tour guide if he might be let off at some place ahead where he could find overnight accommodations.

"Yes", the driver replied knowing of such a place along their route.

Diamond secured the last vacancy at the vast commercial rubber plantation. They called it a cottage, but it was actually a one-room thatched roof hut some distance from the others and a short walk beyond the dining facility, community showers, and recreation room.

"No problem, I like to walk" he told the attendant at check-in. He took a complimentary bottle of water, but declined to sign-up for the next morning's guided tour of the operation, and then he went directly to cottage number six.

For the other dozen or so overnight guests the evening's entertainment was a choice between a stack of dog-eared paperback romance novels, few in English, or the countlessly re-spliced Bogart film classic, *Casablanca*; folding chairs, a bed sheet screen, and film projector were being readied.

It was just after 5:00 PM, but already some of the jungle's nocturnal dwellers were beginning to stir. Diamond brushed away a large spider web barring the doorway of his unit, entered, and flicked the switches for the light and ceiling fan. The space had an unused, musty smell so he propped open the door to help with the ventilation. He placed his suitcases near the table and tried the bamboo-framed bed draped with mosquito netting. Mentally and physically exhausted, but feeling temporarily safe, a short rest was in order, so he lay back and began to contemplate his next move knowing they must be after him. It was so very quiet, his eyelids heavy, the slow fan mesmerizing, and soon he drifted off to sleep.

Just after dark a rat cruised along its twilight circuit between the outlaying cottages searching for food morsels dropped by tourists returning from the buffet. The rat suddenly leapt into the air and scrambled through the torn screen door, quickly making its way across to the safety of darkness beneath the bed on which Diamond slept. The rat's pursuer, one of several skilled vermin exterminators appeared on the doorstep moments later and without knocking he quietly let himself in. Moving silently across the floor he made his move hot on Ratty's trail. However, just as the hunter closed in and the hunted had an end-of-the-line look in its eyes, Diamond stirred, heaved a sigh, turned on his side, continued to his stomach, and his arm slipped from the bed. It dangled directly in the path of the exterminator, at first startled and confused, but then incensed by the interruption.

Diamond did not hear the primal hiss, but he felt the fangs. In a flash, six milliliters of neurotoxic venom pumped into his upper arm. The king cobra's bite is often deadly especially in rural areas were anti-serum is not immediately available and Diamond did all the wrong things in the aftermath. He panicked as so many do and chased the almost nine-foot snake around the room and from under the bed with a chair for several agitated minutes until it finally left the way it entered. Then he mistakenly applied a tourniquet and did not call out for help because he did not want the risk of questions and publicity associated with seeking out professional emergency medical assistance.

In only ten minutes he began to feel waves of pain spreading through his body along with increased dizziness. He sat on the edge of the bed, soaking with sweat, breathing slowly through his mouth, random twitchy convulsions taking over, a sinking drowsiness, and then he toppled to the floor. He tried to raise himself to his knees, but could not do it.

Time seemed to stop and start in a blur as he drifted in and out of consciousness. He thought he heard a voice, voices,

Russian accents, "Mr. Diamond, are you in there? Are you well?" He tried to reply, move his lips, raise a finger, but was unable to do so.

63

Friday afternoon and the US Embassy's cleaning crew was in a jolly mood, singing, joking, and making good progress in the executive offices on the top floor. They had big plans for the weekend with their families, so they hurried to complete the work and depart before the afternoon rush hour. Having finished with the ambassador's office they moved to the conference room. They vacuumed and dusted, removed a carpet stain here and there, cleaned the windows, scrubbed the toilet, and washed a few cups and saucers in the kitchenette as two Marines stood by and watched them.

Chairs were removed from around the conference table and the vacuum cleaner zoomed in and out sucking up every detectible donut crumb and speck of dirt. While hastily re-inserting the chairs back into their positions the ambassador's chair was jammed-in slightly askew, forcing one of the chair's arms under the table's edge. It was just enough pressure to turn the secret radio transmitter on and by Monday morning after more than forty-eight hours of continuous operation the transmitter's battery was dead. Unfortunately for the KGB, without Diamond to change the battery, so was the clandestine eves-dropping operation inside the embassy's conference room.

64

At 1:35 AM Saturday morning the bedside telephone awakened Dirk Eggleston in his flat. A familiar voice, his counterpart from the US Embassy in Kuala Lumpur, Malaysia, was on the line and anxious to talk.

"Dirk, we missed him. We're here at a rubber plantation. A man fitting Diamond's description, but with a different name, checked in late yesterday afternoon off a tour bus. He reportedly didn't have a reservation and was by himself. The people here told us two European-looking men arrived later, around 11:00 PM, and asked if Diamond was an occupant. They showed a photo of him and were directed to his cottage. Anyway, we're here now and searched the place, but nobody's around and it's broken up pretty bad, looks like a struggle."

"Any luggage or personal belongings left behind?"

"Nope, nothing but an empty water bottle. We've got it for prints and we're taking some off the door and furniture too."

"Was Diamond seen leaving the area?"

"No, he wasn't, but the night clerk said he heard a vehicle start up outside the compound sometime around midnight."

"They couldn't be more than a few hours ahead of you, right?"

"Right. I've already alerted our teams back at the embassy and the airport, and we're only on the prowl here for a few minutes longer. We found a spot outside the entrance where a car was parked. There's some fresh motor oil on the ground and footprints. We're taking photos and collecting a sample of the oil. I'll check back with you later."

But Diamond vanished that night and the ensuing weeks

turned into months as the international dragnet continued to come up empty. The evidence pointed to Diamond likely being Bernard as well as the murderer of his own wife, Constance. Speculation was that the KGB had whisked Diamond out of Malaysia. He could be in Moscow or some other hiding place.

Even though the case remained open, the CIA released Kane from the burden of their tasking so he could devote full-time to his official attaché duties. Word passed by Eggleston to Kane was that Janice Crowell was pleased with Kane's participation even though it appeared Bernard had apparently slipped through their fingers.

65

"Good morning, Miss T. Did you have a nice weekend?"
She wiggled her left hand at Kane; a sparkle caught the light.

"Well, look at you! You are breakin' my poor heart, and just who is the lucky man?"

"A physical therapist I met at my sister's wedding" she said, admiring her diamond again.

"When is the happy day?"

"His parents are deciding," she said soberly.

"Do they know what a treasure you are?"

"Apparently not. They think I'm too Westernized."

"What does your fiancé think?"

"He's okay with it, but he is an only child."

"Uh-oh, well, I'm no expert on relationships, but I've got a feeling he is going to be one happy fella. Chin up, you'll be fine."

She held up a fat envelope. "This just came in for you."

Kane went to his desk, tore open the envelope, digested its contents, and read it again to make sure there was no misunderstanding. It was from his intelligence officer detailer in Washington, and it advised him he would soon be in receipt of orders to a career enhancing assignment in Norfolk, Virginia. However, the orders were coming nearly two years early. The letter was apologetic in an official way, but it described a critical situation involving unexpected personnel changes and Kane was considered an integral part of the solution. His billet in Singapore would be gapped for months since the Navy did not have a replacement designated for him in the attaché training pipeline, so the other attaches in the office would have to take up the slack. The DIA and Captain Grusk would not be happy with the news, but it was one of those "needs of the Navy" situations and he knew any attempt to decline the orders would be committing career suicide.

He stared at the photos and memorabilia on his walls and bookcase, pictures of his dad and grandfather in their uniforms, the awards and citations of his own, and he knew he had to go. He had taken comfort in the knowledge he had more time to spend with Aurora, but now he knew it would never happen.

He had decided to ask Aurora to marry him, but he knew there was a good chance she would decline because she was emotionally bound to her family, her culture, and the business. He thought the only way she might be persuaded would involve him resigning his commission and becoming a Singapore citizen, helping in her shop, or seeking employment in the American business community there. He considered the choices and realized he could not do it, so he would have to tell her he would be leaving in just a couple of months. His heart sank.

66

They had developed a form of telephonic shorthand; each aware the other could not speak freely or at length while at work. Kane picked up the phone and dialed her number.

"Aurora" she chirped.

"Dinner tonight?"

"Lovely."

"Pick you up at seven."

After making small talk in the car, they were finally seated at the café and drinks were on the way.

She took a sip and then looked at him without smiling. "I'm glad you called. I wanted to talk to you."

"I wanted to talk to you too, but ladies first." Kane needed more time to think about how he was going to say it.

She spoke softly, finding it difficult to meet his eyes. She told him how much she loved him, and how painful it had been in knowing he did not love her. She made it clear she did not blame him in any way and understood their cultural differences must present a problem for him.

He eyed her with a fixed stare and listened intently. She explained she wanted badly to marry him, but when she realized he did not want to marry her, she had to make other plans. She had called the embassy that morning and inquired about filing the paperwork to go to America.

Kane picked up his glass, downed the remaining contents, and signaled the waiter for the check. Standing, he pulled out her chair, and kissed her cheek. "I'll feed you at my place, we have a lot to talk about."

67

The announcement of Kane's engagement to Aurora Booth was headline news inside the embassy and throughout Singapore's military attaché community. Of course, Kane's parents were ecstatic as well. The wedding date was set for the following summer in Florida and the reception at his parents' home there. Aurora's relatives were also busy making plans for the big event. For some, it would be their first airplane ride and trip to America.

Captain Grusk was only days away from retirement. His replacement, Captain Cross, was busy meeting embassy staff and outside contacts, and learning how the attaché office operated. Several of Kane's colleagues, including Captain Brett, the Brit, were also in receipt of retirement orders. DCM Bass was harder to get along with than ever because of the announcement of a political appointee, not him or another experienced, career State Department person like him to replace Ambassador Lipka.

Eggleston and Kane discontinued their private meetings on Bernard. Overall contact between them tapered off somewhat if not for the weekly staff meeting and questions popping up from time to time about subject matter, which intersected both their offices. They also had invitations to some of the same social events, and everything between them remained cordial, if not as close as before.

They ran into one another again at a large bash hosted by a wealthy Singaporean export entrepreneur. As the party drew to an early close, Eggleston made the rounds to several selected couples promoting a small after party at his flat. Aurora and

Kane were invited and they planned to attend along with the others if the rain would ever let up, but it began to rain even harder. At that point Eggleston decided to make a dash for his car to retrieve and distribute extra umbrellas to those couples without drivers so they wouldn't get soaked getting to their automobiles. Kane decided to splash along and give Eggleston a hand even though Eggleston declined Kane's initial offer of assistance.

By the time they reached the car they were soaked. Eggleston quickly popped the trunk, reached inside, and handed several umbrellas to Kane, kept two others for himself, and slammed the trunk lid shut.

Briefly glancing inside the dimly lit trunk for the umbrellas, Kane saw two bound stacks of letter-sized paper documents. Both of them had what looked like the word "SECRET" stamped on the top pages.

Eggleston undoubtedly had an explanation for carrying classified materials in his trunk and Kane speculated the papers were probably part of some intelligence exchange with the Singaporeans. Regardless though, according to DoD classified material security regulations, it was a violation to transport and store any classified materials like that, and the finding bothered Kane.

Over the following days and weeks, Kane continued his preparations to leave Singapore, turning more and more information and contacts over to Chief Sanderson and the other attachés in the office. It was during this period he also began to detect or maybe it was a feeling of change in Eggleston's behavior; something wasn't right. From time to time Eggleston seemed to make a concerted effort to avoid Kane, getting together only on his terms like when he wanted information, say, a certain classified document on Soviet military forces he did not hold in his own office files. He jokingly commented it was easier to sign them out from the attaché office, if they had them, rather than requesting the documents from the Langley bureaucracy and waiting days or weeks for their arrival.

The classified documents in the trunk incident popped into Kane's mind every time he saw Eggleston. Additionally, Janie

Tan had mentioned a curious spate of copy machine problems upstairs, along with requests from Eggleston's secretary to borrow toner for their copier since they kept unexpectedly running out of it.

Kane had some idle time late one Friday afternoon and out of idle curiosity he felt compelled to drop by Eggleston's office for an impromptu social call, inquire about any news in the Bernard case, and to test his welcome.

When he entered Eggleston's outer office, Eggleston's secretary was standing in his doorway. She glanced at Kane and turned back to her boss. "Commander Kane is here to see you."

Eggleston yelled, "Sorry, Dalton, I'm just about finished here and on my way out, so I'll see you Monday. We'll talk then."

"Sure, it can wait, see you Monday. Have a good trip."

68

Kane returned to his office and sat in thought for a few minutes. Then he called Aurora and told her something had come up and he had to work late. Hurriedly, he locked up and left for his place to change clothes, grab binoculars and a camera, and catch a taxi. It dropped him off at the public park across the street from Eggleston's address. From a shielded location he could see the full front and one side of the high-rise building including the ramp to the underground parking garage.

Kane had no idea where Eggleston might be headed, the airport, across the causeway into Malaysia, or just a meeting or some other event in the city. Eggleston's white sedan soon showed up and disappeared into the parking garage. Kane shifted his view up six stories and waited until he observed the curtains close in Eggleston's flat.

Kane cleaned the binocular lenses then scanned the sidewalk exits and driveway, then up and down and back and forth, waiting and watching. Ten minutes passed before a young couple with shopping bags walked up to the front doors and entered the building. A few minutes later another man approached the building from the rear and disappeared behind it. Then a single individual slowly exited the front door and walked in Kane's direction toward the front curb. If it were not for the characteristic limp Kane would never have recognized the person as Dirk Eggleston. It was definitely Eggleston though, but in disguise; the hat, glasses, beard, umbrella, and a change of clothes would have thrown anyone off. Kane was both surprised and perplexed.

Eggleston hailed a taxi headed toward the city. Kane

bounded from his position, dashed to the street, and stopped another taxi. He incentivized the driver with a $20 bill and they took off in pursuit.

Right away Kane's driver became agitated with the back-seat driving as Kane tried to maintain cautious visual contact with Eggleston's vehicle, "left lane, okay right lane, slower, now faster...." The driver had just about as much it as he could tolerate when Eggleston's taxi pulled to the curb and discharged him. There was no place for Kane's taxi to immediately pull over, so he ducked down in the back seat as they sailed on past and stopped at the first opportunity in the next block. Kane sprung onto the sidewalk and headed back in the direction of where he saw Eggleston being let off.

Eggleston was nowhere to be seen. *Shit!* But rather than spinning around in the middle of the sidewalk, Kane quickly stepped into the adjacent shop and hunkered behind a furniture and drapery display where he could see a little of the sidewalk in each direction through the front window. *Eggleston may have passed through one of these shops and out the back door or he was waiting inside one just to see who might be following him.* Kane decided to stay in place for a few minutes and luck was with him. Incredibly, Eggleston stepped onto the sidewalk, probably from the shop just next-door, scanned left and right, and proceeded on his way. Based on the near miss counter-detection and Eggleston's cautiousness, Kane decided to hang back farther.

At the end of next block Eggleston crossed the street, doubled back a few yards to look into a store window and checked his watch. As soon as he crossed the street Kane faded into another shop. But he knew he couldn't remain stationary for long or he would lose Eggleston for sure.

Kane tugged at his hat and stepped back out onto the sidewalk—no Eggleston anywhere, so he quickly jaywalked through an opening in the traffic and picked up the pace, winding through pedestrians, looking ahead and across. At the next intersection he saw Eggleston standing at the crowded street corner waiting for the light to change. In the next block Eggleston entered a large, multi-story, department store, which forced Kane to make another decision, go inside or wait outside. He had been following Eggleston on foot for about twenty minutes and had a gut feeling something was about to happen, so he went inside the store. As he entered, he wondered if he might be sticking his nose into something way over his pay grade and taking a chance of messing up some high-profile CIA operation.

Kane stayed clear of the escalators and eventually made his way to the rear of the store after a systematic search of the main floor. He was drawn toward a "Deliveries" sign with an arrow pointing to a rear exit. A few steps beyond the exit door he was standing at the loading docks. The entire area was empty and quiet. He jumped off the dock to the ground and walked a few paces toward the alley. A large dark sedan with its left rear door wide open sat idling just around the corner of the building not more than 30 feet away. Kane ducked back out of sight.

An exit door on an adjacent wing of the building squeaked open, then closed and Kane caught a glimpse of Eggleston as he approached the car. Remaining hidden from view, Kane deftly lowered his camera around the corner and held the release button down—the motor drive cranked through the entire roll of film as a car door shut and it drove away.

69

That night after developing the film and reviewing the negatives frame-by-frame with a magnifying glass, Kane could not sleep, but by sunrise he had made up his mind and was ready to take action. He felt certain Eggleston was unlawfully involved with the Russians.

The problem now was how to secretly communicate his concern back to Janice Crowell at the CIA. A plain text message to her was obviously out of the question. Some type of private, personal message would be unusual and draw unwanted attention too particularly since he did not know who else inside the embassy, perhaps someone in communications, might be complicit. It would also be unusual for Kane to send a message outside of the normal chain of command directly to someone like Crowell at the CIA. He concluded the lowest risk was to send a common letter by US mail. He'd merely drop it into the embassy's fleet post office mailbox addressed to his DIA point of contact at the Defense Attaché School. He subsequently crafted the brief note to LCOL Doyle with instructions not to open the enclosed second envelope, but to hand deliver it personally and immediately to Crowell at CIA headquarters.

A week later the attaché office received a priority precedence message from the office of the DIA's Inspector General (IG) stating an IG team was headed to Asia to inspect attaché offices in the region. According to the schedule, Singapore was at the top of the list. Kane, however, knew the inspection was bogus, and he knew Crowell had received his message too because the IG's message included an authentication code word provided to Kane during his initial face-to-face briefing with Janice Crowell.

Late Sunday night before the IG's Monday inspection, Kane received a telephone call at his house. The IG team wanted to meet him at their hotel. Kane immediately agreed when he recognized Crowell's voice on the other end of the line.

In the hotel room, Crowell introduced Kane to the six-man team composed of personnel from the FBI, CIA, and DIA. He was asked to present his evidence on Eggleston, which he did: Eggleston's disguise and the photos with the Russian Second Secretary in the backseat of the car, the stacks of classified material in Eggleston's trunk, the problems with Eggleston's copy machine and the high consumption of copy toner, the several falsified trips, changes in Eggleston's behavior toward Kane over time, and other tidbits of suspicion collected to the present. The information was "interesting, alarming, provocative", but it was circumstantial, not enough hard evidence to make an actual arrest, but enough to initiate an investigation. When Kane finished answering a series of questions, two members of the team were excused, and went into the bedroom where they spent an hour on the telephone. When finished they talked alone with Crowell and then approached Kane and asked, "Would you be willing to wear a wire?"

Kane thought for a moment. "I'll do it." And then he asked, "Eggleston isn't Bernard, is he?"

"No, we're almost certain Steve Diamond is Bernard. Eggleston, if he is what now looks plausible, may have begun work for the KGB following Diamond's disappearance, a possible replacement if you will" Crowell replied.

They discussed details of a trap: what they wanted Kane to say to Eggleston, how he should act, where to sit or stand in Eggleston's office and, of course, a contingency plan, "what we want you to do if things don't go as we would like them to in there." The whole thing was a high-risk gamble to get Eggleston to confess to collusion and espionage with the Russians. A number of careers, including Kane's, and possibly even his life were on the line.

70

The next day as planned, but with understandable trepidation, Kane entered Eggleston's office at 2:00 PM wearing a concealed "wire" along with a manila envelope in hand. He left the office door slightly ajar as instructed.

Surprised by the intrusion Eggleston looked up. "Well, well, I wasn't expecting a visit from you, Dalton. What brings you in? Need a cigar?" he asked as he pushed aside papers on his desktop and tilted back in his chair.

"Oh, no thanks. Sorry to bust in unannounced, but your secretary wasn't out there. Anyway, I won't be long, I just wanted to ask you a few questions."

"That's right, I almost forgot, you probably have your sea bags packed and are ready to ship out of here to where was that again?"

"Norfolk."

"Norfolk, yes. So, what is it you need from me?"

"How long was it after Steve Diamond's disappearance that you started working for the KGB, and did they recruit you or did you just volunteer your services?" Kane asked with as much audaciousness as he could muster.

Unflinchingly, Eggleston stared back. He began to rotate in his chair a little one way and then the other massaging his bottom lip with his thumb and forefinger, assessing.

Kane waited, though not expecting answers.

Eggleston needed more time. "I don't think I heard you correctly. Say that again, would you?" he insisted.

"I said, were you recruited by the KGB or did you just walk-in? Was it for the money? You must be one of their biggest fish, Dirk."

"You know, Dalton, I could have your ass court-martialed for this, tossed out of the Navy, you'd be ruined, broke, sleeping somewhere in a gutter a month from now" Eggleston fired back.

"You haven't answered my questions, Dirk," Kane calmly reiterated.

"You've always had a nose for trouble, haven't you?" Eggleston smirked from behind a false smile.

"Just the answers, Dirk."

"You're in way over your head, Dalton. You're not smart enough for this. You'd need air tight evidence to make such slanderous accusations stick, and you have nothing, nothing at all" Eggleston countered, sounding very self-assured.

"It's right here, Dirk" Kane said holding out the envelope for Eggleston to see. "But don't worry, I don't want to take you down, I just want a piece of the action."

A wary "Ha" escaped from Eggleston lips, nothing more, for once at a loss for words.

"Ha" Kane echoed back, holding his ground.

"So, let's see what you have there," Eggleston said, breaking the momentary standoff.

Kane stepped forward as he extracted the 8x10 inch black and white photo and tossed it on the desktop for Eggleston to examine. It showed Eggleston in disguise about to enter the backseat of the black sedan. Through the back window of the car you could see the head and profile of the Soviet Embassy's Second Secretary, an image good enough for positive identification.

"And just who or what am I supposed to be looking at in this fuzzy photograph" Eggleston replied disparagingly.

"That's you, entering the car. Oh, I've got better ones, but this is one of the better mug shots of your Russian buddy. And by the way where did you get that silly disguise? I saw better beards in my high school's thespian club productions. The KGB surely has better makeup kits than what they've given you. But what really got me started was the cache of classified material in your trunk. Remember during the rainstorm at that party a couple of month ago? No wonder your copier kept breaking down. Your secretary couldn't keep enough toner on hand to make all those copies. And I've got more on your phony little one-and two-day disappearing acts too, your periodic sleepovers with the KGB."

"Shut up!" Eggleston responded in anger as he jerked a desk drawer open, extracted a pistol with a silencer, and aimed it at Kane. "I don't need a partner. So why don't you and I take a little stroll down to my car?" he said, as he stood and motioned toward the door with the gun.

"I'm not going anywhere," Kane answered offhandedly, stalling, his voice wavering at the end.

"Look, Dalton, without your absolute cooperation right here and now there will be a dreadful accident. I hope you realize that," Eggleston threatened, his arm elevating with sight alignment moving to Kane's chest.

The next moment the office door flew open. Three men clad in body armor bounded through the doorway into combat stances with automatic weapons pointed at Eggleston.

"Put the gun down!" an agent yelled as Kane dived behind a chair out of the line of fire. "Lay the gun on the desk, Mr. Eggleston! Do it now! Do what I say right now or I'll have to shoot you!"

Silent, stone-faced, Eggleston slowly raised his hands like he was surrendering but angled the gun toward his head and pulled the trigger. A sharp thud erupted from the gun barrel, blowing his brains and skull fragments across the room. A portion of the bullet slammed into an engraved pewter plate, an award from Singapore's ISD, and knocked it from its wall mount. Eggleston collapsed on his desk and toppled to the floor.

Kane got slowly to his feet. It was over..

About the Author

Tom Cassidy was born in 1942 and graduated from the University of Northern Iowa. He subsequently joined the US Navy, served on several ships, and then he began a career as a naval intelligence officer, which encompassed the Vietnam War, the American hostage crisis in Iran, the US Invasion of Grenada, the Falkland Islands War, and other significant military events around the world. One particularly memorable assignment was in the Republic of Singapore where he was assistant US naval attaché, and thus became the inspiration for this book. He divides his time now between La Jolla, California, and Sunrise Beach, Missouri, with family and friends—often seen with a fishing pole, golf club, or deer rifle in hand.

Curious about other Crossroad Press books?
Stop by our site:
http://www.crossroadpress.com
We offer quality writing
in digital, audio, and print formats.

www.ingramcontent.com/pod-product-compliance
Lightning Source LLC
Chambersburg PA
CBHW022003170626
46808CB00001B/266